DESSA

VAL CREESE

Printed and bound in Australia by BookPOD

Typesetting and cover design by BookPOD

Front cover image iStockphoto

ISBN: 978-0-646-55809-7   (pbk.)

A Cataloguing-in-Publication is available from the National Library of Australia.

1936

Wave to mummy.

Seven year old Alice's eyes were searching upwards over the dark bulge of the liner's bulk as she waved automatically at nothing, while she strained to see the familiar face.

There she is! There!

Edna bumped her up higher.

She's waving to you, see? Look!

Edna pointed with her free hand to an upper deck.

She can see you. She's blowing a kiss. Blow one back.

Alice put her fingers to her mouth as she was bid, but her eyes had not captured the face she wanted to see. Mummy, she called, Mummy. Already, with little warning, the great vessel was moving away. Alice wasn't sure who was moving, she or the ship. Everything was sliding sideways, at once so slow and yet so quick.

Suddenly her wave intensified. Heart, eye, hand, fused with energy. Yes, there. She could see her.

Mummy, she shouted with all her force, and again Mummy, Mummy. But already her breath was dissolving into air, melting into the mists of lost-uttered words, as the ship was turning away from the dock.

Edna put Alice down and took her by the hand.

We'll have boiled eggs for tea, tonight. Your favourite, she said.

Dessa stopped waving, stopped looking. It was amazing how quickly the figures on the wharf side were shrinking. Against the backdrop of the city the late afternoon sun caught the shape of the customs sheds, the cranes, the abandoned railway trucks. Soon the Cowes roads, the Isle of Wight, Southsea, seaward towards the Nab, scenes of a past life: last glimpses, then Escape. Relief.

Agony? Grief? Doubt?

How many times had she faltered, fought, resolved, reneged? Justification? Did her decision need justification? All those years; twenty one years. Give me a child until he is seven, the Jesuits said. Well now Alice was seven. She had waited until Alice was seven. All very well for her sisters Daisy and Maud and even Gwen to criticise and condemn. What did they know about life, swallowed up in their provincial pettifogging?

And then, then Mo!

He was the last thing she wanted to think about.

Mo was something she could never really have foreseen. Something as severing and cruel and as sharp-edged a shard as Jove's lightning. That had been the last, most pernicious blow, one which had very nearly defeated her. A pity, really, that he hadn't died.

What was it about people that made them appear to shrink when you said things like that? A life that could never be a proper life? Surely death was a better alternative? Well? Wasn't it? Think of all those people like Ernest Pardon from next-door to Mother whom the war had reduced to a dribbling half-life, whose needs spread through the family like a crippling disease, leaving Minnie, his main carer crucified daily? Surely his death would have been better for him and her. Life was the problem, not death. Why ever didn't people ever realise that?

Thinking that way had condemned her in her sisters' eyes, but they simply did not know. Had no idea. She had been through enough. They could never understand.

Dessa found herself shivering slightly as she stood leaning over the rails, her thoughts churning with the foaming, creaming whiteness of the wash melting back into the green waters of the sea.

The sea. The sea!

She could see nothing but sea. Miles of sea now between her and Calcutta. Relief. She closed her eyes. All round her she could feel space, sky, sea. This must be what it felt like to come out of prison after having served years of undeserved punishment.

Undeserved?

Well, she had made mistakes, but she had paid for them. No time ever, now, for recrimination. She had made the break. She would not allow herself to think what Alice and Edna were doing.

Alice? Edna?

They would be back at the house. She could smell its biscuity smell and the face-flannel smell upstairs by Alice's little bedroom, and, without really wanting to she recaptured the sight of her own bedroom, the bed barren beneath its tightly tucked dimity bedspread. She had told Edna to move in there if she wanted to, after she had gone. The boys' beds were made up for half-term. Gug's waterproof sheet was on his bed, just in case.

She shivered for the second time.

This wasn't because she was cold but because she had to make a physical effort to divorce herself from the scaffolding of the past years. No use recriminating. Children, babies, the grown boys, their love and incessant demands had eroded her. She, no, not just felt, she was a sandcastle iced shapeless by the tide. Almost. Not quite. Now was her chance to re-animate herself, give herself a life. Forget reasons, arguments, fights, downturns. You have done all you can, she told herself. You must measure up to your decision. They can't sabotage you now. Breathe. Look around you.

You are at sea! At sea.

On board! There was something very exciting about the feel of a ship, a big ship, a ship which sailed regularly half-way round the world. Cold, thick, white rails caramelised with rust, the different levels of decks, the double staircase down to the dining rooms, the brass clock which changed its time with the curve of the earth. She had travelled long distances by sea before but always with the boys and the babies. Without a nanny she had only been able to envy the luxury of passengers who had nothing better to do than play deck golf, or lounge around sipping cold drinks. Well, now she could lie back in her new beach pyjamas, walk lazily round at will, taking in the other passengers, showing off her deck tennis skills or flirting gently with anyone worth flirting with. Pity the money hadn't run to first class, but P&O second class was pretty good. She had already introduced herself to Miss Winthrop, her fellow cabin passenger, not a wildly exciting companion, but she didn't want anyone exciting, she was quite exciting enough for one cabin, and it would have driven her mad to have someone showing off and talking all the time. They would respect each other's privacy, you could tell that from their spark of mutually simultaneous assessment.

Dessa returned to her cabin on deck B to change for dinner. Changing for dinner! White tablecloths, damask napkins, waiters! Dishes brought to the table! It had been years since she had experienced such luxuries. Family meals in her own dining room had, too often, been gale-force events, with the boys racing through their food, arguing between mouthfuls, Gug giggling and knocking over his water, Henry spreading the puddle with his fingers, and Alice silently wiping carrot over her high chair.

Momentarily Dessa smiled at herself.

Stop!

She was doing the very thing she had resolved not to do. Now was now. She shook out an elbow-length sleeved green chiffon dress, suitable for her dining room debut. Yes. Make-up. Hair. She tried to look at herself in the mirror as if she were someone else. It had to be said that the Humby girls weren't bad looking. Dark hair, dark eyes, earrings which complemented the gleaming look she flashed at herself. She would make an entrance as the person she was setting out to be A new life!

She was just about to leave the cabin when she caught sight of her nightdress folded on the pillow. Alice and Edna had come on board to help her unpack. Alice! Saying the name was enough to make her bite her lip. Alice had put it there for her specially. She swallowed. Alice!

Alice! Waving her goodbye.

Stop.

She was doing and feeling what she had made her mind up not to do. She caught her breath. Stop remembering. That was the way to destroy herself. Going over all the pros and cons after all that had happened was self-defeating. Such thoughts had to be put behind her.

She re-arranged the curl behind her ear. The ironies! Major upheavals and she was allowing fleeting thoughts of her little girl to corrode her determination. Little things could sway the balance if she let them.

Elevating her head, and gathering her flimsy skirts together so that they should not catch in the heavy cabin door, she made her way up to the Lounge to smoke a cigarette before dinner. Several pairs of eyes followed her. She presented as a woman of the world who knew her own value. She was going out to India to marry Neil Langford. A slight smile curled around her lips as she made her entrance. She was thinking of Cora. She, Dessa had won that battle at least! Cora would turn in her grave! This thought added spine to her walk as she glanced around her, aware of the impact she was making.

1908

ONE

Dessa's sisters couldn't believe it. And said so. Originally Dessa herself couldn't believe it. As for Cora, it was just as well she had died for she could never have believed that her son had chosen voluntarily to heap ashes on his own head by marrying that woman after all!

Dessa Humby: pushy, common, from a working class background! She, Cora, had seen through her from that very first moment. She, Cora, had watched that girl twist her son round her little finger! Dudley, her husband, was as soft as Neil! That was where the boy got it from! No sense! No ability to see through people! Cora could not believe how naïve they could be. She knew! She could tell what was going on in people's minds. Neil and Dudley had been taken in by the girl's flashing eyes and her confident manner, but not she!

Smiling to herself at such recollections as she entered the ship's lounge, Dessa was right. Cora would not merely have turned in her grave but would have risen from it had she imagined it would ever have come to this. Neil. Her Neil. Her son, eschewing all others to marry 'that girl'.

Neil was Cora's only child and his welfare was her chief concern. His welfare. Her eyes would have hardened and her lips tightened in frustration at the turnout of events. Cora had plans for Neil which he was not always to share. She wanted her only child to grow up to be an English gentleman, a respected professional man of means with a well-to-do wife and family. She knew she would have to part with him at an early age as did anyone who was anyone, for an English Public school education was de rigeur for the sons of expatriates 'holding up the Empire'. Despite Dudley's wanting to keep Neil with them in Assam for as long as possible, she had no intention of sending him to any of those supposedly Eton-style Indian schools which were springing up. 'Her Neil' would be sent to Fortescue's in Hampshire, a decent school 'which she could trust' and which was all the more convenient since it was close to her sisters' for vacations. From Neil's point of view neither of these undertakings was to prove wholly successful, or even bearable, on occasions. He was a quiet, shy, boy and not at all the outgoing prefect type at school which his mother wanted him to be, nor did he ever feel wanted, happy or at home with his aunts and cousins in suburban Bournemouth.

Neil had been born to Cora late in life, as indeed, her marriage to Dudley Langford had also come about late in life. Cora was over thirty when she married him on one of his leaves from Assam. Rather tight-lipped and nervy, she had missed out on marriage at the time when her two sisters and most of her friends had married. She had accounted for this lengthy spinsterhood continually by pointing out her ailing mother's continuing need for her. When her mother did, finally, die her father re-married. It was then that she seized the opportunity offered to her by Dudley for a new life. Going out to India in the latter part of the nineteenth century was no mean challenge for a girl raised in Boscombe, Bournemouth. True, she had come into money at her mother's death and this enabled her to bring out large pieces of Victorian furniture to help her feel at home in Dudley's sprawling bungalow. Such familiar things and Dudley himself, of course. He was a good man, quiet and thorough, and he deserved a good wife. She would certainly be that. She made up her mind. Never lacking in determination, able at last to feel a sense of importance by being needed, she adapted readily to the demands of being a planter's wife.

Back in England, before she had seen 'Tinkharia', Cora had some idea of its appearance from a small watercolour Dudley had brought with him. The double-fronted, gabled house with its wide verandah was set above the neatly trimmed lawns of a lovely garden. Beyond these, as Dudley explained, were the outhouses, barns and drying rooms. Beyond them lay the hut dwellings of the workers of the estate. Whole families, sari clad women, their husbands and children, all in conical 'japi' hats did the work in those pressured hours when the ripe tea bushes had to be picked within six or seven days.

'Running a tea-garden is like running a whole village,' he had explained to her. 'The workers are our responsibility and their welfare, health, sickness, education, birth and death, depends on us.'

He had taken her hand tenderly. 'It's not just me you are marrying. It's all of them as well. You have to think hard before you accept. I couldn't take you half-way round the world to a life you're not prepared for. It's not everyone who wants to be a planter's wife.'

He had smiled. He was a thoughtful, quiet man, who loved the green hillsides of the tea gardens and the muddy red earth paths between the terraced tea bushes, most of which he was responsible for planting. The garden was an in-built part of him, and he needed a committed partner to share his life. Cora would not prove a disappointment. For her part, she welcomed the challenge. She would supersede those sisters who had always relegated her to the role of spinster and would at last be important, a lady in her own right. She accepted Dudley's offer in a glow of happiness.

Cora did most things efficiently. She loved the bungalow with its lofty space, a world apart from the terraced Victorian houses of

Boscombe. The very aura of decisiveness and no nonsense back in England which had limited the numbers of her suitors, was now the very quality which made her a tireless and reliable Memsahib. She ran Dudley's household with zest, enjoying having not just one overworked live-in maid, but two house-boys, a cook and a useful old ayah who did the sewing. Without children for eight years, she took upon herself readily the responsibility for teaching and managing the tea-garden's native workers. Also she was devoted to the Club at Jorhat, which was so essential a centre for the seventeen ex-patriate planters and their families in the area, along with neighbouring British civil servants and professionals. Here, too, she became invaluable. She ran the ladies' lending library, could always be relied on to organise raffles or put together play rehearsal schedules for the drama group. When new wives appeared, she went out of her way to help them settle into 'the Life', initiating them into local niceties and rituals, advising on peoples' relative clout, their idiosyncrasies and social bearing.

It was in this way that she came to meet Ada, young, newlywed Ada Bennett, with whom she formed a friendship which was to last throughout their time in Assam, and which was to continue into their years of retirement in England.

Originally a friendship of need and habit, theirs was a friendship strengthened through an unspoken interdependence of cut and thrust. Ada was quick to see how much Cora needed to be depended on and Cora, who had suffered at the hands of her sisters, was now in a position of authority which she relished. Not that Ada was ever Cora's stooge, far from it! She knew precisely how to stir her friend when it suited her, and did; however, the life, the job, the remoteness of Assam from the 'civilised' world of England nourished their inseparability.

'She's a dear girl in so many ways, Cora confided to Dudley, after their first few meetings, 'but, understandably, she needs a little breaking in.'

'Who better to help her than you?' Dudley had replied with

complete sincerity.

Cora's husband had long been friends with Mervyn Bennett. Like himself, Mervyn, too, had needed a wife when he had been put in charge of the tea-garden at Rituparna. Dudley had been responsible for Mervyn's traineeship with Mason-Webb and Mervyn, for his part, was wholly indebted to Dudley for valuable technical advice. He was also grateful for Cora's interest in his young wife. Wide-eyed Ada asked the questions. Gracious Cora gave the answers. This was a wholly satisfactory situation and one which added a new dimension to Cora's and Dudley's own relationship.

Cora would cast her eyes to the ceiling, smile slightly and sigh just a little. 'Ada,' she would say, shaking her head advisedly, 'Ada, dear Ada, has no idea.'

Dudley would look up, politely, over his latest batch of English newspapers. 'Nothing you'll not be able to help her with, I'm sure.'

This was the cue Cora was expecting, and Dudley never let her down.

Then it would all come out.

'She's nervous, dear girl, about parties. You know, the social thing.'

'And?' The gentle tone of his voice held just the show of concern Cora needed to elaborate her problem.

'Well, we've been invited, along with the Rileys, plus the aunt, and Gordon, who can only ever talk about his mineral collection, and Judith, who always sets out to shock everybody.'

'And?'

'She can't think how to arrange the seating.'

Dudley could always be relied on to be sympathetic. He pointed out genuinely how lucky it was for Ada to have Cora to rely on for the social niceties. This always gave Cora exactly the opening she needed.

'Of course it's understandable, with her background. She comes from Trade.'

The word 'trade' caused her to pause and widen her eyes significantly.

'It's not her fault, of course. She's not used to a social life as we know it. They never had dinner, imagine! Only ever high-tea! A draper's shop in Walsall.'

The casting of the eyes and the shrugging the shoulders in evident pity, said it all.

'You can see why she needs help.' Cora could then speak with the necessary and pleasant degree of superiority which her own background gave her. 'Naturally, I make allowances.'

'Your kindness does you credit, my dear. And Mervyn appreciates all you do. Ada would be lost without you.'

The two couples' friendship strengthened still further when the wives, a year apart, each had a child. Cora was the proud mother of Neil, a thin, nervous, sensitive baby, while Celia, the daughter of Ada and Mervyn was, from the time she was born, bouncing, demanding and self-important, as she was to remain for the rest of her days. Secretly Cora wished that her Neil had some of Celia's toughness, while Ada, somewhat less secretly, was sorry that Cora should have such a timid son.

Eventually in and around 1907, both couples were to retire to England. Their long friendship made them decide to live close to each other, 'back home'. Together they decided on Southsea, the socially 'good' end of Portsmouth.

Neil had just left school and was considering several possibilities for a future career, while the redoubtable Celia was already making her mark at Madame Vehrnes' finishing school in Brussels.

It was at this point in all of their lives that Neil was to meet Dessa.

TWO

In a less well-to-do area of Portsmouth, Dessa's mother, Sarah Humby, stretched up from her weeding. She could smell the change of tide in the wind, and could see the fronds of bright green on the rocks straightening as they dripped their sea-water. The causeway to Horsea Island cleared. Beyond lay the flat, muddy, far reaches of Portsmouth harbour. It was her view, this view of Porchester castle, the view she knew, the sight of which took her away from all those home pressures. Strange, she thought that Roman and Viking ships had sailed here and that now, the other end of the harbour hosted depths enough for massive grey-metal warships, the Dreadnoughts, that her husband, Henry, a shipwright, worked on with such pride.

She loved her garden; the salty smell of the air, the clear sky, her double plot, bursting with lush vegetables for the family. Henry, who could turn his hand to anything, had made her a hut for her tools, a bench for her primus stove, a space by the doorway for a wicker chair when it was time for a bit of a rest and to study the view. This was where she escaped the demands of her ever-burgeoning family and had time to think and be herself.

The sinking sun caught the square tower of the grey castle. Time to go back.

Sarah surveyed her allotment with pride. Gardening was in her blood. Her father had been head gardener on Lord de Vere's estate and she loved and knew how to grow plants of all kinds. Mostly she grew vegetables, but for a hobby she nurtured prize chrysanthemums which she sold to a superior florists in North End and this gave her pocket money for little extras for the children like tennis racquets and hockey sticks.

She took off her apron, locked up the shed, put a large bag of freshly picked beans in her bicycle basket and headed for home. Cycling was something she and Henry had enjoyed before the children came along. They had cycled as far as Rowland's Castle, and even as far as the Forest once, on picnics. Henry always rode his bike to work and she used hers to nip down to the garden at every opportunity. A breath of fresh air. Grass. Trees. So different from those hard, arid bricks of the houses and pavements of Mile End virtually abutting on the high flint walls of the Dockyard, surmounted as they were with foot-long spikes to keep people in and out. Nothing green there. A couple of hours in the garden and she felt fresh again. When Henry retired, she made up her mind that she would leave running the house and all the cooking to him. His turn. Already only three or four of their children still needed looking after. Several were grown up. The eldest, Margaret was walking out with a sergeant from Aldershot, two of the boys were in the Navy, and Maud, wilful and difficult, had run away from home yet again. As she pedalled past the new Alexandra Park, she thought of Dessa. Sarah's hopes lay in Dessa. Unlike the others, she had verve, she had life. Sarah smiled to herself. Big tickets, that one! She'd go far. Sarah remembered the new white dress and the horse-drawn carriage she had allowed her to have to take her to her first communion! That had brought eyes to the windows of every house in Malins Road and gossip to the neighbouring streets! Yes, she did spoil Dessa more than the others, but then Dessa was the kind of daughter she really wanted to have, one who would go places in the world. Margaret was sweet but gentle, 'took after her father'. The boys, nice enough, but they were a bit selfish and lazy, and had little aptitude for school work which you had to have these days if you were to go anywhere. Even Chiver's coaching college couldn't drum anything into Clive. Then there was Maud. Well Maud never stuck at anything and they had wasted far too much money in apprenticing her to Eliot, the tailor. As far as Sarah knew she was now in the Isle of Wight working somewhere behind a Bar, of all things. They had had another row and she had run away again! Self-willed. Not much hope there.

Yes, Dessa was the one!

She had won a scholarship to the Secondary School and was doing very well; in the sports teams, in the school's Shakespeare play (Shakespeare, mind you!), interested in politics, always on about votes for women! Quite right too! There weren't many things women couldn't do better than men in Sarah's opinion and girls needed education and jobs equally with the boys. There was no daughter of Sarah's who didn't have totally equal treatment with the boys in the family. People 'made her sick' who thought girls should sit about waiting on men. Her Dessa had drive and personality. Nobody was going to keep her down!

As Sarah turned into Twyford Avenue she felt a degree of annoyance with Henry. He wasn't much help when it came to urge the children to 'get on'. He was always too relaxed. 'They'll find themselves' he said. 'Their lives. Let them be!'

But Sarah wasn't like that; not at all like that.

Life had shown her that there was one law for the rich and quite another for the poor. You had to fight to 'get on'. Brought up on the de Vere estate she knew how the nobs lived and what was good for them was equally good for her family. The neighbours might buy their children cheap new clothes, but Sarah went to the quiet parts of Southsea, like Marmion Road, where the naval officers' wives sold their children's clothes to second-hand shops. There she bought classy tailored skirts and quality dresses as good as new. It was the same with furniture and jewellery. Sarah would rather have fine, second-hand diamond earrings from the pawn shop, than new trash from some flashy jeweller. She also had a good eye for old mahogany and oak furniture, and haunted the salerooms, rather than buy modern rubbish as did so many of her neighbours. She wanted to bring up her family with a bit of 'class'.

She was now riding past Kingston Crescent and was about to turn into those streets upon streets of brick-terraced houses, whose front-doors opened straight out on to the pavement. There was hardly a time when you couldn't hear some Irish mother screaming at a gaggle of threadbare children, or ride past a group of aproned women with babies in their arms nattering on the pavement. Easy enough to pick out the renters from the potwallopers, her next-door neighbour Minnie Pardon always said.

Like Minnie, in her own way, Sarah was a bit of a snob, though she would be the first to deny it. She was perfectly conscious that her house, Number Forty-one, was at the good end of the street, and that she numbered herself among the thrifty and principled, unlike that widow up the road who was known to sweep the bits under the carpet, yet who always managed to appear in a new hat, even though she didn't have a penny to bless herself with. Such things were hard to tolerate, but it 'took all sorts'.

Unlike the houses at the other end of the street, hers and Minnie's houses had bay-windows. This distinctive feature was the more distinctive in Sarah's house for it was here she displayed a maiden-hair fern of head-turning proportions, that little trick she had of keeping the surface roots dampened daily. She would loop back her Maltese lace curtains, real Maltese lace and none of your cotton factory rubbish, to display her prodigy to advantage.

Moreover number forty-one was larger than the other houses in the street, having four bedrooms. This wasn't just snob value but essential since Sarah at one point, had to take in her dead sister Jessie's three children, in addition to her own nine. The obligation was double since her sister had married Henry's brother and both parents had died within weeks of each other with that terrible scourge, tuberculosis, which hit all too randomly, as Sarah was later to learn to her own family's cost. Fourteen people to feed every day, single handed, it was no wonder that 'the garden' was her haven of escape. Luckily Jessie's children were older than her own and sooner able to step out into the world, so the bulge had only lasted for eighteen months, yet managing everybody had been very tiring for a woman who was pregnant nearly every year. At one stage her husband Henry was advised by Dr. Maybury, to take a job in the West Indies 'to give Sarah a rest'. This accounted for a 'gap' in the ages of the children, which had been a great relief. Initially she had difficulty starting a family. She had six dead babies before she ever had a live one, after which nine came along. When taken with her final illness in her eighties the nurses discovered that she wore a leather strap between her legs, to prevent her uterus protruding. She never ever revealed this discomfort to a soul.

With such a large family the Humby's social life was restricted largely to the home, where kitchen, stairs and bedrooms burst equally with explosions of merriment and outrage. Someone was always borrowing someone else's 'things', and the only place for a bit of peace or privacy was Sarah's 'front-room'.

It was sacrosanct.

Here were all her porcelain and silver treasures, her reflecting crystal candlesticks and the piano. Apart from Czerny's musical exercises, waltz tunes and Gwenny's mezzo-soprano vocal practice, the front room was strictly a 'parlour' for talking with visitors, who were rare and with whom one balanced egg-shell-thin teacups of the best china along with the impedimenta of appliquéd serviettes and fancy plates. Father disliked going in there, but he had his own bolt- hole, the fernery. This was a very unusual feature and one which, again, added considerable prestige to the Humby's standing in the street. The fernery stretched from outside the living room, along past the kitchen window. It had shelves of pot plants, including a dwarf ornamental orange and a grape vine, whose fruit was small, hard and inedible, but whose fanlike leaves filtered the light magically through the glass. Henry had built it originally for Sarah in the earlier days when he had won a large lottery at the Oddfellows club which gave him cash enough to indulge his wife's whims, and which was later to enable him to split mortgages and acquire several small properties which he could keep in repair and rent. This was just as well, since after he was sixty he fathered the two youngest children and needed more cash than a dockyard pension would give him.

Dessa always remembered her father's wicker chair with its old cushion in the fernery. Here he was banished to smoke his pipe. Sarah hated the smell of smoke and tobacco in the house, and Henry liked to get away from the often shrill and argumentative female voices within.

Nothing really disturbed or worried him, in contrast to Sarah who minded about everything and who was fierce, sharp and powerful. She was certainly tough on the family, but she was also tough on herself. In the house she was a perfectionist. She washed, starched and ironed beautifully, fluting and crimping the bonnets and flounces with her goffering iron. She roasted huge joints in her oven, kept a stock pot simmering constantly with egg-shells in it for calcium. Always on Christmas day she fainted after serving roast goose and puddings made black with grated carrot to a family horde squeezed round the table on chairs and benches from all over the house.

It was from Sarah that Dessa inherited passion, drive and determination, and it was to Dessa that Sarah turned when she wanted the little ones taken off her hands on an afternoon or to Sunday school, or put to bed with a story. Dessa invented games, made paper houses, got everyone round the kitchen table at Christmas to create chains and silvery decorations. She had a 'way' with children.

Up at the garden she would take the little ones to fossick among the stones and seashells, and sometimes at low-tide her school-friend, Marie, from Horsea Island would come across the causeway, and they would all go out in a rowing boat. When it came to leaving school and thinking about a career there was no question but that she would be a schoolteacher. Marie's parents could afford to send their daughter away to a residential training college, but Dessa had to become a 'pupil' teacher rather in the same way as boys were apprenticed to a certified tradesman. She, with her lively personality and confidence, was actually sought after for the job. Mother was terribly proud of this 'educated' daughter, who, in her eyes, put her brothers and sisters into the shade.

Removing the large bag of beans from her basket, Sarah brought her bike in carefully through the front door, and set it round behind the coats and the steps to the cellar. She could hear the two youngest girls Daisy and Gwenny, giggling in the kitchen.

'I saw them again,' Daisy was saying to Gwen. 'Just by All Saints' church. I couldn't exactly hear what they were saying, and I didn't want them to see me. But he's got a really posh voice and kept smiling! Dessa was putting on her snooty look. I think I heard her call him "Neil."

THREE

Cora's and Dudley's retirement from Assam coincided with Neil's leaving school. He had passed his Senior Oxford exams adequately but didn't feel academically-inclined enough to go to University. This was shattering for Cora who had high hopes for her son, but Dudley persuaded her that Neil's best interests would be served by letting him choose his own career.

'It's his life, my dear, and he's the best one to find out what he's best suited to. Allow him to work it out for himself. He knows that we will help him all we can.'

Cora found inaction difficult, particularly since in those first months back in England she had been looking forward with relish to what she regarded as her necessary interest and advice on her son's every action. Used to keeping himself to himself, Neil behaved, according to her, in a 'secretive' way which frustrated her dreadfully. He was a seventeen-and a half-year old, an only child with elderly parents who had just set up house in a part of the world with which he was not at all familiar. No longer away at school he was isolated from his friends and out of kilter. From Neil's point of view his mother was as omnipresent as she was controlling and had no idea about the kind of things which interested the young. All the time he felt he was not living up to her expectations, and took himself off to escape her attentions.

Cora wrote to Ada, her only confidante, who was still in Assam for a few remaining months.

'We love the house and garden. Dudley has decided to have a hothouse built to raise orchids, which will be a great hobby for him, as he misses the green spaces of 'Tinkharia'. Just to re-assure you when you come home, you won't regret buying in Southsea, it has so much to recommend it and we are so looking forward to having you here with us, just around the corner! The south coast has a far milder climate than north Wales, which Mervyn favoured, so just as well you talked him out of that! You will be only five minutes from the sea, as indeed are we, and the sort of people we have met to date are rather 'our' sort, (if you know what I mean!) There is a first class railway service to Town and if you've time to spare there is nothing more pleasant than to take the little steamer over the water to Seaview from the newly-established, and very attractive South Parade Pier. They have an assembly room there, lovely for tea in the afternoon and there's always a string trio, so it's quite elegant. I can see us walking along the promenade, taking tea, watching the liners sailing to New York which, of course are on their way from Southampton. They put up notices to tell the public which ships will be sailing past, and at what times, according to the tides.

What else can I tell you? The shops. Well, they are excellent, if rather expensive, but then they have a good class clientele. As for household shopping, it's all delivered to the door, as you would expect. Ponton, the grocer, comes round on Thursday mornings to take my order, and it is delivered the same day, ready for the weekend. The vegetable man comes round with his cart, twice a week, as does an excellent fishmonger, and milk and bread are delivered daily. A bit of a change from our expeditions to Jorhat!

The only thing that's worrying me at the moment is Neil. He seems to be at a bit of a loose end. I make suggestions for him and urge him to come to the South Parade Pier with me, or to take a trip to the Isle of Wight, but nothing I suggest seems to please him. He's never impolite exactly, but he spends far too much time in his room or going for rides on his bicycle. Nor does he show any signs of making up his mind about what he wants to do for a career. My solicitor said he'd be pleased to take him for Articles, so that's a possibility which we are considering. It worries me that he keeps himself to himself too much and that he doesn't seem to come in contact with people of his own age. He did go and stay for a weekend with an old school friend, Julian, but he is off to Cambridge, and that means they are not likely to see much of each other in the future. To tell you the truth, I really hoped that Neil would go to Oxford or Cambridge. It does give you such a good start in life, but that wasn't to be. Neil doesn't seem to have any interest in that sort of thing. The only thing I'm having a bit of success with is getting him to join the Craneswater Tennis club. He's a pretty good player and it will make him meet people and gain confidence. It's a pity he's not more like your Celia, who is so resourceful and self-reliant. You don't know how lucky you are! If only Neil could be a bit more like her!

We both miss you and the months can't go by quickly enough until you retire. The naval officer and his wife who rent your property seem very nice, but I can't wait until you are here.

Give our love to...'

Yes. Neil was lonely. Yes, Neil did go for long cycle rides, sometimes taking his bike across the ferry to Gosport and Alverstoke, sometimes to Hayling Island, sometimes over the 'hill', Portsmouth's sloping chalk ridge, behind its island. He did try working in Thorndyke and Williams' law firm in King's road, but found the atmosphere and the people he worked with to be solemn, silent and slow, and couldn't think of anything worse than spending four years, (four years, Mother!) besieged by unreadable law books filling ledgers in his enviable copperplate writing, and tramping daily to the titles office.

After six months he told his parents that he really didn't feel suited to the law. Cora was embarrassed by this, because Mr.Thorndyke had been doing her a favour, and Neil, she had to face it, had let her down.

She felt an uncontrollable flush mounting her neck. She pursed her lips and breathed heavily.

'What, then? What do you like? Remember you can't keep chopping and changing. It's not a question of liking, but being prepared to stick at something. The law is a very good career. You're turning down an excellent opportunity.'

She harangued him in vain.

Neil went off on even longer cycle rides.

It was on one of these rides that he spotted a group of prep school boys under the charge of a young master, setting themselves up to play a cricket match. He stopped and watched. That was more in his line. He could do what that chap was doing easily enough. Yes. Teaching. He could be a prep school master. You didn't have to have qualifications. It wasn't particularly good pay, but it was quite a decent sort of life.

He mentioned his idea to his father.

Dudley, kind as ever, brightened at Neil's making a suggestion of his own. 'Sounds good,' he said. 'I'll have a chat with John. He knows about schools.'

As it happened Dudley's interest in orchids had caused him to make friends with Councillor John Courtenay, who lived just up the road. Besides doing his best to grow orchids, Courtenay was, conveniently, a member of the Portsmouth Education Committee. Having met the 'nice young man' and heard about his indecisiveness, he offered to help.

'Don't go in for teaching until you've got some real idea of what it entails. You've got to be cut out for it. A friend of mine runs a local Junior Boys' school. He's always glad of a bit of extra help. Try being a pupil-teacher for a term or two and you'll soon see if it suits you.'

Which was how, some weeks later, Neil found himself on playground duty at Seymour Road, Junior Boys' School, walking up and down, looking, he thought, au fait with his situation, whistle in pocket, enjoying the sunshine, but really rather oblivious of the constant scream-levels of playtime and the cavortings of the boys, who were running round insanely, or bouncing balls violently against the wall, or roughing each other up a bit, not always good humouredly.

Suddenly he was struck by a compelling voice.

'Please stop your boys throwing apple cores at my girls!'

The voice struck again, this time nearer.

Neil raised his eyes to confront the source of the trajectory issuing from the forbidden side of the iron railings. Instead of a tight-lipped, narrow-eyed schoolmarm stood an attractive young woman, challenging him, with, what he considered, looking back, to be a distinct sparkle of amusement in her expression.

'Isabel's been hit in the face. Her friend says those boys did it.' The voice, now reinforced with a forthright gesture, indicated a gang of ten year-old boys trying, with difficulty, to keep serious faces.

Neil had straightened up and advanced towards the group of four. He remembered trying to put on an official look.

'Is this true?' he had asked, rather pleased with the sound of his tone.

'They started it,' said one of the boys. 'They threw their apple core at us.'

'All we did was send it back,' said the boy next to him.

Except for Isabel, the girls were giggling and making the most of their supposed innocence. The boys were smirking.

'Away from the railings, all of you,' Neil now said with confidence in his newly acquired schoolmasterly voice.

'That goes for you girls, too,' said Dessa firmly, 'and pick up those two apple cores.

There's a place for rubbish over there.' She pointed to the bin.

The Junior- Girls' bell rang to seal the moment. Simultaneously the whistle blew on the boys' side, for line up. Silence reigned. It was death to talk in line for boys and girls alike.

Dessa looked back over her shoulder straight at Neil, and smiled dazzlingly. Neil never forgot that smile, nor could he ever get it out of his mind.

The next week after school, when Dessa was about to get on her bike to go home, she found she had a flat tyre. As she leaned her handlebars awkwardly between the railings, her string bag of exercise books fell out onto the pavement. Neil happened to be wheeling his bike out of the Boys' gateway at that exact time.

Bending down to retrieve her books, 'Allow me,' said a voice. Dessa looked up to see Neil gathering together her books for her. She stood up with surprise.

'Flat tyre,' she said.

'I'll pump it up for you.'

'Thanks, I can manage.'

But Neil had already produced his bicycle pump.

'I'll put enough air in it to get you home. Looks like a slow puncture,' he said.

'I've got a brother who'll fix it,' she replied.

Both stood up and looked at each other for a moment.

'Thanks,' and she had gone.

Neil's eyes followed her. The apple-core teacher. She didn't look old enough to be a teacher. To date any of the female teachers in the Junior Girls, of whom he had caught sight over the divide, were distinctly older, sterner, grumpier-looking or stared back at you under their eyebrows. This young woman, no, this girl, was fresh-faced, smiling, pert; she looked straight at you. Well? Everything and nothing about that. It was the way she had looked. In his mind's eye Neil kept seeing her as she looked back at him when the whistle went.

He found he was constantly on the lookout for her. Two or three days ago he had thought he had seen her hurrying, late, perhaps, to park her bike, to get to prayers in time. He didn't much care for the ritual of formal prayers in the morning, with the staff leading in the solemn-looking lines of boys, who stood to get a whack if they so much as coughed. Also he felt very self-conscious standing among the proper teachers' cohort and didn't quite know where to look when Mr. Banks sounded off twice as loudly as necessary, both to show off his own deep bass voice as well as to show up the puny attempts of teachers like himself who didn't sing very well, along with the meagre efforts of most of the mumbling, breadcrumb-voiced boys. He could only think of her. When he should have been considering 'Death's dark vale' he found his mind wandering off and in the middle of the Principal's reading of Isaiah, Chapter sixteen, about the daughters of Moab, he was wondering what might be going on behind the wall at the back which divided the boys' hall from the girls'. Was the headmistress reading the same passage from the Bible at the same time? Was she, like he, trying to focus on 'the lamp burning dim before the sacred ark'?

Prayers was followed daily by twenty minutes' Bible study followed by sums, geography, then playtime! Perhaps she, like he, would be on duty again.

He gulped down his tea and hurried outside where he slowed down not to look as if he was hurrying. Pacing the tarmac he deliberately walked diagonally from where she might be but all he saw was a disappearing grey skirt and boots which might only, possibly, have been hers. He had a stroke of luck a couple of days later when he had to fetch some sports equipment from the store and he spotted her among a group of girls who were all smiling at something she had bent down to tell them. They were looking at her admiringly, he could tell.

Meanwhile, although he would keep finding himself watching for her, he was seriously doing his best to see if he was any good at this job. At least he was another person around and could be a bit of help with this class of forty six, he tried to tell himself. Not that Mr. Lineham needed much help. He was impressive. One look through those spectacles and there was neither twitch nor breath in the room. Neil dreaded the moment when he might, despite all good advice, be left totally alone to keep order.

'Don't give them an inch, Mr.Langford. And don't ever turn your back. Boys will be boys, and in my class I can always hear a pin drop. Keep your distance too. The school nurse says there are enough nits in any one class to populate Africa.'

Neil smiled to himself at the thought of the effect this remark would have made on his mother. Her idea about his teaching was confined to private schools, prep schools with gold-braided uniforms in large houses with ample grounds. She had been distinctly sniffy when pupil teaching in a state school had been proposed, but Dudley had overcome her objections with the temporary nature of the venture and the good sense it made for Neil to take a look at teaching of any kind.

'He's brightened up a lot, doing this job,' said Dudley. 'He's always up early in the morning to be on time, and there's some structure in his life, at last, don't you think?' Cora admitted that, she, too, was surprised. Neil was always well into having his breakfast before they ever came down, and he certainly was far less morose than he had been.

As the days passed, Neil found himself whistling on his way to school. Instead of working out how many weeks it would take Tom to save up 2/6 if he saved at the rate of 3d per week he was thinking whether he would see...? Why, he didn't even know her name.

It was finally at the combined Junior School Sports in the park that he came to speak to her. Out of doors! The sky the limit! A sunny but fresh day. The park was green as only England can be green. The tracks had already been marked. Neil had instructions to measure the long jump, to organise the batons and the relay, and to fire the starting gun. These were things he was fully confident about, and when he spotted her at the trestle table which had been set up with cups of tea for the teachers and enamel jugs of water for the teams, surprising even himself, he held up his head and issued instructions in an unusually clear, precise voice.

Dessa looked up. She looked towards him. That was no common, ordinary Portsmouth voice, but a posh voice, the kind of accent used by her headmistress at the Secondary School and by posh people, and the vicar. Yes, that was the young man who was pupil-teaching at the boys' school, the one who had helped her with her bike. Yes, of course he had spoken to her then, but she had hardly noticed how he spoke, nor at the time was she specially interested. She wasn't at all smitten by boys, like some girls. Boys were no mystery to her. If she wanted to pick up a boy, she did, no trouble. It never occurred to her that there could be anything particularly interesting about this rather shy young man who didn't seem capable of keeping order in his own playground. Well, he had come on! He wasn't bad looking either! Slim. Thin-faced, tall, but not too tall.

She caught his eye and smiled!

Delighted, Neil nodded back.

Reinforced with excitement, he elaborated on his instructions and positively electrified the relay teams into action, emphasising the total importance of passing on the baton, and indirectly causing one of the runners to make a false start so they had to do it all over again.

The races were over. The cups had been presented. The team bands collected. The hurdles had been stacked inside a trolley. All the while Neil kept his eye on her, determined not to make his way back with the boxes of equipment until he saw her do the same. She was carrying the tea stuff in a large washing basket, and he caught her up. This was the chance he had been waiting for.

'Perfect day for it. The sports, I mean.'

(That accent again)

'The kids have had a good time.'

'So have I.' He looked at her and smiled. He was feeling venturesome, even a bit cheeky.

'No more apple-cores, I hope.'

She smiled. 'I really think it was the girls' fault. Tulip told me on the quiet that Joan did it on purpose. Girls are far from innocent you know.'

'I'm only just learning how to deal with boys!'

She gave him a sideways look, and flashed her eyes. 'I learned that a long time ago.'

'Would you think it rude of me if I asked you your name?'

Dessa smiled again. 'I was wondering when you would'

'And?'

'It's Dessa, if you must know, short for Odessa. My mother in a rush of blood called me after a Black Sea port.' She paused, 'Well?'

Neil took time to look at her. He saw the look behind her dark eyes, the depth of her personality, her poise.

'It's a nice name. Certainly an unusual one.'

'And yours?'

'Mine's Neil. Neil Langford.'

FOUR

'Hey, Dessa!'

Dessa turned her head to see who was calling, and recognised Neil cycling down Commercial Road, just as she was turning in from Peel Street.

'Neil!' She pulled over by the kerb and took one foot off the pedal to wait for him.

'Caught you up! I spotted you the other day, but I was too far back and a horse and cart got in the way. We can ride together!'

He had in fact been keeping his eyes skinned for Dessa once he realised that her journey to school was along this part of Commercial Road. To-day, Success!

'Okay!'

They pedalled along in silence. Dessa was in no hurry to make any overtures. Neil on the other hand was brimming up inside and not quite sure how to do the right thing.

'Are you enjoying school?' That, surely, was a pretty safe gambit.

'Wouldn't be there if I didn't. What about you?'

'Mmn. I'm just trying it out to see if I'm any good at it. There's a lot to learn.'

'It's common sense, surely.'

'Yes and no. Perhaps for you. You seem to have the knack, every time I see you with the girls.'

'I've had kids around me all my life.'

'That must help.'

Dessa laughed. 'Give the boys the strap and make the girls cry!'

'Seriously?'

'Seriously.'

By this time they were at the school gates.

'We should do this again,' he said. 'And I could ride you home from school.'

'Think I can't manage?'

He was a bit embarrassed. 'No. I mean—'

She softened. 'Perhaps.'

'Where do you live?'

'Where do you?'

'Southsea.'

His word dropped a bomb. Southsea! That was a posh area.

'Too far. Out of your way.' Dessa used the most dimissive of tones to cover up her social embarrassment.

'Still, we could meet at the corner, like we did to-day.'

'Why not? Now and then.' And she was gone.

In school that day Dessa kept turning over a number of thoughts, possibilities and prejudices.

Did she like him?

Yes.

What was it about him she liked?

He was different from the boys she knew in and around the streets where she lived and the friends her brothers brought home. His politeness, his gentlemanliness. The way he flushed slightly when he spoke to her. The accent. But now, Southsea! He lived in Southsea! She might have guessed. That made things difficult.

Used to being the king-pin of the family, used to feeling one-up among the less-fortunate inhabitants of Baker street, Nelson street and Charlotte street, suddenly having to confront social barriers raised by Neil in the shape of Southsea and Palmerstone Road gave her pause.

She was out of her element. She wasn't used to feeling out of control.

There was no question of his seeing her home. That would end everything.

She had already had to survive the scalds of snobbery from girls at the Secondary School and she had hated being made to feel inferior. 'Scholarship girl' they called her as an insult. Etched into her memory was that first day in her new school uniform, her family so proud of her for winning a scholarship, and she had suffered withering looks because her father was a 'tradesman' and her family too poor to pay fees. And where did she live? Mile-End. Well! She still smarted at the thought. Mile-End was a social stigma. She wished her family dead. Why was she so unlucky as to have been born in Malins road? Why wasn't her father a doctor, a lawyer or a professional of some kind! What luck! Why didn't her family, why didn't she, 'speak posh'?

Two girls were holding up their hands patiently, and she had been looking round her class without seeing anything, thinking defensively about herself and this very real social chasm. Finally her eyes focused. She gave the nod.

'I've got on too many stitches, Miss.'

Back to reality.

Mrs Lander, the widow of the black knick-knocks (schoolgirl joke, never proved) had put Dessa wholly in charge of the knitting class, and the room was stuffy with forty two pairs of knitting needles coping with spider stitch, making dish-cloths with cotton yarn. Dessa had already had the girls in pairs winding the unbleached skeins into special balls round their thumbs, a trick her mother had taught her to stop the balls being hard and tight. It was a great game to stick your finger into the hole and the kids loved it. She never had behavioural problems in her class, young as she was. The girls loved her, stayed behind after the bell went, vied with each other to carry her bag. No problems there.

Neil was a wholly different sort of problem. And she didn't know best how to manage herself. Yes. She wanted that sort of boy-friend, someone who would help her go up in the world, but how could she have enough confidence to bridge their social-gap and not lose face?

Another thought struck her.

What was someone like him doing in a place like Seymour Road Junior boys? He didn't belong. He stood out distinctly from the grey-suited, dour, jaded middle-aged male staff like a Christmas decoration among withering holly. The boys had already picked Neil's meek manner, how he was out of his element and a bit of a pushover. She could tell that instantly on the apple core day, by the way they smirked, and hadn't stood up properly as they certainly would have for Mr. Lineham. There was a whole lot she had to find out. Slow down, she told herself. Unfamiliar territory.

Mrs Lander came back into the room, glad for having had a quiet half-hour. She smiled appreciatively at Dessa. 'Everything all right?' Dessa nodded. School was fine. It was the Neil problem that wasn't fine.

The bell went. The class packed up for the day and each girl stood in the aisle by her double desk.

'Hands together. Eyes closed.'

'You say the prayer for us tonight, Miss Humby.'

'Thank you for the world so sweet...'

Looking back, that summer had been as sweet as it had been catalytic. Neil and she had fallen in love. Dessa was in no hurry to fall in love but where among her family and their friends would she be likely to come across an upper-class type?

For Neil it was love at first sight, for Dessa a slow, practical progression. She had to be sure of him. She wasn't going to be used. Her caginess was not merely coquetry. It was her class insecurities which made her play for time.

On the school day that ended early, he invited her to have tea. Tea! In a tea-shop!

'The Harlequin' in Cosham,' he said, 'it's run by a pair of rather unusual ladies. My mother's friend describes them as 'arty'. She goes there because they know about tea.'

Dessa had never been invited out to a tea-shop in her life.

'Why not?' She said, secretly rather pleased.

There were two or three occupied tables when they arrived, but a table in the window was empty, and Dessa wanted as much to be seen by passers-by, as to be interested in what was going on around her. A grey-haired lady, her hair in a bun and wearing a woven, hand-printed smock in shades of blue and purple, brought them a menu artistically hand-written on artistically hand-made paper.

'Scones with home-made jam. Sticky lardy cake. Gingerbread. French cream sandwich.' On the opposite side it said, 'Choices of Tea; Indian, Ceylon, Assam, Chinese.'

'Tea's tea,' said Dessa doing her best to look nonchalant. 'It's all the same to me.'

'That's where you're wrong,' said Neil, smiling politely.

Initially Dessa was taken aback. She sat up straight and blinked. Neil's spontaneous reaction put her in her place. She was used to being the catalyst of most conversations but Neil was now on his own ground. He had things to tell that she knew nothing about. What followed took her directly into Neil's background, to India, Assam, and 'Tinkharia', where he had been brought up. Another world!

Dessa's eyes were being opened; she didn't want Neil to know by how much.

'You probably drink Indian tea at your home, with milk. Assam tea is large-leafed and delicate. Milk spoils it in my view. Try some.'

Dessa wouldn't try, but she was definitely impressed.

⚶

Bit by bit she became more and more, sure of Neil. They met whenever they could, for picnics or for cycle rides together. Her defensive playing it cool increased Neil's ardour, and his pursuit gave rise to more and more meetings and deeper and deeper discussions. His experiences abroad captured her imagination, limited as she had been to a single visit to Mother's sister, Aunt Annie, a strong lady with three sons, who ran a pawn shop solo in East London, and a journey to Plymouth, by sea, which was hardly anything compared to sailing to India.

While Dessa's imagination had soared into saris and elephants, Neil, for his part was impressed by the practical fact that Dessa's going to sea was in a sailing boat borrowed and sailed by her father!

'Quite a rough sail, down past Portland lighthouse, and that rocky Dorset coast! Your father must know a lot about boats.'

'Course he does,' Dessa had replied 'He's not a shipwright for nothing! It's his trade. And I was the only one of my sisters who wasn't sick! We had to go because Father's brother died and the inheritance of the family farm in Devon had to be sorted out To get a wife and five children down to the west by rail cost heaps, so we sailed.'

The more Neil told Dessa about his ayah, his pony, his childhood, and the tea-garden, the more she was intrigued. She, who had never been away from her family ever, thought it was awful that he had been sent all the way back to boarding school in England, during which time he only saw his parents for a few weeks on one of their furloughs.

'Boarding school! Posh, perhaps, but I should hate it!'

'Normal,' Neil replied. 'Everybody did.'

'How terrible for you,' she said. 'Children need their parents.'

Neil, equally, was intrigued by the complexities of Dessa's large family. Her youngest brother was not much more than seven, while her eldest sister was married and nearly thirty. And there were so many of them without the three extra cousins. He wanted to meet them all and said so.

It was a Saturday and they had cycled all along the Southsea front to Eastney, where the road became a track and the grasses grew tall and coarse in the sand. The little ferry boat took them and their bikes over to Hayling Island, where they could be together, away from everybody, for Southsea 'front' was a formal promenade where people dressed up to impress each other, or sat in chairs, taking stock of the passers-by. At Hayling, you could lie on the jetty, mesmerised by the configurations of jelly-fish, or, better still, let your hair down in the dunes.

Dessa had.

Tucking up her skirts she had run full tilt, along the edge of the shallow waves. She had splashed herself, she had splashed Neil; she was a hooligan, dragging ribbons of brown seaweed behind her. He had chased her up the beach to the dunes, where she stumbled and fell laughing into the warm sand. He had wanted to kiss her very much but did not know how. He ached to kiss her. Her eyes dared him. Her laughter teased him yet the thought of touching her was too much.

Suddenly she stopped. The change made them both stand stock still and swallow. At that point he had stepped towards her deliberately and kissed her gently, sweetly, his heart overflowing.

Sand; spinifex; sky; flesh and breath dissolved. Their eyes spoke what tongues could not. Then she had kissed him. He could never forget. He had never before been kissed as she kissed him. Then she had grabbed her shoes and run off, leaving him stunned. They never spoke about what happened, but from then on, they were inseparable.

Dessa and Neil. Neil and Dessa.

Their thoughts and actions fused.

The weeks passed. They rode together to school. They met afterwards. Neither made an arrangement without the inclusion mentally or physically of the other. There were weekend expeditions, but the most ordinary things were now significant as long as they were shared. Neil was amazed how Dessa seemed free to do anything she liked.

'Your mother's a pretty go-ahead type, isn't she? If I had a sister I couldn't see my mother letting her out of her sight like yours does. My mother likes to govern the household. I guess it's all those years in Assam, being responsible for everybody, the workers and their families. She likes to know what's going on all the time. Now, I suppose, because she hasn't much to do, she's always wanting to know where I am.'

'And do you tell her?'

'Not always.' He smiled.

They had swum together and were lying on their towels in the sunshine, drying off. The sand sticking to them turned to fine blond grain between their toes. Dessa was lying on her back with her eyes closed, Neil, on his front, looking at her and thinking how relaxed and beautiful she looked.

'You'd never guess you're a schoolmarm.'

'What do I need? Horn-rimmed spectacles and a bun?'

'You don't act like one.'

'Should I?'

Neil stroked back the hair from her face.

'I really want to be one; a schoolmarm, as you call it. Mother's very proud of that. She never had any education to speak of.' She opened her eyes and sat up on her elbow. 'You see, my family isn't like yours. We're ordinary working people. Your family is,' she paused, 'well, different, richer, upper class. I feel embarrassed about it sometimes.'

'You! Not really! I can't believe that! That's stupid!'

'When I hear all about India, and you going to a boarding school and living in Southsea, well…. It's a fact. Why ever should you want to go out with me? You could have posh girl friends, girls who stay at home and help their mothers. Girls who don't have to work for a living. Social girls.'

Neil laughed. 'You're the one person I do want to go out with. It's such an amazing co-incidence that we ever met! I think about it every day. If I hadn't packed up that job in the lawyer's office... Well would I?'

'You'd have met someone else. Some one of your own class.'

'Stop all this 'class' stuff. It's only in your head. What difference does it make to us?'

'Nothing to me, but it might make a difference to you.'

Neil instinctively put his arms round her. 'I never think like that.'

Dessa looked serious.

'I mean it. I'm not like that.' He was lost for words. Feelings took over. Without any preamble or explanation he held her, stroked her, embraced her. She, equally, returned his kisses.

For Dessa those real insecurities which had haunted her gradually melted. The more she got to know Neil, the clearer it became that he found her special and loved her for herself. Class didn't enter into any of his thoughts. Softly she leaned her shoulders into his embrace, with relief and triumph.

She could feel safe, really safe. No barriers. For her this changed everything. When Neil asked to meet her parents and brothers and sisters she knew he meant it. He wanted to be part of a family, something he had never had, a family. Better still, her family. All of them.

He had looked straight into her eyes.

'I love you for what you are, not for what you're not, you silly.'

'Same.'

They had laughed together.

She gave him a huge hug.

The very next weekend she invited Neil home to meet everybody and mother insisted on getting out her Minton china.

FIVE

Neil sat smoking on his verandah, sipping a long whisky. In three weeks' time he would be setting off to meet Dessa. Full circle? Life begins at, -- well, in his case forty-three. After all those years! He patted his spaniel, Spot, lying at his feet. Beyond him lay his treasured garden, beyond that, disappearing down the slopes, the tea gardens, tiered and tended, and in the distance, the steeper foothills of the Barail Ranges. What would Dessa make of their life together here? How would she like the rambling bungalow, too full of his mother's large furniture which she had shipped out from England, when she had come into family money? He had grown up among these sideboards, linen presses and ancient desks, which he had moved from Tinkharia, when he had been made manager of Rituparna and then moved back again when he had been promoted to his father's original and larger garden. Sentiment; why not?

'Stuffy,' was Celia's comment when she first looked round. He smiled as he remembered that chapter in his life. 'Needs a woman's touch,' she had said. True, it did, but as it turned out not Celia's. To think that he had nearly married her! He snorted inwardly. On second thoughts that wasn't putting it correctly; she had nearly married him! How pleased his mother would have been! He and the incomparable Celia! And it would have happened but for......He paused. Well, he wouldn't be here now, about to make the journey down to Calcutta if he hadn't heard about Dessa.

Dessa.

What would Dessa do with it all, himself included?

He rose, strolled into the sitting room, the more sombre for its high-ceilinged darkness, in contrast to the light outside. This house, this place, was home to him far more than England had ever been, but, he reflected, that was before the war, and so much had changed since then, not least himself. And he needed a wife. The Company preferred their senior employees to be married. It was only the dearth of suitable people available, caused by the war, that had given him the opportunity to be put in charge of Rituparna unmarried and so young.

He had a very good idea of what his mother would be saying if she knew that he and Dessa had actually got together again after all that had happened. What a pity it was that she had never taken to Dessa. Hers, his, everybody's lives would have been totally different.

He strolled over to the mantelpiece and looked at a photo of Dessa and himself together, when he had last been in England. It had been taken on the beach at Bembridge in the Isle of Wight, back in 1934. They were both laughing and happy, leaning against an old rowing boat, with the lifeboat runway in the background. That had been a wonderful week-end. No children. Just each other, and it was soon going to be like that here, again.

Definitely no children. His only proviso.

He might have put up with the little girl, but certainly not the others. Besides they were at boarding school; nothing unusual about that. The two who made him feel wholly uncomfortable were Mo and

Austen, particularly Mo. It wasn't only the way they looked at him silently, or the way they went past him as if he didn't exist, he had actually heard their conversation accidentally, one afternoon, on one of his leaves. He could still hear that note of accusation in Mo's voice.

'First Uncle Morris and now him. We never come home without him here.'

'Uncle Morris is all right'.

'S'pose.'

'He bowls for you and chucks balls. Come to that so does Uncle Neil.'

'He isn't our uncle, that's the difference.'

Neil had never forgotten. He had felt very hurt. Now there wouldn't be a problem. He had waited and she had waited, and both the older boys now were safely at University, and able enough to look after themselves. Mo, apparently, had proved to be a brilliant linguist, and won an open scholarship at sixteen to an Oxford college. Austen, who had always felt intellectually inadequate in Mo's wake, had proved quite clever in his own right and won an exhibition in P.P.E. With both of them grown up, Dessa's and his new life was going to begin. Those eyes in the portrait he need never see again. That portrait over the stairs in Dessa's house. All that was over and done with.

He strolled out on to the verandah to drink in the wonderful view which had stayed much the same as he always remembered it over the years. Dessa would soon be making it her own, soon, at last.

Vikram, his house-'boy', who was in fact only five or six years younger than Neil had been with him since he was fifteen and now ran the whole household. They had a wonderful relationship. Too wonderful for some of the women in the club, but these small communities loved rumours and created gossip, equally, along with their care and concern for each other. Vikram had given Neil the support he needed not only when Dessa's terrible letter had arrived, and, to add misery to devastation, when his first spaniel, Gypsy, had disappeared without trace, never to be found.

That was all a long time ago, now, well behind him. At last, his life was going to work out as he wanted.

He lit another cigarette.

What a dreadful pity his mother had been so bitchy to Dessa! It could have all been so different.

He strolled across the verandah and moved into his garden. Everything was going to change now.

In a way, he reflected, it was his fault for being the kind of person he was, and not what Cora, his mother, had wanted him to be. He had drifted through school and had disappointed her time and again. Never a prefect, never a House Captain, never anything that 'counted', in her eyes. She had never been able to accept him for himself. He wasn't the sort for University, he was bad at making up his mind. In her eyes he had 'no ambition', unlike Celia. How often had he heard that!

He remembered the endless cut and thrust between Ada and his mother. Cora's long-time closest friend, never missed a chance to salivate about her own Celia's success, which was anathema to his mother. How ironic that he had nearly ended up marrying her!

Celia, the popular Celia, was a girl with aplomb. Celia was the kind of girl who knew exactly 'what was what', as his mother frequently told him. During those first months in Southsea, she had never stopped telling him how he ought to get out to meet people, people 'of his own class'. Look how well Celia had done for herself, meeting all those interesting and important families connected with friends at finishing school! In comparison, what his mother none too silently considered to be his own dreadful inadequacies, continually worried and irritated her. To make things worse, she had to put up with Ada's litany of Celia's triumphs. Ada! He could see Ada now, small, smug and ebullient, sitting among the chintz cushions in the morning room of 103, St. Stephen's Road, telling his mother how Celia was out and about with people who were 'very high-up'. She had made friends with

Fleur, the daughter of the British Consul in Rome, and was to spend the holidays there.

And what could his mother say about him? That he had got a temporary job, trying himself out as a pupil-teacher.

Ada never actively denigrated Neil's preliminary efforts in working in a state primary school, but she hadn't been interested or impressed. Cora hadn't been impressed either, but at least she thought that Ada might have acknowledged that Neil was at last trying to do something. Cora resented 'that snide side of Ada', she told Dudley, which enjoyed doing her best to make her feel inferior.

'I can always see through her oblique forays,' she complained, 'which are wholly unkind and unnecessary, when you think of all the things I've done for her. I know what she's getting at. She's always making comparisons between Celia and Neil. She never misses an opportunity to point out how her Celia is going up in the world, hardly disguising the fact that Neil isn't.'

Neil didn't need much imagination to see how his mild and supportive father would do his best always to smooth his mother's disappointment. He could hear his voice, trying to calm her down.

'Don't make yourself miserable by reading too much into Ada's way of talking, my dear,' Dudley would reply, trying to mollify her. 'Think of Neil. He's doing very well. He's been a changed boy since he took up at that school. You've said so yourself.'

It was at this point that Neil introduced Dessa to his parents.

How excited he had been! Dessa, lively, fun, special to him in every way! His mother would surely be impressed that he had found a young woman of her calibre!

Alas! From his mother's point of view he had allowed himself to get tied up 'with a no-body'. Cora so badly wanted something which would impress Ada, and what did she get? A working-class girl from Mile End, 'of all places'.

Cora was full of frustration and disappointment. Not because Dessa wasn't lively or attractive or bright, but because she was.

People from her social class in Cora's mind, had no right to claims of any kind; it showed presumption. Neil smiled to himself as he remembered. Humby by name but not by nature! Inadvertently Dessa had added wholly to his mother's chagrin on account of her natural self-possession, outward-going temperament and sense of humour. Had she been a mousey, quiet, dependent schoolmarmy type, needing support of the kind of special understanding only his mother could give, Cora might actually have liked her.

So sad and so stupid that Dessa's own keenness to meet his parents and to be a success with them had been fouled from the start.

Their meeting had come about through the Tennis club's under twenty-one mixed doubles tournament. How intrigued Cora had been when he told her that he had entered! She had blinked her eyes very fast and had pursed her lips into a little smile, as she always did when she had something special to announce, or got excited about something.

'Mixed doubles? Did I hear you say 'mixed doubles' darling? Well you are a dark horse! Dudley, did you hear that?'

But Dudley hadn't worked out what she meant and Neil had had to explain it all to them both as they sat round the dinner table.

'A young lady! How exciting, Dudley! Did you hear that? Neil's found a partner for the tournament! A young lady!'

Dudley widened his eyes.

Cora couldn't stop.

'You must invite her to tea, so we can meet her. That would be nice, don't you think so Dudley? On Sunday. A young lady! Where did you meet her? What kind of family does she come from?' She had smiled her widest kind of smile. 'Presumably she's good at tennis!'

'She loves tennis. She was in her school tennis eight. We've been having a few hits at Alexandra Park after school in the evenings.'

'So that's where you've been! All this time, and to think I was quite worried about you!'

Then the questions had poured out.

'How long have you known her? Where did you meet? We don't like to pry, do we Dudley? But we guessed something was up, didn't we Dudley! Well not your father exactly, but I guessed because ---well, mothers know about these things, and ever since you took it into your head to consider teaching you've been a different person. Where did you meet her? What is her background?'

'She was working in the Junior girls' school,' he had told her. 'She still is. She gets her teaching certificate at the end of next year.'

'A teacher?'

'Yes.'

'Oh.'

There had been a slight pause.

'Well! Dudley, what do you think of that! We would like to meet her as soon as we can.'

That Sunday Neil remembered feeling pleased, happy and proud to be introducing Dessa to his parents. He met her at the bus stop by the Canoe Lake, and she was looking summery and particularly fetching in a blue linen skirt, a flowery cotton blouse, and a large straw hat with a blue ribbon round it, not like the proverbial teacher at all.

'They're sure to like you,' Neil had been saying in response to her questions. 'They both played tennis in India and they're delighted about the tournament. They are going to come along and watch.'

By this time they had reached St. Stephen's Road, where the houses were large Victorian semi-detached impressive buildings with mullioned windows, steps up to a porch-way and a grand front door. Dessa had opened her eyes wide and smiled.

'Grander than I thought!' she exclaimed. 'Bit of a contrast with Malins Road!'

He squeezed her hand. 'So what!' he whispered in her ear.

The hallway was square and panelled, with a parquet floor and Indian rugs. There were two dark portraits on the wall facing the entrance, whose pictures, Dessa was to learn later, represented Cora's mother and father. A wide solid oak staircase with a carved banister rose to the floors above. A door to the right opened, and Cora, neatly dressed in a formal grey dress with a high neckline and a cameo brooch at her throat, emerged erect, hand extended to meet Dessa.

'Introduce us, Neil.'

Dessa had thought the formality a bit unusual, she told Neil afterwards, but he had warned her that his mother was 'old-fashioned'.

They had proceeded into the drawing room. Dessa's eyes opened wide again at the massive gilt mirror over the fireplace. Then her eyes had widened still further, but more with amusement than anything, for there stretched on the floor, flat, but for its raised head and open mouth, baring ferocious un-drawing-room-like–fangs, was a tiger. He had forgotten to tell her about the tiger! Neil laughed to himself as he remembered Dessa's feigned astonishment. He'd had that tiger round him as long as he could remember! People who had lived in India went in for that sort of thing.

'Is that to keep the evil spirits away?' she had asked.

'Cora wanted us to bring him back with all the other stuff,' said Dudley, rising, smiling, to greet her. He indicated an elephant's foot table and a row of ebony elephants in diminishing size on the mantelpiece. 'You can't come back from India without a few trophies, can you Cora? See here, that's our bungalow.'

'Tinkharia?'

His father was pleased at Dessa's knowing the name.

'I've told her all about it,' interrupted Neil.

'It looks wonderful,' said Dessa. 'How many years were you there?'

'Best part of a lifetime,' replied Dudley.

'You must have had a very exciting life. To me everything that Neil has described has sounded thrilling. All that travelling, so far away! The furthest I've ever been is Devonshire. Father hired a sailing boat and sailed us there himself.'

'He sailed a large boat single-handed, with all the family,' added Neil, keen to impress.

'Oh, so you sail!' Cora, gratified, was keen to take over the conversation.

Having a private yacht was something she approved of.

Dessa had laughed. 'Not exactly! That's an extravagant sport for the rich! No, Dad's a ship's carpenter, or was. He's retired now. He knows all about boats, and it was the cheapest way to get the family back to the farm, when his brother died. I've often thought how lovely it would be to be a passenger on a liner. Sailing to India must be so luxurious!'

Cora's affability started to diminish at this point.

Dudley, however, was obviously taken with Dessa and her friendly, easy manner, and Neil was pleased to see how well she and his father were getting along. He knew how much Dudley liked thinking back to his past. He'd certainly sailed to India and back a few times.

'The Canal made all the difference,' his father went on. 'Cut down the journey by four thousand miles. That's a long time at sea, I can tell you. And remember, when you get to Calcutta, it's a heck of a long way by rail to Jorhat, and then you're still not there.'

Cora, sidelined by this conversation, was itching to take over, but Dessa was talking again. This girl wasn't backward in coming forward.

'It must have been difficult leaving such an interesting life and coming back to England to live in a,' she sought about for an appropriate word, 'an ordinary sea-side town. Apart from the Navy,' she added.

'You have to retire sometime,' Dudley had said, nodding. 'Cora's choice, but we're both happy to be here, aren't we, my dear? I've got my greenhouse and orchids. I'd be lost without those. You must come and take a look at them.'

'I think my mother must be a bit like you,' went on Dessa. 'She has a fernery with a grape vine, but she also grows prize-winning chrysanthemums and heaps of vegetables on her allotment.'

At the word 'allotment' Cora had made a noise which could have been compared to a cough. She half covered it up by suggesting they all sit down. Neil hadn't properly noticed, because he was so keen to show his parents what a splendid girl he had managed to meet, but Dessa felt instinctively that Cora was less interested in her mother's gardening skills, than shocked to think her family didn't have their own proper garden and told Neil so, afterwards.

'Well, shall we all sit down?' invited Cora for a second time. Usually used to making the running she had been put out a little by Dessa's initiating conversation and 'not being in the least bit shy', as she told Ada, later.

They were no sooner settled into armchairs than she made it clear that she was taking over.

'Dessa you must tell us all about yourself.'

Neil had felt worried that his mother would start a third degree cross examination and sure enough she was. This hadn't worried Dessa in the least, because she was used to being the sort of girl people liked, although from the first she sensed that Neil's mother had not taken to her.

At this point Ellen had brought in the tea on a trolley. Silver teapot, a spirit kettle, Coalport china, dainty embroidered napkins, all very impressive. Dessa was just about to say how much her mother would love the cups and saucers, when she realised she knew Ellen, she told Neil afterwards.

Naturally she spoke, and wholly spontaneously.

'Ellen Hollins! I had no idea this was where you were in service! Hello! What a coincidence!'

'Well I never! Dessa Humby!'

'It's a lovely house to work in,' Dessa had said to Ellen, pleased to be friendly.

Cora's face had tightened and Neil had caught his mother's expression. No explanations afterwards about Dessa's father being the Hollins' landlord could assuage her 'embarrassed' disapproval. He saw his mother close her eyes for a moment and he read her thoughts. His tennis partner, a friend of their maid! Something she could never tell Ada.

On the way back to the bus stop Dessa had said plainly, 'Your mother doesn't think I'm good enough for you. All those questions about my family, and where we live. Your father, well, he's different. He likes me. And I like him. But, I have to say it. I think your mother despises me and is a snob.'

Neil had tried to assuage the protest in vain. Cora and Dessa had got off to a bad start, and, as Neil always admitted, through no fault of Dessa's own.

Neil thought back, regretfully The pity of it. It could have been so different.

Over the years it worsened. In Neil's eyes what were to him Dessa's special talents and charm, were, increasingly, anathema to his mother. She would turn in her grave if she had guessed that he and Dessa were at last to marry after broken engagements and all those years of mess, anguish and heartbreak.

And the tennis tournament! Not even their success in the tennis tournament had helped improve Cora's attitude. Neil and Dessa had been among the youngest in the competition. Dessa had done wonders at net, and her strong, low forehand scored nearly every time. Amazingly, they had got to the finals, surprising themselves to have done so well. Neil hoped that at least this success might give his mother something to redeem herself with Ada, but it was never enough to improve relations between the two chief women in his life.

Alas! He realised that he had got himself the kind of girl who turned the heads of everyone except his mother.

SIX

'He still doesn't see through her,' Cora told Ada. 'What is it about men? Women can run rings round them.'

'Pity. Great pity.' Ada smiled irritatingly, with a self-satisfied smile. She was carefully removing the cherry from her cake and nodding approvingly at the bow flourishes of the intense female 'cellist. They were taking tea together as they often did in the tea rooms of the South Parade pier, where afternoon tea on Wednedays and Saturdays was elevated by the efforts of a string trio from among a forest of potted palms.

'It's two years now.'

'More tea?' Ada was humming. 'I love this one, don't you? Percy Elliot. "A Toi."'

'Infatuation. Not love.' Cora, persistently, was referring to her continuing frustrations with Neil and not at all to the strains emanating from the podium.

Ada shook her head gently as she nibbled at the cherry. 'Who can say?'

The trio had paused for applause. Cora frowned involuntarily as her friend raised both hands high in front of her face, tapping her right fingers gently onto the palm of the left, ostensibly to indicate her pleasure with the music, although Cora knew perfectly well that this was Ada's means of establishing her presence. Ada always 'showed off' and on this occasion Cora had little patience with her because she wanted her to focus wholly on her, Cora's, continuing predicament.

'She changes jobs. He follows. First it was that Prep school. I had hopes that he might meet a young matron on the staff there, or a suitable girl of some social standing, but no. And now of all things he's got himself a different job at Petersfield, even further away.'

Ada was trying to catch the waitress's eye and was refusing giving Cora her full attention. 'Oh dear,' she said with little conviction, 'what is it this time?'

'He's working for an estate agent.'

'Business? That's a step in the right direction, surely? There's a future there.' Ada widened her eyes knowingly. 'Especially with a bit of capital.'

'Over my dead body if he's counting on me.' Cora drew her skirt firmly across her knees. 'As long as he's tied up with her, I'm not interested.' Her mouth shut tight and small.

The string trio had disappeared for their break. Glancing around, Ada could see no-one of any real interest at the other tables. Time, now, for her to expand on Celia's successes.

'Such a shame you have all these worries with Neil. I'm so lucky. Celia's always in such great demand. You know she's been teaching etiquette at Madame Vehrnes, well now she's on the brink of getting a very sought-after hostessing job in Paris, her French is so good. Madame Vehrnes is begging her to stay.'

While this conversation was in progress, Cora's unfathomable son, Neil, was lying on the grass by the Meon River enjoying the watery sounds rippling below its banks. He was not alone. Dessa, the unsuitable Dessa, was lying close by. For both of them it was a day off. The sun was shining. Her arm was crooked under her head. She was letting out a breath in protest, half smiling and opening her eyes.

'You've asked me that before.'

He had broken into her reverie.

He persisted.

'Why don't we?'

'We don't need to.'

'I need to.'

'We're too young.' She shut her eyes.

'You're not listening to me.'

'I am.'

'We're not too young. You're twenty two, nearly.'

'So?'

'We love each other.'

'Yes.' Dessa gave Neil a sly, amused look and stroked his arm.

'I want to be sure of you.'

'You are sure of me. Anyway, what has love to do with engagement? Engagement has to do with marriage.'

He looked down at her with his very blue eyes and said nothing.

'Well?' she teased, 'what has it?'

'You know as well as I do.'

'But now? To get engaged? It's not going to prove anything. It's not as if we don't see each other a lot.' She propped herself up on her elbows, looking at him through half-closed eyes.

'Yes, but...' He was thinking about her bed-sit above the ironmonger's shop, the rag rug. It's story. Their story.

She read his thoughts and traced her fingers softly down the back of his neck.

'Neil, darling, you have to be sensible. Getting engaged means you're seriously considering marriage. Marriage is a contract. It's about houses and settling down and money. Be practical. You earn even less than I do. If we get married I have to give up my job. Teaching rules are No Married Women. Only widows, remember? My seventy five pounds a year would be sorely missed. It's not as if your mother is likely to help out if you marry me! Now's not the time to start an engagement. You've only been a few months in your new job and they pay you a pittance!'

'I'm not saying get married now. I'm just saying let's get engaged to make me feel I've got something to work for. I've only taken this job at Petersfield to be near to you.'

She gave him a hug and laughed.

'A ring's not going to make any difference to us. You know that. We're having a great time, away from our families, doing what we like.' She hugged him again. 'Come on, I'm starving. 'Let's get something to eat, and we can spend the rest of the afternoon back in my room.

He looked at her quizzically.

'Relax! The Macdonalds are away visiting.' She gave him a knowing look and pulled him up from the grass. 'Our day off. Let's make the most of it.'

They got on Neil's motor-bike, Dessa riding pillion. Neil's total pleasure was zooming to West Meon from Petersfield at weekends, when they would meet up to have picnics, go for walks, and yes, that, as well. That, especially.

Dessa's bed-sit was right in the middle of West Meon over 'Macdonalds, General Ironmongers.' She had been teaching in the village school for eighteen months, lodging with the family, but with a room over the end of the shop, its access up an outside wooden staircase. The Macdonald family liked Dessa and she, them. She made her own breakfast, but had a cooked midday dinner with them on days when she wasn't on duty. She also took her weekly bath with them, 'en famille' on Friday nights in the large tin bath got down for the occasion onto the stone floor of the scullery. Grandmother went in first, then the two children, 'then me, because I'm a visitor,' she had written to Neil.

'Mrs Mac keeps two large preserving pans on the boil on her stove, and at intervals, with a dipper, ladles out some of the cold water, to fill up with hot. You should see us all, in the big family room by the fire, our heads wrapped up in towels or brushing wet hair for each other. When Mr. Macdonald goes in, the kitchen door is firmly shut, but the hot soapy water invariably makes him break into song in his deep bass voice, and we can't stop laughing to hear where 'his caravan has rested', or 'silver threads among the gold.' Then Mrs Macdonald brings us all hot cocoa and date and walnut cakes! They really have taken me into the family, which is lovely, and the school is right over the road. It couldn't be better.'

Dessa's letters punctuated Neil's week. She enjoyed describing everything to him and she wrote so naturally, it was the next-best-thing to being with her.

As for her job, it wasn't easy at first, because she had to get used to having the headmistress sitting at her desk up the other end of the 'hall' where she taught. 'Try that!' she wrote. 'I call her "Hawk-Eye" because she watches everything! She pops up every five minutes to say "we don't do it like that here." I realised pretty early on I had to suck up to her and the other two old biddy teachers, neither of whom were keen to accept someone young, (underlined) from the town, (underlined). But that's all past history. A few voluntary chores, running a stall in the church fete, singing in the church choir and they're all as nice as pie.' Then, just to tease Neil a bit she added, 'Even the curate has taken a fancy to me, but don't get worried, he's gangly and spotty, not nearly as handsome as you and not my type at all, (the 'not' was underlined twice.)

The letter then went on to tell him at great length, how she enjoyed her room. What luxury! Having a room to herself, after sharing a house with so many siblings, really mattered, 'something you, probably, can't understand.'

It's large, really large, compared to the bedroom in Malins Road where three of us shared, two in the double feather bed, three, sometimes. You only graduated to the single bed if someone like Maud quarrelled with mother and moved out! Now I have my own washstand, not cluttered up with Maud's bits of cucumber and olive oil (beauty aids) but you wouldn't know about that! The black iron bed creaks a bit and goes down in the middle, (but there's always the hearthrug!) I've got a desk under the window, a rounded padded armchair, a bow-fronted chest of drawers and a cupboard in the wall. It's bliss!'

Originally it had been the idea of a room to herself which had persuaded Dessa finally to move away from Portsmouth. Despite all Neil's agonised protestations she had taken up the offer of a job as governess with Colonel Parson's family. That had been a room! A grand room in a grand old manor-house built of soft, ancient red brick and flint. Rich people were lucky. The house stood in its own spacious grounds, with tall woody cedar trees emphasising the curving drive. Another attraction had been the pony and governess cart, but it was the room, mainly, which had decided her to take the job, that, and the need to get away from the same old places where she had lived and worked all her life. It wasn't that she didn't enjoy being with the family, exactly, but she was young, she felt confident, energetic and adventurous, and there was no rush for love.

Neil could never quite understand how much she needed new experiences. He did not want to be separated from her at all. She on the other hand had not been anywhere.

'Darling can't you see you'll be too far away from me. I want you nearer. I'm trying to see it as you do, but I'll be stuck in Southsea and you'll be out in the country and we'll never get to see each other.'

But there was no holding her, she was determined.

'Bishop's Waltham isn't very far. Of course we shall get to see each other. If we're to have a future it's not just me you should be thinking about, but you. You've got to think of your career. You're not facing up to things. Are you going to be a teacher? Do you want to be a teacher? If you really do you'll have to go away to Exeter to get a proper training. Your parents can afford it, and you're not too old. Good heavens! I'd have given anything for a chance to go away to a proper training college! You don't know how lucky you are!'

Neil looked down and picked a hair off his sleeve. Two years away in the West country and Dessa could so easily meet someone else. She was attractive, vital; he couldn't risk it. What could he best do?

Ada, of all people had come to the rescue. Her eagle-eyes had spotted an advertisement in 'The Times' for a 'live-in house tutor, teacher of younger boys and sport at all levels' at a prep school. Applications to the Headmaster, Julian Lloyd-Jones, M.A.Oxon.'

'How's that?'

She had dropped in for her usual morning chat, this time, newspaper in hand.

'I was about to throw it away when it caught my eye, quite by chance! Just the thing for Neil, I thought, after all you have been saying. This will get him away from you know who, with her up in the country in one direction and him in another. Why, he might even meet a nice young matron , or a boy's sister, someone more of his own class!'

Cora had been delighted. Ada was a good friend who understood her problems. If Neil could get this job he would be in a different milieu, and 'this', meaning Dessa, could all 'blow over'. Such things apart, it was definitely a step forward. It was a good prep school. She sat back in her chair, blinking her eyes at this new prospect. Through the window Dudley's terraced garden was looking exceptionally attractive this morning, and, she noticed, Ada was wearing the new skirt she had bought her for her birthday. A stroke of luck at last! What relief! And there was something at the back of her mind. The name of the school. Yes! Something really positive. St.Bartholemew's! Of course. It rang a bell! Hadn't Ada remembered that Judith's two nephews had boarded there? The boys wore a distinctive dark green and gold uniform and boaters. If only Neil would do his best to apply for the position! She would draw his attention to the advertisement with casual tact.

Ada and she exchanged mutually significant glances. They indulged in second cups of coffee in anticipation.

Unbeknown to his mother Neil was as keen to get the job as she was keen for him to get it. From his point of view the prep school was near Havant, far enough away to escape Cora's interference yet close enough to Bishop's Waltham to see Dessa.

Qualifications? In privately owned prep schools the best qualification was being a 'good chap' a public-school type 'who knew the ropes'. From Julian Lloyd-Jones point of view a candidate without qualifications was an advantage. The new man would be at his mercy and couldn't claim top-bracket pay. Neil was ideal. He spoke the King's English, he looked a gentleman, and was young enough to do plenty of dog's body jobs as well as being suitably 'sporty'. He had references from own housemaster, Roger Carter, whom he, Julian, remembered from Oriel College. They had been in the same year, as well as in the same rugger team. The deal was done.

Cora was overjoyed.

If Neil was starting a new job in a new place, she didn't doubt but that all the nuisance business with Dessa would soon blow over. Definitely 'a step forward', she remarked to Dudley. 'It was high time Neil started to create a proper future for himself. St. Bartholemew's couldn't be better.'

'If that's what the boy wants, then that's fine,' Dudley said.

'He's showing a bit of determination at last,' remarked Cora with relief.

For Neil the ironies of his new job were multiple. Freedom and imprisonment at the same time.

'Darling it is so difficult to meet! Your days off and my days off hardly ever coincide! Old Lloyd-Jones is as mean as hell. Saturdays are full on with classes and matches and boarding house evening duties, and on Sundays there's only about a couple of hours free in the afternoon after morning chapel and a horrible mid-day formal Sunday dinner and I'm hardly ever getting to see you.'

Those weren't Neil's only troubles. At this stage he hadn't even considered the hazards Dessa's own job might create.

Initially she was as pleased with her new position as he was fed-up with his.

'Stop moaning, darling. It's because it's all new. Be patient.' She was enjoying herself.

Her room was 'beautiful and historic'. Mrs. Parsons was gentle and frail and 'never interfered'. Tristan and Lucy were adorable. She was getting a taste for 'county' living! The manor house had a stunning library, which she was free to use, also two nights each week she had formal dinner with the family in their splendid dining room.

The only trouble proved to be the Colonel himself.

A young, dashing, dark-haired woman flashing energetically about the place could not be resisted.

'He, what!' Neil had exploded. 'More than once!'

'Don't worry, I can handle him,' Dessa re-assured. 'But if his attentions don't stop. I'm leaving. Such a shame! No wonder the last one only lasted five months! I love the children and Mrs. Parsons, but I won't have his hot breath in my ear at the end of every dark passage and I've told him so. Poor lady, married to a randy bastard like that!'

She left after three months, with two extra months' money.

Neil presumed that after her experiences with Colonel Parsons Dessa would want to fly back to Malins Road, but not Dessa. Before he could get over the shock of that man, that old man, assaulting his girl, his Dessa had already taken another job, this time even further away.

'Dessa No! Not West Meon!' he exploded. 'There isn't even a railway and there are only two buses a week!'

'Neil, darling, it isn't as if time and distance will make any difference to us! We've got each other. But we've also got to make our way in the world. This is only a tiny bit of our lives.'

'But, West Meon!'

'Be practical! Remember I'm the one who has to be there and do the job, and I shall enjoy the experience. It's the best on offer. I like the country and the village and the only other alternatives are Alresford, which is miles away, or coming back to Fratton, which I would hate. Be reasonable.'

'I am being reasonable. You've got your certificate and can pick and choose where you work, whereas I haven't. I'm stuck at Bartholemew's. The chances of me finding another prep school nearer to you aren't great. I don't like you being so far away.'

'Being in West Meon won't stop us writing, silly. I love your letters. Neil, it's not for ever. Don't spoil our times together by arguing. Kiss me.'

He kissed her.

'More.'

They made love in the dunes.

'Slowly,' she said. 'Relax. Slowly. Not so fast.' She, smoothed his shoulders, made him lie on his back, gently stroking away his anxieties and tensions.

Renewed and made whole he lay on the sand, thinking. They both lay in silence together, looking up at the sky, the wisps of cloud, hearing the gulls.

Raising himself on his elbows and looking straight into her eyes, he brushed the sand from her hair. He stirred, hesitated, and stirred again. A slight smile moved across his face. 'I've been thinking,' he said. He sat up fully, still fixing his eyes on her.

'If the mountain won't go to Mahomet, Mahomet must go to the mountain.'

'Meaning..?' She queried, through half-closed eyes.

'I've an idea,'

'And?'

Neil's ideas were often charming, delightful, but not very practical.

'Guess.'

'I can't guess.'

'Guess what I'm thinking. You'll like it.'

'Hmn.' She stretched and folded her arms under her head.

'What? Tell me.' She was waiting for the sky to fall in.

'I'll get a motor bike.'

From comatose to sparkling eyes and a huge grin in a moment! Dessa flung her arms around him. 'A motor bike! What fun!' She hugged him violently.

He kissed her, but she was too excited to be kissed. 'I can ride pillion! You can zoom up to West Meon in no time! You see! I knew there would be a solution!'

The spontaneous idea of a motor bike contrasted heavily with the reality of buying one. Saving up on the pittance Julian Lloyd-Jones paid Neil when nearly half his so-called salary was deducted for 'board' was not a quick process. Increasingly Neil found himself getting fed up. The more the Headmaster hailed him with smiles and praise, for winning the cricket against Medhurst, or for painting the scenery for the school play, the more he seemed to load him with extra responsibilities. In the boarding house he was at the mercy of Matron and the Housekeeper, both perfectly nice, middle-aged women but they, in turn, loaded him with requests he found hard to refuse. Would he 'keep an eye' on a boy in the sick-bay, would he sort out some terrible 'tuck' mix-up; it was never-ending.

He was taking prep one evening in the stuffy dining room which smelt equally of 'boy' and the evening's kedgeree, when suddenly an idea came to him.

Action. Take action! Simple! Do something! It was up to him to do something about his increasing malaise!

He didn't have to stay at this school.

St. Bartholemew's could manage perfectly well without him. And was he cut out for teaching?

Those grubby exercise books, those sad little boys, as he himself once had been, that bullying, toneless, obtuse ruffian, Fitzgerald. Sure he enjoyed the sport, but all the rest! Most members of the staff were bachelors and that was the last thing he wanted, to be stuck in the staff room, smoking, complaining, tied to the notice board, his life governed by lists and chalk, and fighting for the newspapers. He could find another job. First things first! Dessa was his life and he hardly ever saw her, tied down in this job. The only snag was that he was paid terminally and he would have to stick it out for a bit longer. But then!

'I thought you were happy here' the head told him when he gave in his resignation. 'What is it about St. Bartholemew's that you don't like? I should like to know.'

'It's not the school, Sir. It's private reasons.'

'And I can't persuade you otherwise? A rise in salary, perhaps?' He cast a sidelong look at Neil.

'No Sir, thank-you. I have plans.'

Neil was amazed at his own self-possession, his determination. There, he had done it! Dessa was even more amazed when she received the weekly letter in his steady, regular, copperplate hand, telling her the news.

'You should have seen the expression on his face when I told him that I thought there were alternative lives to Bartholemew's! He was 'disappointed in me', was how he put it. He was the one who was disappointed. He'll have to find another dog's body. The worm has turned!'

Neil's usual letters were predictably gentle, loving and sometimes wry, but there was nothing predictable about this one! Neil was suddenly springing into life!

'Mahomet's mobilising fast' he wrote. 'I shall get a job in Petersfield come hell and high water!' And he did.

Lying back on her chaise-longue on board 'The Britannia' Dessa remembered everything. She remembered Neil's surprising and sudden decision to get out of teaching. Thinking back, he had only probably gone to St. Bartholomew's in the first place because of her and now, because of her, he was changing jobs again. What, this time?

Butler and Cooper were Estate Agents, and how useful the motor-bike was, in this, Neil's new job around farms and country properties. She still had an old sepia photograph of 'The Enfield', Neil sitting astride, grinning, one foot on the ground! What fun they had, swooping along country lanes, skidding through puddles, she, learning from experience not to burn her calves on the exhaust pipe! How old were they then all those years ago? In their early twenties, carefree!

A hundred thoughts could whirl through the memory in seconds. Dessa found herself smiling, relaxed, at one with the throb and motion of the ship. What a contrast with that ghastly journey back to England from Port Elizabeth! No. Not that. She wasn't going to spoil this ocean sunshine and the welcome cocooning of this long sea-journey with crippling memories of the past. She massaged her arms and the backs of her hands with coconut oil. She was tanning nicely. Luckily her olive skin didn't burn and she would be looking good and feeling thoroughly rested by the time she reached Calcutta. She had caught the eye of more than one man, too. That gave her confidence! All those child-bearing years hadn't neutered her as they had some women! She had chummed up with a small group who had nightly cocktails together. There were dances! She found herself fox-trotting easily and rather well, even though she had almost forgotten that she knew how! She had won a prize for deck-tennis. Her cabin companion, as she first guessed, proved interesting, reliable and friendly without being a nuisance. How lucky for them both that right from the start they shared a mutual understanding about when to be social, and when not.

She was massaging the back of her left hand when she noticed her ring, Neil's ring. Yes! Christmas, 1912! Who could ever have believed all that would happen between then and now! Too many experiences for a single lifetime. Not that she or they had had any idea then. Just as well, perhaps. Survival. It was all a matter of survival.

Neil's whole future had shaped itself at the start of 1913, after he left the job at Petersfield when they, finally, had got engaged! She turned the ring around on her finger, as she thought back. At last, after all the attempts at teaching and experiences in a law office and with an estate agent had come the chance of a career which would really suit him. Of all things, in India!

Out of the blue had come his chance of working back in Assam.

The Bennetts and the Langfords had been at a Christmas party! In her mind's eye, Dessa could see Cora and Ada gossiping away with Mervyn. His on-going boutique tea business put him in constant touch with Mason-Webb, and apparently the Company was scouting round for a new, suitable trainee out in Assam. Unexpectedly, Graham Riley, a friend of theirs, was seeking early retirement for health reasons. All this had cropped up over the hot punch. It had changed everything!

'Sounds right for your Neil, if you ask me,' Mervyn had said. 'He hasn't exactly liked any of the jobs he's done to date. This will be perfect for him. In the steps of his father!'

Dudley rarely interfered in Neil's life, but he felt that this might be too good an opportunity to be missed. He and Neil had always had a tacit respect for each other and it had been next day, when he was showing him round his orchids in the greenhouse, that he raised the question casually. Had he ever thought about going back to India?

A green-fingered move! Like father, like son. When Dessa had heard about it she was convinced that it was just the chance Neil needed. Running a tea-garden!

A brainwave! An opportunity not to be missed! Why had such an idea never struck their minds before! Neil was so suited to that kind of job. It made such good sense!

For the only time in their lives Dessa and Cora were in agreement.

Dessa remembered being wholly wrapt in the idea.

'You've never really taken to any of the jobs you've tried', she said 'But this is perfect! It's in the blood!'

She could see herself as a planter's wife, out in India! Servants! A tea-plantation to run!

'You've only got to train for two years, and in any case you're halfway there already. People know you and your father! Why it's the best thing that could ever have happened ! You've got to go for it darling! And we'll get engaged. Of course we'll get engaged!'

Everything had fallen into place so quickly, Dessa remembered. Neil got the job and was to sail out in the March.

They became engaged in the New Year. Dudley gave them his blessing.

Neil had bought her this five-diamond hooped ring of stunning stones, the envy of her two younger sisters, the same ring which was now reflecting the ocean's sunshine. She had always kept it.

Dessa admired it on her hand, and smiled. At last! It was all coming to fruition. She put the cap back on the bottle of palm oil. She glanced at the time. Soon time to change.

As she made her way along the deck and down the two levels of staircases to her cabin, she remembered those final good-byes, and just how final they proved to be.

Neil had kissed her with silent intensity, and she, who was rarely moved to tears had felt emotionally out of her depth. He had whispered that he was going to prepare a place for her. She wasn't religious but those Biblical words had struck home. Neil's own eyes were streaming and she had had to bite her lip not to make a fool of herself.

Well, now at last she was on her way to make a new life. It was all, finally going to happen.

What Dessa hadn't known for sure, and could only ever have guessed by instinct, was Cora's own reaction to the engagement. Her eyes hadn't been moist at all. She had accepted the goings on with a curious equanimity.

'It's the best thing that could have happened,' she had told Ada later. 'With any luck he'll meet a decent girl out there. Someone of his own class. Two years is a very long time. This engagement will not last. Mark my words.'

SEVEN

'I began work yesterday morning,' he had written to Dessa.

It was the tenth letter he'd written to her since leaving Southampton. 'Again there's so much to tell you I don't know where to begin.

I had little idea of what was expected of me, but The Johnsons have been terribly kind and have set me up in an establishment of my own, my own little bungalow! I have a boy to look after me called Vikram, which makes me feel rather spoiled, but that is quite usual here. His family works on the property. There is a settlement of workers. The company provides them with housing and stores. Compared to the city people they are pretty well-off. Calcutta, for example, is horribly unchanged as I remember it, swarming with half-starved Indians scrabbling in rubbish tips, begging and sleeping on the streets, while cows roam around and are made a fuss of by everybody. Our workers here are far better off, local country stock, used to the local terrain, tough, good people.

Mr. Johnson wants me to stop calling him 'sir' all the time, although I find that difficult. I'm trying .

I'm writing this at the table of my living room in the light of a paraffin lamp. It gets dark quickly and I can hear the wings and shards of beetles, bumping against the blind. Things are going to work out well for us here, I know. Everything has been splendid from the moment I left the ship.

At the weekend the Johnsons are taking me to the Club in Jorhat. That's where everybody goes. I expect there are even one or two people there who remember my parents! Might be embarrassing! You can't believe how many new people I've met. Canon Ashcroft called especially to meet me. I told him all about us. He's in charge at Holy Trinity, our church. Coincidence! He comes from Petersfield and was very pleased to talk. Also he knows the Butler family. (Butler and Cook, remember!) If you were here then everything would be perfect ('perfect' was heavily underlined). This little bungalow would be quite big enough for us.

I picture you back home in West Meon with Miss Rickards keeping an eye on you in school, the Macdonalds feeding you up on cakes, the curate visiting you a little too often for my liking, and you singing away in the church choir on Sundays. I can even hear the creaking of the eaves in your bedroom! With any luck I might dream about you to-night!

'All my love, Neil.'

Much to Neil's delight, a fat first letter had been brought over from the big house unexpectedly by Vikram. The strong, clear handwriting stood out on the bulging envelope containing sheets and sheets of blue notepaper. 'I wish I could say I wasn't missing you,' Dessa wrote, 'but there's a lump of me inside you, so I'm quite hollow. No point in dressing up. No Enfield at the weekends. The only good thing is that I'm saving all my money, and, imagine, if you can, me, on dark winter evenings with Mrs. Macdonald teaching me to crochet lace to put round table cloths, for our 'bottom drawer!'

Dead easy for him to visualise where she was. Nothing had changed. But the only picture she could summon regarding his surroundings came straight out of the eleven year olds' school geography books, and not a very good picture at that. He had to send her some photos soon. Mother wanted one of him in a topi to put up on her parlour mantelpiece. The vicar had enquired after 'our young Empire builder', 'that's You', she underlined. And she was sure it was no coincidence that twice recently they had sung about, 'India's coral strands,' not that he was remotely near to anything but hills and mountains, according to the atlas. Her only mind's eye picture of beaches of any kind was.... Well! He knew where that was!

She was lying on her bed, writing, 'enveloped!' she put in inverted commas, not by 'you' but by a solidity of dark shadows. If she closed her eyes it was almost as if he was there with her; she could feel the gentleness of his fingers, and the comfort of his arms round her. She hoped all the women he met were old, boring and with faces like horses and teeth like tombstones. She ringed his name with little kisses.

'All my Love'

This letter raised Neil up and threw him down. It excited him and it depressed him, yet overall it made him purposeful and ready for work, because he was doing it for 'them', their future.

What else could he tell her?

He paused, looking at the darkness. What would Dessa make of it all; the night air, the smells, the quietude. How different from the busy streets of Portsmouth, the elegant shops in Palmerstone Road, the plays on at the King's theatre. With any luck, by the time he had completed his apprenticeship they would have a bungalow of their own, and one day, manage their own tea-garden. Yes , He would tell her about tea.

He dipped his pen into the ink.

'There's far more to producing tea than you'd imagine,' he wrote. 'There have been a number of important changes even since Father was here. Tell your class there's at least a hundred things to be done before they can drink a cup of tea.'

Photographs of Neil, four months into his new life show a confident, smiling, bronzed young man. Beatrice and Rodney had written to Cora and Dudley to say how well their son was doing and how 'everybody likes him'.

'You see' Cora told Ada, 'It's just the change he needed. What future was there for him, tied down to that girl? Now he's learning auction bridge at the club, he gets invited out to dinners and apparently he's playing tennis with cracks like Peter and Quentin!'

Ada smiled. 'I'm sure it won't be long before,....well, you know what I mean, anything could happen!'

Reading from Beatrice's letter Cora's face beamed with an expression half-way between surprise and gratification. 'Imagine! He's even got a part in the dramatic societies' play, a Shaw play, "Arms and the Man."

'He is branching out!'

'And Eulalie's taking him under her wing, Beatrice says.'

Ada winked. 'She'll liven him up if anyone could!'

At that moment more or less, eight thousand miles away, Eulalie was in this very process. She was the play's producer, and working away very hard. The opening night was in a few weeks.

Frustration had caused her to take a break and share a cigarette with Verity, the wardrobe mistress.

'So difficult to get Neil to relax! He's not a natural actor. He's supposed to draw Pamela to him and slip his arm dexterously round her waist, and he does it as if he's facing a firing squad! She's doing her best, poor girl. She has to say, 'Let me go sir, or I shall be disgraced' and Neil no more looks as if he's making a pass at her than taking Holy Communion.'

Eulalie drew on her cigarette. 'If you ask me, she fancies him a bit.' She widened her eyes, knowingly. 'That might do the trick!'

'Does he realise?'

Eulalie resorted again to eyes rather than words. She smiled. 'He's about as aware of women's charms as St. Francis. If you ask me, he prefers his dog!'

The evening of August 4th had been scheduled for the dress-rehearsal of 'Arms and the Man' but the rehearsal never took place.

Britain declared war on Germany.

The news plunged every expatriate in and around Jorhat into consternation.

Uproar struck.

The D.C. brought the neighbourhood together to the Club to announce the news officially. His face and voice were grave.

A wave of tension silenced the room.

'It is with great regret that I must inform you that Great Britain has been obliged to declare war on Germany. As you are aware, recent events in Bosnia have upset the balance of power in Europe. Germany's decision to force Belgium to give passage to their warring troops against Belgium's own wishes has meant that Britain has had to uphold the rights of her ally. We have entered this war for moral reasons in support of our long standing Treaty of London with the Belgian people.'

All were dumb. Friends clasped each other in shock.

War.

The silence was broken by a single voice.

'God Save the King.'

A second and a third voice joined in.

All members of the Club found themselves singing spontaneously. This was a moment of history.

Nor was that enough for such news and such a moment. The national anthem was followed by a rendering of 'Land of Hope and Glory', everyone singing with fervent solemnity.

Like a relieving downpour after a clap of thunder, came a deluge of clamour and disbelief.

Cacophany.

Germany? Had the Telegraph Office got it right? There had to be some mistake. Why, Germany and Britain had just made a joint agreement about the Baghdad railway. The proper enemy was Russia. It was a Serb business anyway, and Austro-Hungary's affair. Why should the news of the Archduke and Archduchess' death have lead to this? No-one could condone, nor had condoned, such shocking violence by a bunch of schoolboys with home-made bombs, but what had this to do with England? Ever since the Turk had got the boot there had been countless troubles in Thessalonia, or was it Bosnia, places you'd never heard of and could hardly find on a map. Diplomacy was one thing, war quite another. It certainly wouldn't be a war to last long, just a flourish, sabre-rattling. A question of honour. Serious, too. Britain hadn't been to war since the Crimea, not counting the Boers that is. But Germany! Queen Victoria's own grandson!

Arguments, Questioning, Indignation.

The clubroom was at boiling point.

Peter Rutherford couldn't understand why the enemy wasn't Russia. They'd got it wrong. Quentin had read, only yesterday, that 'Germany wanted to expand commercially and grow in wealth'. How could war do that! Old Gordon was bristling and thought it right that Britain should teach somebody a lesson, 'which was exactly what they were doing. They had to drink to that.'

They did. Great Britain, France and Russia, allies against the Kaiser, Austro-Hungary, Bulgaria and the Ottoman Empire.

Before the DC left he told everyone 'to continue as usual'. As yet he had had no communication concerning their community's best response to such shattering tidings. As soon as that came he would let them know 'immediately'.

James, swayed off course by the day's news, had clapped Neil on the shoulder and confided 'that within no time, the Germans would be kicked in the teeth on one side, and in the arse on the other.'

That night the Club members made their way home 'proud to be British'. What no-one realised at the time was that German submarines were to keep England and India well apart for all of four years.

1914

ONE

'Never seen anything like it! Eighteen frickin' miles of warships! The whole bloomin' Navy.'

'Couldn't see the Island for them! And all those reservists called up!'

'Should've thought it was plain enough when the King came down here! Definitely something up'.

'An'they've got the cheek to march through Belgium like they owned it.'

'They've brought it on themselves'.

'Those weren't yer ordinary summer manoeuvres, don't kid me. They was on purpose, just to give Jerry the abdabs.'

'The Kaiser's only got one thing in mind, and that's to 'ave a quick go at the bloody frogs an' put them in their place so's not to muck up their real go.'

'We should just let them get on wiv it. Don't get involved. Aint got nothin' to do with us.'

'That's just where you're wrong you see. That's wot's got up our nose.'

Henry and his friends at the 'Green Post' were both less and more surprised about Britain's declaration of war than the members of the Jorhat club. Something was certainly going on right before their eyes in The Solent, when, on July 10th, 1914, the Grand Fleet's new C-in-C, Sir John Jellicoe mobilised the 'most unprecedented and complex collection of warships' anyone had ever seen.

'Those Jerries won't dare to take on our Dreadnoughts. We all knows that.'

'But we can't just let them do what they like marchin' their troops through Belgium.'

'That's the point. War it is. Wot's that gonna mean, I ask you?

'Won't last long. We'll show 'em!'

In August 1914 no-body was quite sure what war was going to mean or how it would affect ordinary people. Four Humby members had already been involved in the July naval manoeuvres: two of Dessa's brothers, Maud's husband, only recently returned from a naval tour in Shanghai, and Daisy's handsome fiance, who had recently been promoted to the officer class as a sub-lieutenant on account of his sister's snobby husband's strong family influence. The flourish of naval power and presence had been a deliberate anti-German threat. The fact that it had little immediate result in deterring the Schlieffen Plan threw the British Empire into a war which scarred the world. Lack of co-operation between French and English generals, along with ill-conceived military engagements against the Gemans at Mons and on the Marne, served only to create the deadlock and inhumanity of the Western Front, yet at this early stage of this terrible war there were huge and unparallelled upsurges of enthusiasm and patriotism which infected all layers of society.

The Humby family was no exception.

Daisy joined the W.R.A.C.s, much to Maud's disbelief.

'Her contribution to winning the war is tarting herself up in uniform, fluttering her eyes and laughing a lot. She's technically in 'communications' but never actually tells us what she does. The only person she communicates with as far as I can see is her darling Desmond. They really are mad about each other, but Daisy always was over-enthusiastic and extreme.'

Dessa's version of that message never actually reached Neil, because it had been blue-pencilled out by the censor. Neither had the news of the German Zeppelin which circled over Portsmouth taking reconnaissance pictures of the dockyard. Everybody had been as scared as they were fascinated. It had been a great monster thing, like an enormous shark, bringing war to the air.

'We can never feel safe again,' said Sarah. 'We know where we are with the army and navy but now things can drop out on us from the sky! Whatever is the world coming to?'

'I read between the lines, ' Neil wrote, 'because it seems to me that Humby family news from Portsmouth is T--S---- apparently. But, Dessa darling, I'm glad to know that you have returned home at such a time. You all need to be together. Besides you're just the person to take on boys so that the men can enlist for the war. I have already tried to enlist here, but tea-planters are on reserve, as are rubber planters and teak planters, because, apparently, we all contribute to essential British supplies (Where would our Tommies be without their 'cha'?)

Letters between India and Britain became far from regular since the war didn't come to its presupposed swift end. Nor was the Zeppelin the only surprise weapon. The sea, too, had lethal hidden threats below its surface in the submarine. Jules Verne's and H.G. Wells' horror stories about the depths of the sea were taking on sinister meanings.

This technological weapon was responsible for changing the rules of war. The submarine relied on stealth. It ambushed its victims in an underhand way. The idea of underwater ships originally went back as far as the sixteenth century, but already in America and especially in Germany, their navy was taking up the idea very seriously. Initially the British regarded such warfare as pure piracy and were furious to think how the Bosch was stealing a march on them, shutting up their precious Battle fleet safely in the Kiel canal whilst damaging Allied shipping so effectively in such an underhand way. The usual British routes to India and the Far East were threatened seriously by U-Boat bases in the Mediterranean. British ships now had to settle for the long way round. For Neil and Dessa the chances of seeing each other were increasingly remote, and communication by letter, a matter of luck.

In the early months of 1915, Dessa missed Neil so much she had every intention of sailing out to Calcutta. 'This war shows no sign of coming to an end,' she wrote. 'I'm stuck here and you're stuck there. None of this was part of our plan. Whenever will we see each other again?'

U-boat damage to British shipping was getting increasingly alarming, according to several family members working in the dockyard 'in the know', and that was even before the controversial sinking of the 'Lusitania'.

Neil wrote very strongly 'On no account are you to consider sailing out here. The risks are far too great.' This was underlined doubly. 'There is nowhere now which isn't a war-zone. It would be suicide. Imagine how I would be, isolated among these hills without you. It doesn't bear thinking about. No, no and no! Be patient. The war can't go on for ever. We love each other. Nothing can take that away.'

War went on. Its creeping fingers spread in all directions from Turkey to Poland to Russia.

Back in Portsmouth, the most important base of the Senior Service, skilled workers were in great demand irrespective of age, as so much shipping needed repair and maintenance. The workshops bristled with activity. 'Father was glad to be re-called,' wrote Dessa. 'He feels that it's something positive he can do.'

In her letters she made hints about blackout and food shortages. If it hadn't been for mother's allotment, the Humby family would have been forced to eat those disgusting artichokes instead of potatoes. You'll be pleased to know too, that your father thinks like my mother, for he has turned some of his lawn at the back into a vegetable garden. Your parents are O.K. but Ada was with your mother when I called, so I didn't stay long.'

War affected everyone, including the Malins Road household, two of whose members had already died with tuberculosis, the eldest, Margaret, and the young fifteen-year-old William. For Dessa coming back home was a wholly different experience from pre-war. Her two eldest brothers were away in the navy and Daisy, Gwenny and even young Morris now ruled, taking up everyone's time and space, and exploding about in a way which made Dessa feel middle-aged.

'You're barely twenty five yet you carry on like a maiden aunt!' teased Daisy. 'When did you last go out? I never see you wearing anything but that boring old navy blue woollen skirt. For heaven's sake put on something a bit fetching and come out with us to the South Parade Pier. Just because you're engaged doesn't mean you have to sit at home every night crocheting traycloths. And if you're not doing that you're marking kids' books like a proper old schoolmarm!'

'That's what I am,' Dessa replied.

'Rubbish! You're not! Anything but! Neil wouldn't want you to mope about. You don't know what he gets up to out there anyway!'

'I'll forget you said that,' replied Dessa.

'Mind your tongue,' said Mother.

But it was true. Dessa rode off to school every day, managed her own class of boys which was sometimes doubled with yet another group, and brought home a basket full of exercise books to mark every night. She would sit with Mother in the evening crocheting for her bottom drawer. Neil's photograph looked down on them, bronzed and smiling among the Barail Hills.

'I feel like "The Lady of Shalott",' she said to herself, 'and there isn't even a mirror.'

※

One evening, sometime later, Daisy's head came round the door.

'De-ess!'

Dessa looked up.

'Could I, d'you think, could I?'

'What?'

'Borrow your fox fur.'

'Where are you off to now? Who do you want to impress this time?'

The white fox fur had been a special parting gift from Neil. Dessa kept it in the cupboard upstairs, safe in moth balls in an old pillow case.

'Tonight I'm meeting Desmond's sister. She's very posh. I don't want to let Desmond down. She lives in one of those huge apartments in Southsea Terrace. May I? I'll look after it.'

'Mind you do.'

'Is that a 'yes'?'

Dessa nodded. 'You'll find it—'

'I know. I've found it.'

Daisy drew it out from behind her back, snuggled it flirtatiously round her shoulders. 'How do I look'? She said.

She did look very pretty.

Dessa felt like an old maid.

'Desmond's picking me up in half an hour. Thanks Dess!'

Not only was Daisy whirling about now, but even Gwen. Although she was still at school she was casting her eyes around the boys, sharing her energetic singing practise with the whole household, and threatening to 'sing to the troops'.

'Poor troops!' commented Morris. 'Imagine their last impression of England! Gwen warbling "Torn from my heart as twilight closes/ Love sends a little gift of roses!"'

'There is a war on,' she had retorted. 'It's my singing teacher's idea. She thinks I'm good. Besides it's rotten for them, going over there to all that. Some of them aren't much older than you. I want to cheer them up.'

Morris did his best to suppress a smile. 'I guess there's more than one advantage of being too young to join up.' He added.

The life of the street, as of most streets, had been changed by the war. Any men around were either young or old. It was the women, now, who were setting off on their bikes to work in the morning, and places like the corset factory, even, had been turned over to munitions. The publican's wife of 'The Green Post' shared running the pub with her daughters, and old Mrs Hicks had come back from the country to manage the general shop on the corner.

And there were the dreaded telegrams, which crippled and wounded everybody.

'You're lucky,' Maud had told Dessa. 'You've only got to wait until the war's over for your man. He may be stuck in India, but at least he's safe. I never know where David is, or whether I'll ever see him again. You've got nothing to grumble about.'

Daisy had even less to grumble about. For her the war was a romp, it was fun, it was exciting!

The next day, she returned the fox fur utterly triumphant from having met Desmond's sister.

'It's all so posh, there, and she's absolutely stunning, Dess! She was a dancer on the London stage before she married! Her father was on the Halls, and her mother had been a dancer too. The theatre's in their blood, not that you'd think it with Desmond! She absolutely thinks I'm right for her baby brother, her only brother, her only relation, really, because her mother died. Your fox-fur impressed her, I could tell. I knew it would. I told her I had borrowed it from you. She wants to be introduced. She said you sounded interesting. I told her you were the brainy one, and that you weren't like me a bit. And Mother.' She looked at Sarah across the kitchen table, Sarah, who had been taking in everything with reservations. 'Mother, she wants to meet you, too. She wants you to visit.'

'She can want!' retorted mother. 'I'm not going out to meet anyone. Whoever she is, if she wants to meet me she can come here.' And that was that.

'Of course, she'll come, but that's not the point, now. The point is, she's having a few people round this Saturday evening and insists that Dessa should come. She wants to get to know the family.' She put her head to one side smiling her most enchanting smile, so well practised recently. 'I said I'd ask you. You've got to come, Dess. O.K.?'

TWO

I t's not as if I could possibly forget. It was an evening which changed my life. For the better? For the worse? Who can say? What makes us do what we do? Accident? Choice? What comes to mind especially was Daisy's aplomb. She was the one who knew her way around! My younger dotty sister! She was in charge! Naval officers! Parties! Sutherland Heights! Jauntily she stepped out of the taxi, with Desmond guiding her elbow. I followed. She set the pace. Standing still she directed my eyes upwards. She was excited to see my reaction.

'Second floor. That huge bay-window. There's a lift.' She said this casually as if she had frequented lifts and smart living all her life.

We were inside the hallway.

Desmond dealt with the lift's heavy diagonal iron bars, pulling them backwards. He pressed a button! We rose, magically. As we stepped out we could hear a mingle of people noises, talking, laughing.

'Sounds like a big party,' Daisy's eyes sparkled. 'Fun, Dess! Fun! Wait till she meets your sister, Desmond.' She turned to me. She is...

(words failed her)... Well, you'll see for yourself.' Her eyes widened with delight at the thought of my reaction.

The chairs in the panelled hallway were heavy with coats and wraps, as was the hall-stand. Exuding from the doorway was the scent and sight of tobacco smoke curling around the sounds of a gramophone and the crescendos of merriment.

'She'll have folded back the partitions and rolled up the rugs I bet!' Daisy was full of excitement. 'I told you she was a professional dancer in the West End, didn't I?' (This was said to me) Then she hugged Desmond's arm and whispered loudly in his ear 'You're not such a bad dancer yourself, are you, darling!'

We entered.

I hadn't expected anything like this. People stood around in groups, chatting, smoking or moving casually to help themselves to drinks or delicacies unprocurable in wartime. It was exactly as if the war had stopped at Daphne's flat. This was the sort of party I had only ever read about. My social experiences with Neil had been limited to gatherings at Ada's or Councillor Courtenay's or Cora's, and those occasions had been devised by seemly silent social rules consisting of sipping sherry politely or 'supper' after a theatre, discussing the performance. The other kind of parties I was knew were hardly elegant in any way; sing-songs with the Macdonalds, family get-togethers round the piano, pencil and paper games, or teachers' tea-parties in the All-Saint's church hall alongside a trestle table. As Daisy knew, this party would open my eyes. I tried to give out an impression of being in my own element, but for me this party was like going to a foreign country for the first time.

I stood looking round me moving only my eyes. There was Daisy, swimming about, perfectly at ease in this lake of islands of excitement. People were saying 'Daisy!' as if she were worth knowing, and she did little waves across the room, or winked saucily and squeezed her shoulders.

'You've got to meet Daphne, Dessa. That's why we're here. Look! She's seen us.'

There was movement on the far side of the room.

I waited.

She rose.

Moving elegantly through her guests who backed to let her pass, she extended her hand towards me.

'At last! Dessa! The clever sister! Daisy's told me all about you. It was time we met.'

This was Daphne. I couldn't take my eyes off her.

Tall, beautiful, with perfect features, her fair hair looped cunningly into a careless bun at the nape of her long neck, she presented like a Burne-Jones goddess. Her clothes complemented her elegance; a grey-green crepe de chine ankle length under-dress surmounted by a paisley-patterned over dress looped over one shoulder, and secured by a diamond pin. So wrapt was I at this vision, it never occurred to me to feel the ordinariness of my own plain cream silk.

I stepped forward to meet her. She was speaking to me. I smiled. 'See what I mean,' Daisy was whispering to me as I moved. I did indeed. She hadn't exaggerated one bit.

Already Daphne was talking, taking me by the hand over to a far corner.

'Over here,' she was saying. 'Let's sit on the sofa so we can become acquainted. She looked around her.

'Far more people have turned up than I was expecting,' she said. 'It started off by being mostly a few close friends, then it occurred to me that some of the boys especially were needing a party because they are soon to be on alert. All Navy, of course, but what else would you expect?'

By this time we were both seated and once again she had taken my hand. I could feel her visually digesting me. She looked at me as you would look at a picture. I was looking at her too.

She was talking.

'You couldn't look less like your sister! She's delightful, all froth and bubble. Just the girl for Desmond. So lucky for him that they met! But you,' she leaned back slightly, 'you are very different.' Her eyes twinkled. 'Not the run of the mill; too thoughtful, too organised?' She looked at me teasingly. But,' she paused, quizzically, biting her lower lip, 'there's something of the gypsy in you, I would say, darling, which you can't quite cover up!' She squeezed my hand and laughed. 'I'm known for my fortune telling! I don't have to look at tea-leaves or palms of hands, I just look at people!' She patted my hand and then let it go, 'What do you say to that?'

Her question didn't require an answer, for she was smiling across the room, as she caught sight of other guests.

I was amused, pleased, because she so obviously liked me, but, I was also sceptical. I had set out to meet Desmond's sister with what I can now only call a degree of hauteur. All Daisy's enthusiasm I had put down to the usual inane Daisy railings, for to me, all the time she was growing up I felt her to be giggly, stupid and trivial, well, just a younger sister. Now, her earlier descriptions which I had dismissed as exaggerations were patently only too true. Daphne was rivetingly beautiful and she had created around her an atmosphere of raffish sophistication totally new to me.

She turned her attention to me again.

'Desmond's my only brother, you know. Our mother died when we were young. Father gave up the theatre to bring us up.' She smiled a ravishing smile, not at all rehearsed, but which lit up her face with warmth and genuine gentleness. I was disarmed. Despite the wall I had put up before meeting her, I found myself liking her. Really liking her.

She was still talking.

'You're looking too serious. No wonder with a fiancé miles away and the war on. Well, you can relax here tonight. Forget the war for a little while.'

'Daisy has been talking.'

'You know Daisy, she never stops. Desmond adores her. They're both as silly', she corrected herself, 'no, as delightful, as each other.'

'Looks like my younger sister will be married before me.'

Across the floor, among other couples, were Daisy and Desmond tap–tapping away stylishly.

'Desmond, drinks!' Daphne raised her hand to catch her brother's eye. 'Dessa needs a drink! She hasn't come to the party just to meet me.'

At that moment two young Naval officers who had been talking to each other by a thickly curtained window behind us, leant over to the back of the sofa. One bent forward to speak to the hostess. I couldn't help noticing how Daphne turned her long, slim legs sideways with the grace of a gazelle. Her earrings were dangling, her bracelets tinkling amid a breath of exotic perfume. She raised her hand. One of the men took her fingers and kissed them. He whispered something in her ear in response to which she opened her eyes wide and said something like 'as soon! Indeed!'

I stood up. I didn't want to intrude.

Daphne caught my arm.

'Don't disappear darling, before you've met Ginty and Guy.' She looked up to the two men.

'This is Dessa, Daisy's sister. Look after her for me. She hardly knows anyone here.'

Ginty clicked his heels, German fashion. 'Enchanted,' he said as he took my hand and kissed it.

'And I'm Guy.'

I inclined my head towards him just at the moment Desmond appeared with a tray of drinks.

'My special party cup. You must try some. I won't take 'no' for an answer.' Daphne took a glass and put it into my hand. 'No, don't just hold it, taste it.'

I blinked, not used to alcohol.

'Now have another and you'll get into the party mood! Fill up her glass, Desmond!'

He did.

'I'm taking Dessa over to have a look at your records,' he said. 'We'll do a spot of winding.'

I suppose at this point I might never have talked to Guy again, for as we were making our way into the large room a distinctive voice said 'Dessa Humby?'

I smiled vaguely. 'Yes?'

The owner of the voice introduced herself. 'Celia, Celia Bennett. Surely you're Neil Langford's fiancé. You're the teacher.'

'Yes.'

'We have met. My mother's Neil's mother's friend!'

As if I didn't remember all that Cora stuff about the incomparable Celia. And here she was! I had to admit she was very attractive and wholly self-possessed.

'Fancy meeting you here!' Her tone of voice suggested that she was really asking why someone like me could possibly be at the same party as herself. I told her about Daisy.

She laughed. 'Impossible! Daisy your sister! Small world'.

She was quick to tell me that her name wasn't Bennett any more, but Ackroyd. The man standing alongside her was her husband, Lieutenant Adrian Ackroyd. She introduced us, spelling out the words with particular emphasis not only because of the noise in the room but because Adrian was looking extraordinarily blank. 'Darling, you remember mother's friend Cora? Well this is her son Neil's fiancée.' She turned back to me, with a measuring look.

'Of all people!' She went on. 'How is dear Neil? I gather he's stuck out in Assam and missing all the fun and can't enlist even if he wants to.'

I nodded.

'He's stuck and I'm stuck. He won't hear of me trying to go out to join him.'

'Quite right. Far too dangerous. You'd be mad to try, darling, wouldn't she, Adrian? Those U-boats are no joke.'

She was smoking as she was talking and, while raising her chin to blow curlicues of cigarette smoke upwards, her eye caught sight of Ginty and Guy. 'They can tell you, can't they Adrian, they're in subs.'

Submarines. I knew a lot about what was going on with submarines because of Father. He'd been on about 'Diesel' and eight new J class submarines being constructed not only at Portsmouth, but also at Devonport and Pembroke, 'to get back a bit of initiative', he had said, and not before time. 'Our secret weapon,' he had added, with a quizzical look.

The conversation stopped at this point because Desmond had been at work with the gramophone and the opening bars of a tango were filling the room. Everyone's attention was focused on Desmond's announcement and he was banging a fork on a silver salver.

'Just watch this!' Daisy had dropped back beside me, laughing. 'You'll love it! Daphne's party piece. She never does it when Miles is around, he's such a snob.'

'Miles?'

'Her husband,' she whispered briefly, 'She usually gives parties when he's away.'

At the far end of the room, where I had been sitting beside Daphne, Ginty was standing with one hand behind his back and the other extended towards Daphne. Applause and foot drumming accompanied her rising. Riveting their eyes on each other with powerful passion, they took centre stage as the party guests flattened themselves against the walls to make room for the performance. Perfect. Heads back, features haughty and composed, their dance began.

You could see that Daphne was a professional dancer. She coiled and uncoiled herself with controlled ease, shoulders, hips, arms and fingertips tensely elastic, dramatic, rhythmic, proud. Her skirts swirled sinuously enhancing her movements. Ginty paired her remarkably. The dance ended to rapturous applause, with him on his knees before her. I think I clapped more than anyone else in the room. What a performance! What a party! Where had I been living these last months?

Desmond came round with more drinks. Daisy came up. 'See! Enjoying yourself? Bit of a change from marking books! Here eat something. Can't think where Daphne gets all this delicious food. You certainly wouldn't know there was a war on.'

We sat down beside each other.

'Didn't know you knew Celia!'

'You must have heard me talk about her. The formidable Ada's perfect daughter, remember? She and Neil were brought up together in India. She's married to the man she's standing by. Over there,' I indicated.

'Oh Adrian!' Daisy nodded, her mouth full of sandwich. 'Yes. Desmond knows Adrian.'

By now the atmosphere was smokier, the tempo of the party more intimate. Couples were moving back nonchalantly to dance, the tune was a slow waltz, and I was dancing with Desmond. Out of the corner of my eye I sensed that other naval officer looking at me. I pretended not to notice. As the dance came to an end he came up to us.

'Hostess's orders. My turn now, Desmond.' He inclined his head courteously towards me and took over. It was all so natural, 'I'm Guy,' he said.

I can hardly say we danced. There were at least ten couples moving sleepily round the floor. I can't even remember the tune. What I do remember was the comfort of his arm and the smell of his neck, a male smell. He held me close. It felt wonderful. I didn't want the holding ever to stop. Instinctively, against all of my intentions, I nestled into his body. This was something I had been missing for a long time, a very long time. He kissed my forehead imperceptibly, speech spared.

Whatever the music was it faded and we moved to a corner with filled glasses. We talked about Daphne and London, and all the while

I could feel his look, penetrating me. The silence made me talk too much. I found myself explaining about Daisy and Daphne and why I had come.

'Nonsense,' he interrupted. He leaned back and half-closed his eyes. 'I already know why you came.'

I was taken aback. 'I've told you,' I said naively. 'That's why.'

He silenced me with an authoritative look.

It was compelling. I was intrigued.

Dilating his nostrils imperceptibly, he sat back even further, the better to absorb me with his eyes.

'There's only one reason you came here tonight.' He was motionless, save for a slight twist of his lip. 'And that,' he continued, 'was to meet me.'

Somehow what he said seemed wholly irresistible. I fell for his charm despite myself. I think it was the way he took over. His assumption, his confidence. His taking over was a new experience for me. I was always the one to make decisions, yet here I was welcoming his overtures utterly and unprotestingly. I shook my head very slowly and looked straight into his eyes.

I was outwardly trying to say 'no' but my eyes said 'yes'.

'I'm engaged,' I protested, unconvincingly.

'You make it sound like a disease.'

I had to smile. Thinking back it was his humour which shattered my waning resolution.

'Someone's lucky,' he had replied. He picked up my left hand, contemplated Neil's ring, and kissed my fingers. His eyes challenged me. He was studying my face like a map.

'All's fair in love and war.' He gave me back my hand, shrugged and breathed reflectively.

I didn't have to reply, for at that moment the grandfather clock in the hall struck four.

Cinderella! He saw my reaction.

'I'll take you home. It's late.'

I was searching through the coats and wraps in the dim light of the hallway, when he came from behind, sliding me into the opposite doorway where his arms encircled me and he kissed me as I had never been kissed before.

In the taxi we sat side by side not speaking, my head on his shoulder, his arm round me. He helped me out into the silent street when the taxi reached home.

'You kissed me back,' he said. 'I shan't forget.'

Before I could reply he was gone.

THREE

T he following week I was pushing my bike through the front-door after school when Gwenny came rushing up to me. I was putting my bike away, as usual, and taking out the usual bag of exercise books when she followed me down the hall and stood stock still, beside me. She didn't speak, but looked at me in a very cheeky way.

'And?' I queried.

'Who do you know called 'Guy'?' she said.

'Why?'

'His name's on the card. They're on the kitchen table. It's a huge bouquet. The whole street knows. The boy on the bike delivering them was so swamped his bike fell over!'

Sure enough, on the kitchen table, utterly flamboyantly wrapped in shiny paper and ribbon, for all the world to see, was a massive bunch of red roses.

Gwenny eyed me. 'What have you been up to?'

I didn't reply. I was reading the card. All it said was 'Greetings, Guy.'

I caught my breath and smiled. Guy! Surprise! I felt pleased and flattered but Gwenny was still looking at me.

'So?' I looked at her straight, pretending to be composed. 'Aren't they beautiful!'

'And ...?' She queried.

'Someone I met at Daphne's party.' I tossed off my reply in as casual manner as I could, but inside I was in turmoil. How to cover it up?

I was as excited as I was embarrassed. Guy. Neil. Flowers. I knew what Gwenny was thinking.

My first instinct was to put them straight into the dustbin. If I felt like this about Gwenny, what on earth would I feel about Mother? Mother would be a real worry. They weren't exactly hideable. They were utterly magnificent. In any case Mother would find them wherever I put them. Then, well then!

I knew the 'then' alright.

I was feeling marvellous and guilty all at once.

'Just one of the people at the party. Daisy will tell you. A chap who took a shine at me.'

'Some shine!' Gwenny uttered incredulously. 'Must have cost a packet! They're from 'Fortescues' in Palmerston Road.'

Attack was the best means of defence. But what was there to defend?

'We'll put them in a vase in the front room.'

'If you can find a vase big enough,' Gwenny added.

We had to find a space. Every surface in Mother's parlour was crowded with precious knick-knacks, a tortoiseshell snuff-box, a Minton dish, an iridescent paua-shell from New Zealand, a carved ivory trellis of flowers, all amidst a forest of cameo frames of photographs. She didn't like anyone 'touching her things'.

'The occasional table,' I said, decisively, glancing round the room. This was an occasion alright. Set up in their vase they trounced the maiden-hair fern, and there was Neil's photograph on the mantelpiece looking at us all the time.

I needed a space.

Guy.

I hadn't sorted out my thoughts about him.

How could I have any thoughts about him?

I was trying not to think about him.

I needed privacy. I hadn't wanted anyone to know, least of all Mother.

When she came back from the garden she reacted exactly as I knew she would.

She who loved flowers, stared at the roses with the maximum of hostility.

'Large enough to cover guilt?' she demanded. 'Do you think I'm stupid or something? Coming home at four in the morning with some bloke you've never met before! I might have expected such gadabout behaviour from someone like Maud, but you, Dessa! You must be out of your mind! You've got the nicest, most gentlemanly fiancé in the world, doing his best to create a life for you both out there and you do the dirt on him. Going to parties with other men indeed! You had better watch yourself!'

'I didn't go out to a party like that, mother. You know I didn't. You didn't want to meet Desmond's sister. I went to meet her for the family. You know I did. I told you all about her.' I felt myself protesting a bit too much.

'But you didn't tell me about a man who has sent you a mass---she accentuated the word mass--- of roses. Why was that, might I ask?'

It was Daisy, ultimately who came to my rescue.

She did her best to calm mother down, reassuring her with a series of 'thats'. She and Desmond knew Guy quite well; that he was a favourite of Daphne's; that he was much looked up to in the Service; that he was a colourful sort of character; that it was just the sort of thing he would do.

Mother was not convinced.

'Besides,' Daisy added, 'he's not around anymore. He's on some special dangerous top-secret mission. He just admired Dessa, that's all. And why wouldn't he? Apart from me, and Daphne, of course, she was one of the better-looking girls there! Don't get too worried, Mother. For all you know, as we speak, he might be stuck on the bottom in a frightful submarine, winning the war for us.'

My heart missed a beat.

I picked up the scissors from the kitchen table where I had left them and dropped them clumsily on the floor. They sprawled up at me open and ugly, still with a bit of rose stalk caught in them. I could feel my mouth tighten.

Mother could think what she liked. She no longer counted.

Stuck on the bottom? Winning the war for us?

I was seriously worried. Daphne had been talking to them, those two, Ginty and Guy. I was trying to remember. What had she said exactly? Something about being on alert? And what had that woman Celia said? Submarines? And now, Daisy of all people, 'dangerous mission?'

Despite all the news from the Western front, the deaths, the wounded, no members yet, of our immediate family, in so far as we knew, had been involved directly in anything in the war labelled 'top secret'. So far we had been lucky. Mother's nephews were still alive in France. Our two boys in the Navy were somewhere 'up north', with Admiral Beattie's fleet. Maud's husband had not yet been blown up in the engine room of the 'Triumph' at Gallipoli. Now, here was I, shaken beyond measure by the thought that this man I had met only once, might be suffocating slowly in some terrible confined space in the depths of an icy silent sea. Roses! His roses. What ironies! A wreath to himself. Submarines spelled danger.

At that stage I had no idea how much I was to learn about them. I was to learn how the snobbish Senior Service regarded submariners as a rogue branch of weird volunteers, those 'unwashed chauffeurs'.

I knew Father's pre-war jokes about them having to be escorted by a surface vessel waving a red flag. But this was now. Submarines were serious.

All I could surmise from Daisy's words was that the unusual man I had met at Daphne's party might have disappeared forever, which made me feel intensely sick.

We went upstairs. There were things I wanted to ask her. There were heaps of things I wanted to ask her.

'Thanks,' I said, 'for getting mother off my back. You realise, don't you, I had no idea he would send me flowers.'

'Just the sort of thing he would do. He's got an eye for the girls. He and Ginty live it up to the hilt. But that's submariners for you. Guy's one of Daphne's favourites. He's so amusing and dashing. She likes that. Mind you, he does drink too much, but so do all the submariners. They're known for it. They live on their nerves all the time.'

'And is he really on a mission?'

She nodded. 'All Desmond said is that he and Ginty went flying off to Chatham and that is bad news. The navy's searching all over for the German High Seas Fleet for a fight. They've gone into hiding.'

'So Guy and Ginty....?'

'I guess.' She nodded.

'When will they get back?'

She shrugged. 'Don't ask me! That's in the lap of the gods.'

I hesitated. Somehow I didn't want our conversation to come to an end. Daisy was my only possible link, and I wanted to go on talking. More than anything I wanted to be talking about him, Guy, that man. It couldn't just end like this. What could I say? How might I innocently contrive some sort of link? It came to me. The flowers.

'Do you think I should thank him for the roses?'

She gave me a knowing look. 'That's for you to decide.'

'Just a brief note. But where to address it? And, come to think of it, I don't even know his surname.'

Daisy burst out laughing.

'Hall. Guy Hall. He's one of the bright boys. An engineer. What's more a Lieutenant, Lieutenant Hall.'

'And his address?'

'Daphne will find him. Write a note and I'll give it to her to give to him. She'll track him down.'

But Daphne hadn't. Even Daphne hadn't managed that. It was Daisy who brought the news from Desmond. Lieutenant Guy Hall was missing. Posted Missing. His submarine had been reported well overdue.

Numbness, gloom, anxiety. No colour anywhere. The heaviest of hearts.

War had invaded number forty-one, along with other households in the street and scores of houses all over the country.

FOUR

When I came home from school one day, after Daphne's party, and before I had any significant thoughts about the war and Guy's safety, waiting for me on the kitchen table was a letter from Neil: the familiar blue envelope, the regular copperplate handwriting, the fat pages of love and need squeezing through the chat of his daily routines. He wrote of the local happenings. I tried always to visualise the collection of workers' huts among the hills, the outhouses, the drying sheds, which I had only seen in geography books, and which for me were all rather like indeterminate stage scenery, but it was the best I could do to feel close to all he described. He wrote of the latest antics of his dog, his visits to the club, the tennis parties, naming intimately people I didn't know. I supposed I would get to know such people and be part of their way of life one day. But distance and the war increasingly made tea-gardens in Assam seem like a fabled Xanadu, rather than a reality, all worlds apart. Genitive of vague time,

'Eines Tages.' I remembered my schoolgirl German lessons. Nobody learned German now.

For the first time I felt out of touch. Seriously. This was a new feeling, a feeling which was as involuntary as it was persistent.

What was happening to me? Worse, what had happened to me?

My head no longer seemed in control.

I wanted to meet all these people. I did. Where Neil was, I wanted to be. That was the plan. Our plan.

But where was the irrepressible excitement of a letter? Why was I feeling blank?

Reading this letter that day was like looking at an alien photograph album, trying to give substance to shadows of unknown people. None of the paper kisses and words of tender affection were working.

I took it upstairs to the hidden shelf in my wardrobe, as I had done with all Neil's letters, but this time I found myself adding it directly to the shoeboxful. Usually I first wrapped it in my nightdress and put it under my pillow to touch it re-assuringly and evocatively before I went to sleep.

I stared at this jam-packed file; envelope after envelope ranged in the historical order of my life for the past two years, a boxed chronology of pressed flower passion.

How was I allowing such a thought?

The harm was done. I had thought it.

What I thought was me, was no longer. The ramifications would not bear probing.

The war. That's what it was, the war. Whenever would it end? How would it end? The war was everybody's problem. It had escalated beyond any reckoning, the war, but could I blame it for my malaise? Nothing was working out well. On top of everything the war hadn't turned out to be the straightforward moral flourish it first promised. Russian initial successes had proved a flash in the pan. The Germans were now sweeping through Poland and Galicia. Horror upon horror, and against all codes of war, the Germans had used gas at Ypres. And then, the debacle of Gallipoli; a disaster which struck our family directly, as well as the families of all those Australians and New-Zealanders who had crossed the world to fight. Until now, who had ever heard of Gallipoli? We had to look it up on the map in our efforts to prop up Maud, who had had to face the terrible telegram with the news that David had gone down on 'The Triumph' at the Dardenalles.

What did I have to worry about, in comparison?

Nothing.

She had been right. My man was safely playing tennis in Assam, my man.

But was he my man?

I thought about all those young men who were far from safe, and of those who had already suffered. Mother's sister's son had been badly injured at Ypres; two boys down the street whom we had played with as children had died in the first months on the Marne. And then, well, there was Guy. No wonder Daphne gave such parties. The times created an atmosphere of now or never.

I tried again to concentrate on my letter to Neil.

Should I tell him about Guy?

An awful thought ran through my brain. There was no need.

If... If... No.

No need to mention anything about Guy, especially if... I shrank from the reality. Nothing had happened. Neil needn't know. He'd prefer not to know. It had only been a party. It didn't really concern him. It had just been a happening, an accidental happening. The roses were dead. Perhaps, and at any time, working in submarines, Guy himself might be dead. It was wartime. Life and emotions got accelerated in wartime to make up for...all the risks.

On with my weekly letter.

I wrote on a regular basis, despite the hazards of wartime gaps, which made me shudder when I thought of all those terrible inroads the Germans were making on our shipping. What had I last written to Neil about? That had been aeons ago. Before...?

Before I'd told him how we'd had to economise in paper at school and how there were only three men left on the staff, and how I missed him. I'd written how the boys were all keen to get into the army under-age, and how the sports had to be cancelled, and how I missed him. I'd told him about Gwen's singing and how I'd just finished reading 'The old Wives' Tale'. Now what? My mind was a blank.

Something safe. Yes. His father. Dudley.

Dudley was always pleased to see me and I could report how his war effort was growing vegetables, which he gave away in basketsful. He'd dug up a large part of the back lawn and grew celery, peas, carrots and beans in abundance. That was it, the garden, safe ground, the garden! I smiled to myself. And Cora. Yes I would tell him about Cora. In all seriousness I had done my best not to irritate her and we were on speaking terms.

'I was lucky to catch your mother in with all the work she does on the Lady Mayoress's Committee.' I wrote. 'She and Ada have thrown themselves into the war-effort, organising knitting bees, bandage-rolling and raffles for the wounded. Their good work has put them in touch with new friends. They really are part of the establishment now.'

That was alright.

Normally I never had to think what I would write about. The ideas flowed. Writing to Neil was my greatest pleasure, a high point of the week. I liked settling down on the kitchen table when everyone was out.

I found myself pushing the hair off my forehead. Now, what had I written?

I re-read from the beginning.

'Dearest Neil'.... Yes he was dearest Neil. He was kind, he was good and he needed me more than anything. Mother was perfectly right. He had gone out to Assam to make a life for both of us. It wasn't his fault that the war had intervened and it couldn't go on forever... I diddled around with my nib. It was trailing ink. A hair caught in it perhaps. Yes. I eased it out and continued.

'What else can I tell you that's interesting?' Yes. News of Daisy and Desmond.

'Daisy and Desmond are shortly to be married. No fancy wedding, but with the war on and Desmond in the navy, they're not going to wait any longer.'

It was then that I realised that I would have to tell him about the party after all. I bit my lip. I had met Celia, and she was sure to gossip to her mother and in no time the news would get to Cora.

I twiddled with how to do it. Yes. Tell him about Desmond's sister! Nothing wrong with that!

'Desmond's sister is an amazing woman, very (underlined) good looking and very talented. She was on the London stage. A week or two ago Daisy took me along to meet her. She gives very sophisticated parties. Champagne, if you please, and everybody seemed to smoke (not me, of course!) Now here's a surprise for you! (Good idea!)

'Guess who I met at the party? Of all people, your mother's friend, Ada's daughter, Celia. She recognised me and asked after you. She's married too! It seems everyone's married except us. She introduced me to her husband Adrian, a Lieutenant in the Navy, but I expect you have already heard about that from your mother.

What else is there to tell you? Well, Clive's been on leave and brought his wife and little boy around to see us. Maud's son Philip, is the same age. I took them both to Alexandra Park together to the swings, because, as you know, understandably, Maud is pretty low at the moment...'

At that point I was interrupted by a knock on the door.

I answered.

Guy was standing there, his shape outlined by the white light exploding round him in the doorway.

I could scarcely breathe.

Not a word. He took me in his arms.

'I'm back,' he said.

And nothing was ever the same again.

FIVE

'Of course I will' I answered. 'My boys are off all day at the football rally.'

The famous Mrs. Lander of the black knick-knocks, who was never away from school, had bad 'flu, and I was taking her class in my old classroom. Ironic that, but it didn't occur to me until later, but it was in that room with forty two ten-year-olds crocheting cotton loops round beads for milk-jug covers that it happened. The realisation.

Pregnant. I was pregnant.

Lasting only about three seconds I experienced a faint wave of nausea and what I can only describe as a hot flush; a queer sensation that I had never felt before.

My period which was as regular as the Isle-of-Wight ferry hadn't come. And?

'You're panicking,' said sister Maud.

'I've never been so late before,' I answered.

I had gone round to Maud's not because we were especially close, but she was my sister and reputedly 'a woman of the world' though that wasn't mother's name for it. Also I had been helping her a bit with Philip, since David's death on the 'Triumph'.

'Well, we'll try to bring it on,' she said, not asking any questions, which was decent of her.

I still had the picture in my mind of the rough, splintered, wooden class-room floor and how, in shock, I had jogged the tin of coloured glass beads so they had skittered everywhere.

Nellie and Violet had seen my look of annoyance, as the beads tinkled down in dozens in their reds and blues and greens.

'Don't worry, Miss, we'll pick them up for you.' Dear girls, I wanted picking up, not those ridiculous beads.

Pregnant.

I had never given such a thing a thought.

I had always been so careful.

Never, after those seized, tumultuous moments with Guy, had I ever left nature to chance.

Again, I felt myself swelling with heat.

The beads mesmerised me.

Some were stuck between the boards and needed dislodging with knitting needles. Horrible thought. Some were never gouged up, but eventually most were restored to the tin.

Total disbelief. Could this be happening to me?

All those daring exploits with Neil on that rag rug, in that sagging iron bed! What I didn't know then and know now, was that Neil had never got anyone pregnant. No-one. Not even Pam or, later, Celia, and certainly not me. There had never been any risk.

Maud's voice was saying, 'Only six days? Nothing to get worried about. I've got some of Eedie's pills. A really hot bath and a good stiff gin might do the trick.'

I don't know how I let her talk me into it.

I was walled up in her shiny modern bathroom.

To have a bathroom as a regular feature in a house, was modern. Dad had started to turn our back bedroom into a bathroom ages ago, but never got round to the plumbing. Maud's bathroom in her new house was state of the art, with fancy snowdrop tiles and a dark green frieze of leaves round the entire wall. You didn't have to cart the hot water upstairs either, for facing me as I lay sweating, was a copper monster of a gas geyser which could create it on the spot. Its gas blue-eye flickered as it hypnotised me with its power.

'This isn't funny. It's terribly hot.'

'You've got to have it as hot as you can stand it.'

'Don't put any more in or I shall faint. I'm already suffering third degree burns.'

'Five minutes more and I'll give you a cold douche.'

'Why?'

'Shock. Shock works wonders.'

'I'm shocked enough. The whole thing's a terrible shock.'

'Not that kind of shock,' Maud said scathingly.

I must say she never asked questions. I have to give her that. She didn't probe. It was just as if I had had a bad fall off my bike. If only! I lay scalding, in the hard Portsmouth water, my skin red and corrugated with the handfuls of soda crystals which softened it.

'Now drink this.'

'What is it?'

I didn't need to ask for I could smell it from where she was standing. Dutch gin.

'I've put a bit of water in it and here's a couple of Eedie's pills.' Eedie was mother's niece, daughter of our uncle and aunt who had died. She kept a pub down at the Hard where all the sailors went, and she and Maud had always been friends. Eedie knew her way around.

'Should I take them?'

'Eedie says they're pretty reliable, but it's up to you.'

'You know what mother always said.'

'I said it's up to you.'

'Could they damage the baby?'

'They're supposed to wipe out the baby.'

Until that moment, I had given little thought to the reality of a baby.

A baby was a person. I was trying to get rid of it as if it were a disease. The shame and disgrace of a daughter getting pregnant before marriage would kill mother, particularly since I was her favourite daughter, the one who was going places. What chance of going anywhere now? Even Maud, mother's unfavourite daughter was married safely to David before she got pregnant, whatever had 'gone on' before.

Mother! Her disappointment! I could hardly bring myself to think about it. She'd have been devastated if it had been Neil's baby, now, how much more devastated she would she be to know it was Guy's! I wasn't just letting her down, but Neil, of whom she was so fond, Neil, faithful and devoted in faraway Assam. In her eyes it was the worst, the very worst thing I could have done.

What had happened to me?

What was the best thing to do?

What was the proper thing, the decent thing to do?

Why wasn't I the person I thought I was?

It's strange that when something utterly catastrophic happens you see everything, every detail and problem in an instantaneous flash. When the beads fell all over the floor that's exactly what had happened. My reaction? Desperation. How to undo the past weeks. As if I could.

I had gone to see Guy whenever an opportunity arose. Hell, it was wartime, he was involved in dangerous expeditions, life-threatening. He needed the totality of wild sex as much as I did. I didn't like to admit that I was in love with him, but he had me in thrall. All those things which Daisy said Daphne liked about him I liked, and he was such an erotic lover. Those years with Neil had been fresh, simple, fragile but now I could hardly recognise myself. Guy filled me with fire, tantalisingly, he made me laugh with his irreverence and impertinence. I had taken good care to do all the things you do to avoid pregnancy, but I had been too clever by half, and was drowning in my own disbelief.

'Right down.' Maud was standing over me, holding out the glass and the pills. 'You're in a jam as I see it. This could fix everything.'

If only, if only.

Looking back I thought it was probably the stupidest thing I had ever done in my life.

I swallowed down the pills, washed with gulps of revolting hot-gin water. Not much water either and I hated the taste of gin.

'I'm feeling sick. The heat, the smell.'

Maud put a wrung-out cold flannel on my forehead. It was marvellous. She was telling me to get out and it was burning her skin, trying to pull out the plug. However I got out I don't know, but before I knew anything I was standing in a tin bath of cold water and Maud was dipping it all over me with a dipper.

'I'm...' I stumbled to the side of the big bath and vomited. That was relief, temporary relief, but then the awful upheaval again. Curdled yellow mess spreading like a jellyfish was mixing into the disappearing water. Strands of my hair were caught up with it. Holding the side of the bath, I sank back onto the floor. Another cold flannel on my forehead, and Maud wrapped me round with a towel.

'Hope some of it went down,' she said. 'Vomiting was about the worst thing you could have done. You ought to take some more, to make sure.'

'I can't. I feel dreadful. I couldn't do any of that again.'

'We'll just have to hope then.'

I hoped.

I hoped just about as hard as anyone can hope, but all in vain. They were days of great anxiety. My 'queer time' didn't come.

Sounds funny now, but that was what we called it. Back then with five girls in the family and a mother who would never dream of wasting money on things you could buy in the chemist, we all had our bits of cotton towel and sheeting to deal with our monthly bleeds. These rags which were kept soaking in covered buckets in extraordinary places were washed by mother and hung out to dry. Sometimes she would soak them in diluted urine to help remove blood stains. Boiling in soap and water would do the rest.

'There's always proper medical abortions, if none of this works,' said Maud, trying to be re-assuring. 'That kind of thing's better done away from here where people talk.' She opened her eyes, knowingly, then stood thinking for a moment. 'Aunt Annie's your best bet. Costs a lot, of course. But how are you going to explain this away with Neil in India?'

How?

Those ensuing days were dreadful days. I didn't want to contact Guy, even if I could. I had to resolve this by myself. In any case he was back on duty in Chatham and away for several weeks at a time on hazardous underwater operations. That first time when he had been 'missing' the 'J' class submarine on which he was chief engineer, had actually been on reconnaissance around the Kiel canal, total enemy territory, spying out the enemy fleet! It made me shudder to think of the iron nerves that crew had to have with such risk and tension. One of their diesels had broken down and they had hit bottom in an emergency dive, not realising how shallow were the waters. The heavy merchant traffic in and around the Baltic Sea at the time meant that in addition they had had to stay on the bottom, hiding, and were days behind schedule. No wonder they had been posted missing. (bel. d.) Guy eventually was to win a DSC for his part in fixing things. Pity nothing could fix me.

Nothing worked. All that horrible, unnatural, unhealthy torture and nothing worked. Those days of hoping, investigating, imagining blood traces were in vain. I must have the reproductive system of a Hydra to stand up to such bombardment. And the ironies did not escape me then or now, that my poor dead sister Margaret had only still-born children and Daisy was never ever able to get pregnant.

This baby.

Some baby which could survive the Scylla and Charybidis of Eedie's pills, gin and scalding baths. What could I do next?

I knew all the stories about kitchen table abortions, fake doctors and shifty people in the know. Aunt Annie, who knew everyone in and around her pawn-shop in Bethnal Green was a possibility, but something held me back.

Whether the baby survived or not, I was no longer the same person. I was not the woman Neil had fallen in love with. I had done the worst thing. I had chosen to go off with another man. How unrealistic had I been supposing getting rid of the baby would preserve our status quo.

But how was I to tell him?

Every one of his letters held me as being the most precious thing in his whole life. I knew all too well what this would mean to him. The social disaster of pre-marriage pregnancy was nothing compared to his grief.

How had it all happened? I knew, of course I knew.

I had fallen for Guy.

These were very sad, desperate weeks. Dessa the confident, Dessa the ebullient had undergone a total metamorphosis.

Suddenly and unexpectedly events moved and whirled me along with them.

Guy re-appeared.

'I'm back! Aren't you going to ask me in?'

He stood smiling, looking very dashing in his uniform, and before I could utter, he kissed me full on the lips and stepped inside. Father was in the fernery, smoking. Mother, mercifully, was out. Father reported him to Mother later as a 'fine-looking young man, fighting for his country' with 'some sort of connection to Desmond and Daisy'. He was very impressed, too, for outside Forty One stood a dashing, shiny, three-wheeler car, another cynosure for the eyes of the street.

'Hired it for my leave, so we can get about together,' he said. 'I have plans for us. It's high time you stopped fighting against my charm!'

It was then that I burst into tears.

We had driven up and along the hill. Portsmouth, its harbour and Porchester Castle lay below us. He pulled in and put his arm round me.

Very gently he took out his handkerchief and wiped the tears from my cheek.

'What's been happening? Tears? You? Anything wrong? Tell me.'

I did.

Everything.

I think it was the spontaneity of his reaction which bowled me over. The last thing I expected was that he might be pleased.

His eyes widened and shone. His face was breaking out all over in a smile. He was laughing and squeezing me tightly.

'My lucky day!' he exclaimed, giving me an enormous hug, still laughing, utterly delighted.

I was wide-eyed in disbelief.

'Terrific! Two at a blow! Nothing like long hours under the sea to make you realise what's missing in my life, darling! You! I love you!'

I was more embarrassed than anything. I didn't want him to think I was pointing a pistol at him, and I was so at odds with myself I couldn't get out a proper sentence.

'I don't want you to feel....'

'That I have to marry you!' He laughed all over again. 'That's exactly what I want to do. And now couldn't be a better time!'

I was still fumbling for words, and very tearful. 'I'm not sure whether...'

'You love me?' he interrupted 'Is that what you were going to say?

I didn't realise that I was shaking my head. I wasn't meaning to.

'Don't worry,' he went on, 'if that's all it is you soon will. I'm a very loveable person.' He smiled broadly, putting his finger across my lips. His eyes really asked the next question.

Slowly I nodded.

'See! It wasn't that hard, was it!'

I felt an enormous relief as I drew into him closely.

'I think I'm pretty lucky,' he said. 'And a baby! No putting things off in wartime! All's fair in love and war, remember?'

He lifted my hand gently to his lips and kissed it, looking closely for my engagement ring which I had taken off, disgusted with myself. Again, his eyes said it all. He asked no questions.

'Wedding ring soon, for what it's worth. Besides you've no idea yet what the ten days leave is about. I'm being drafted to Scotland, Rosyth, to carry out trials on His Majesty's secret naval weapon. We'll be married as soon as we can. Agree?'

SIX

Pregnant. Married. Scotland.

Even now I don't like to think too much about those frightful weeks preceding what I can only describe honestly as treachery, my treachery. I had let down mother. I had let down Neil. I had not been able to resist Guy's overtures and I had deliberately played what mother called 'fast and loose' imagining I was scot free to persist with my original plans of marrying a tea-planter, having had all the fun, indulgence, excitements and flattery of those exotic moments with someone more exciting.

'You can't eat your cake and have it.' Those were mother's warning words when the roses had arrived, even though at that time I had technically done nothing wrong.

Wrong! It makes me smile now that I know so much more about life and its double standards. Believe me I mourn for all those sad girls whose lives were ruined because they 'had to get married' and for those even sadder, more desperate girls who died having abortions. I could write a book about 'Sex and Society'. Having had five children I know how comforting it is to have the re-assurance of a partner. Managing on your own is very hard. I know that a huge weight fell from me when Guy actually wanted to have our child and it wasn't simply a matter of obeying a social code. We loved each other. Did we? I think we did.

Sex or love?

Mother would have said 'sex', except that was a word which was never used in those days. She never let on what her feelings were in that regard, but her provocative eye and passionate nature certainly attracted father, if only evidenced by the fact that married at seventeen, she had twenty one pregnancies.

Certainly I never realised the full depth of my own sexuality until Guy. His confident sophistication, sensual originality and humour swept me to thirst for his teasing embraces. The hyperbole of war, danger, weapons, and top-secret experiment, meant that we couldn't get enough of each other in those exciting weeks in Rosyth, newly married. He could never pass me without touching me, arresting anything I happened to be doing. 'Lineaments of gratified desire'. Blake got it right. We made whirlwinds of love on kitchen chairs, against available walls, in the well of the stairs. Such moments of assuagement were perfect in themselves, but, like a drug, primed with the worming current which urged more. I found myself fixated and bowled over by such love. Thoughts of Neil, Mother, guilt, faded into insignificance. Besides I was several months into my pregnancy and physically involved in a growing visible future. Up in Scotland, away from my family's critical eyes, the immediate weeks were a continuous honeymoon, that is, until the Admiralty had put together the final touches for the K class submarine, and Guy was posted again to Harwich.

We put together the bits and pieces which underpinned our life and Guy went on ahead to find a furnished flat for us in Dovercourt, where eventually Mo was born.

Once down in Essex I found myself on my own for the first time ever. Malins Road had always been bursting with children, babies, the comings and going of brothers and sisters, neighbours in and out; it was, and always had been, a hive of living activity. I remembered how much I had wanted my independence and a room of my own, how I had loved my job at West Meon and all those weekends with Neil and the motor bike. Somehow, Dovercourt wasn't like that at all. I had too much time to think. There was nothing to interrupt me, and there was the guilt of unfinished business.

Neil.

Guy would not be away just for a few days at a time. Harwich was the Naval base for operations in the North Sea, the Baltic Sea, and even as far away as The Gulf of Finland. I was on my own and with plenty of time for reflection and concern.

Mother.

I had only ever seen Mother cry once, and that was when William died, aged fifteen, despite all her efforts to combat his tuberculosis. She would wrap him up in scarves and send him off on the tram to the hill to get the fresh air he so badly needed, for she heard that sanatoriums were built up in the mountains and 'air' helped. She had him sleep with her in bed at night, to comfort him, wracked by his bone-shaking cough. She gave him little nips of brandy to keep him going, but all in vain. When he died she would not bring herself to have him buried, but kept his body in the parlour surrounded by Madonna lilies for more than ten whole days. Lovely as lilies are, I cannot bear their scent without seeing my pale cadaverous brother in his coffin, so young and so ravaged, lying in mother's front room.

Yes. She had wept then, not with sobbing hopelessness, but what was worse, a moist dampness of tears which kept her eyes red and sore for weeks behind her pebble-spectacles. When I summoned the courage to tell her that I was going to Scotland to marry Guy, she had the same reaction.

Past grief, fury and disappointment, she had risen quietly from her chair. The silence was worse than any reprimand. She stood and looked at me. Her watery eyes obliged her to take off her glasses as she took out her handkerchief to wipe them. 'I hope it will be for the best,' was all she said, then, after a pause added 'you'd best tell your father.'

She had guessed everything.

There had been nothing I could say or do. She had waved her hand slowly across the air in front of her, dropped her arm uselessly, closed her eyes and took in a deep breath. That was all.

On my own in the flat in Dovercourt I went over that moment again and again.

Guy had done well to find anywhere for us to live. In 1916 with the swollen importance of Harwich, naval wives and families as well as ancillary staff swamped the area because it was close enough to the power-house of the port, yet sufficiently removed to be comfortably habitable. Dovercourt had originally been a modest Victorian sea-side settlement, rather like a small-scale Southsea. The houses along the sea-front were three or even four storeys high with sea-views, gables and wide windows. The naval officers' wives who lived there were largely pretty rich and snobby, with nannies for their children and upper class accents to delight Professor Higgins. My introductions into this new Naval social world brought a renewed, vulnerable schoolgirl flush of feeling, the same as I had experienced when being denigrated as a scholarship girl, of not being 'out of the top drawer', as they used to say. I didn't feel this at all when Guy introduced me to his fellow submariners who largely were an odd mixed breed, but I certainly felt it when introduced to Commanders' wives who wanted to know family 'background' and called the Red Cross the 'red crawss'. Celia Bennett would have been in her element in such a social milieu, along with Cora and Ada but I wasn't as 'au fait' as I would like to have been, and I needed to adjust.

What had happened to my proverbial panache? What indeed! Guy had enough 'panache' for two; part of his attraction, I guess, who prior to knowing him had always been the one to make the running for the entire family. Although I braved it out, I think that the social pressure of 'having to get married' undermined me. I can't impress on you enough how black a mark it was at that time. I had to salvage myself to 'take on' these 'socially conscious' Naval people who seemed more interested in prying and snobbery than making friends. Looking back, I must admit that my entry into this new life was a baptism of fire.

Besides the compulsory ladies' social tea and coffee parties and the intermittently wild, spontaneous drinks gatherings when crews got safely home after reckless brushes with the enemy, I spent a lot of time alone in the flat. It consisted of the first floor of a three-storey house, with a lodger who lived in a bed-sitter up in the attic, with whom we had to share the bathroom. Mr. Newman was a bachelor about fifty, who worked in the post office in town. He was silent and quiet and to my surprise, hardly ever seemed to need the bathroom at all, but he would nod on the stairs and would always help me carry down rubbish when Guy was away. The landlady, on the other hand, was quite the opposite. She always 'caught you' just as you were hurrying off. She was the kind who wanted to know 'the business' as mother put it, and if any mail came she brought it up not so much out of kindness as to have a sniff round. I once caught her coming out of our bedroom, saying she had shut the window for me because she 'thought it was going to rain', not that I had seen any signs. However, she was the landlady and she lived on the ground-floor and I think she was lonely. Every now and again I bought her a few flowers to get on-side and that worked a treat. Guy chatted her up wonderfully when he was at home so we passed muster as 'good tenants, so much better than the last.' Never having had children herself she was thrilled at the idea of a baby being born in the house.

'Call me Mavis' she said. 'No more of this Mrs. Pyne.' What had happened to Mr. Pyne we never knew, but she and I stayed on first-name terms and kept in touch right up until the time we went to Africa.

The flat consisted of our bedroom, a very small box room, a kitchen made from another small bedroom and the bathroom, the same. Mrs. Pyne, (Mavis) had gone one step further than Father, and actually had put plumbing into this converted bedroom, including a geyser all too like the one Maud had in her house. There was a washbasin and the china indoor lavatory, with a curling blue and white design round the pan. The best feature of the flat, however, was the living room, which was sunny and bright and large enough for a round dining table, as well as easy chairs. In the bay-window was an old-fashioned sofa with a curled end, and in those weeks before Mo was born I would put his weight and my legs up and look out onto the street and the gardens. It was here I did my thinking. A lot of thinking. But it had to be done. I couldn't put it off any longer.

I had to face telling Neil.

I had never thought of myself as being the kind of person to let others down yet I had let Neil down in the worst possible way. All his trust. All his love. I had done everything in absolute inverse proportion to all the depth of feeling and emotion he had invested in me. The question which troubled me was if I had managed to get rid of the baby, could I really have gone on with Neil as before? Was I that same pre-war person? I had to face up to myself, no messing.

The straight answer was 'no'.

I had 'gone off' with another man. The better the situation had worked out for me the worse it was for him. I knew him well enough to know that not telling him was adding daily to his misery.

Frailty was too polite a word for what was cowardice.

I had to write. If the first letter didn't reach him because of all the wartime hazards, well, I would just have to write again. Punishment? Yes. I would write to Cora as well. She would be over the moon.

'Dear Neil,' I wrote. 'I have tried to write to you innumerable times, but I can't get the words right. They never will be right. I have only myself to blame for what has happened and I am very conscious of the terrible hurt it will cause you.

I am pregnant.

I am ashamed to admit that I tried to get rid of the baby, something only my sister knows. It was as unsuccessful as it was stupid. I couldn't have pretended to you for the rest of my life. In the circumstances I felt that the only thing I could do was marry the father, since he seemed to want me. Somehow I thought this would do you the least harm and leave you free to start again with better luck.

I cannot, and do not, forgive myself for the harm I have done you. I didn't mean it to end like this.

Forgive me if you can Dessa.'

If only I had written straight away!

What a coward I had been, and in a way, still was because I couldn't put into words the fact that I was in love with someone else. I simply couldn't tell him that, not after everything.

This time I didn't re-read the words and tear them up, but went straight to the Post Office. There the letter-box swallowed them for better or for worse, to regurgitate them half-way round the world.

I felt sick at the thought of the misery Neil would feel when he read the contents.

The next day I wrote briefly to Cora and Dudley. Dudley was heartbroken I learned later, but apparently Cora told Ada that it was the best piece of news she had heard in years.

'What did I tell you!' she had exclaimed with satisfaction.

SEVEN

'Guess what, Darling! Yours Truly is the right man in the right place at the right time! I've been offered the management of 'Rituparna' for the duration! If only you were here so we could move in together. I've got a whole lot of stuff over from Mother and I think it needs a woman's touch to arrange everything in this great bungalow. It's not as rambling as 'Tinkharia' but huge for the two of us! As for the master bedroom, well I mustn't think about that! I leave it to your imagination!

Oh, this war! And you there and me, here, alas! The news, however, still seems pretty gloomy and the chances of bringing it to an end seem as far away as ever. No good moping, darling, we've got to make the best of it. At least we've got each other.

Picture me, your own silly old Neil, sitting in a large armchair, surveying the world from my, *our*, verandah, smoking, yes! A cigar! To celebrate my promotion in your absence I bought myself a box of Havanas! (Is that two 'n's or one?) There's only one thing missing to make everything perfect, and that's you, my darling. Gypsy is lying at my feet, dying to have you here as much as me! If only!

The next thing on the list is to get a car. Absolutely essential .How will you like that? Remember the old motor-bike? What fun we had together.

I'm even allowing myself to think about our wedding! What do you think? Better for me to come home or for you to come out? Sentiment or money? Three fares against one, and the girls here at the club would lay on a super reception. Nothing they'd like better. But it's your choice.'

I couldn't read any more.

Gwenny had come to stay with me for a week for company, while Guy was away. She had brought a suitcase full of my things, including a packet of letters from Neil, which had lain, unopened, on the chest of drawers in the back bedroom. I had opened the top one.

I drew breath and stared at the wall.

This is just what I didn't want to read or think about. The ironies were too hard to bear. My own letter with all its finalities must have crossed with this one. No. Not crossed. Was crossing. I simply couldn't face opening any of the others. I must have looked peculiar because Gwenny asked me if I was feeling funny. The baby? Twinges? Faintness? Morning sickness? Certainly not the last. Our family never seemed to have sicknesses in pregnancy of any kind. Then she cottoned on, not surprisingly, because the envelope had fallen to the floor, and the sheets of paper were still in my hand.

She didn't say a word but just looked at me.

'Put them away' she said, 'or better still, burn them. If you don't want to do it I'll do it. It's water under the bridge.'

Even at the time I remember being surprised that my baby sister was standing by me giving me advice: she, whom I had pushed up to mother's garden in the old pram with the even younger Morris up the other end.

'Come on out,' she said. 'A walk by the sea will do you good. Aristotle advised pregnant women to walk every day to the shrine of the goddess of childbirth to pray for a safe delivery. If that was good enough for the Greeks it's good enough for you. Come on! The past is the past.'

'Is it?' I remember thinking. 'In my case it seems endlessly to shape the present, and at considerable cost. At the time of course I didn't realise how profound that was.

Over in Assam, Neil was feeling inner, darkening tremors. He had made the move to Rituparna. 'The girls', Pam and Eulalie had helped him make the change. They had been marvellous, but, increasingly he felt something was wrong.

No news.

'No news is good news,' he told himself unconvincingly. He tried to feel how he had been feeling only a week or two ago. He had no reason to feel any different. Dessa was always in his mind, especially now. How would she arrange all these rooms? She had flair. How she would love 'Rituparna'. The excitements! She'd make a great Company wife. He tried to bring to mind the teasing expression on her face when she tilted her chin challengingly to provoke him, or the sound of her spirited laughter. There was no-one remotely like her, confident, fearless, challenging. She'd take on Eulalie, even. And they'd make a great pair at tennis. He could see her, full of initiative, entering into everything, friendly, amusing. He was sure all the people he knew would like her and pretty sure she would like them.

He could teach her Bridge and with her sharp mind, she'd soon be expert. They would give parties. She'd be so good at everything! She could act in plays, (he smiled to himself as he remembered his own agonies in 'Arms and the Man'.)

Yes, all that, but why no letter? What could be wrong?

It was in the middle of such thoughts that he realised that Gypsy was no longer lying at his feet. She usually lay on his feet and he couldn't move without disturbing her. Now he was the one being disturbed. That evening, pre-occupied, he'd neither noticed her coming or going. He had thought no more of it, but needing a breath of night air he walked from the verandah into the garden, whistling for her casually. She always came with him if he went for an evening stroll. Strange. She didn't turn up. He whistled again.

Again, no doggy, bounding rush; nor, as sometimes when she got up to tricks of her own, a return with slow, slinking compliance. Perhaps she was round at the back? Cook, maybe, was giving her an extra treat over from dinner.

Neither Vikram nor Lila had seen her.

He strolled along the roadway where lights and dying fires and the aftermath of cooking smells indicated that the workers were settling down for the night.

'Any sign of Gypsy?' he asked Ravi, Nishan and Karn who were sitting smoking on some steps. They shook their heads.

He wandered over to the sheds and the office. Ravi called out that perhaps she had come over to play with the children.

'Naughty girl with the pi dogs,' called out Karn, laughingly, his white teeth shining in a flicker of firelight.

Neil gave up. Silly to get worried unnecessarily. She'd run off once before when they had first come to this new place, but she'd come back stinking of something dead she'd rolled in and he remembered how woebegone and bedraggled she had looked with all her fur soaking wet as he scrubbed the smell off her. That night he thought he heard scratching sounds underneath the house. He had strained his ears, hearing and not hearing. The quivering silence reminded him when, as a small boy, he was sure he had heard Father Christmas' sleigh. Again he could swear he heard a noise, but nothing. Maybe she was trapped. He went outside to check under the house again; nothing. Nothing. No Gypsy.

Neil was wholly unnerved.

His dog. He and his dog were inseparable. She helped make up for Dessa's absence, the distance, the war. No letters. They were a lifeline. Gypsy was a lifeline, and now? Weeks with no letters, and no Gypsy.

Despite searching the property with two of his workers, probing animal holes, the dam, old sheds, no sign. Neil whistled his lips dry. Any excitement in moving to Rituparna had evaporated. Later that week he had to go into Jorhat. His first call was at the post office. Hari, the clerk had known him from a boy and called him Mister Neil to differentiate him from 'Mr. Langford' his father. They always had a bit of a chat.

'No jerry blow-up this time,' smiled Hari, handing over the mail.

Neil's flash of remission tailed off in disappointment as he fingered through the envelopes rapidly. One from his mother, various business letters, but nothing from Dessa. The next week, nothing. The next week, the same. Neil couldn't comprehend what was happening. Everything that mattered was falling apart. No Dessa. No dog. Was she all right? The war. Portsmouth. Zeppelins. Accidents.

He bumped into Pam.

'Whatever's the matter with you?' she enquired. 'You look dreadful.'

'I feel dreadful,' he confessed. 'Nothing's going right at the moment. Gypsy's missing and no mail.'

She looked at the envelopes in his hand.

'Nothing from Dessa.'

'Anything could have happened.'

'That's what's worrying me.'

'And your dog?'

Pam knew all about Neil's passion for Gypsy whom he had chosen as a gift from one of her spaniel's litters.

'That is worrying. Let's have lunch together and you can tell me all about it.' She put her arm round his shoulders and gave him a re-assuring squeeze.

That night neither present letters, nor letters saved from long-ago, nor whisky, could ease Neil's mood. He smoked a couple of cigarettes. He got out a cigar, but after a few puffs, allowed it to burn into aromatic ash beside him. Those iconic photographs on the mantelpiece looked paper thin and hollow. His mother's large furniture menaced. No Gypsy to weight his feet. His helplessness and impotence was crippling. He had never known before what it was to feel so sad.

A scratching sound suddenly brought all his faculties into action. Gypsy! He undid the door catch on the verandah. As he peered into the darkness a gust of wind flung the second door back against the wall. Nothing.

A week later Dessa's letter arrived.

He froze in disbelief at its news.

He could not even weep. Dessa had brought him to life and now Dessa had killed him.

What was left? He did not know.

EIGHT

Tribal Arab women take over the corpses. The Club women, as Cora had foreseen, took over the walking corpse of 'Poor Neil'.

'He couldn't be in a better place,' Cora told Ada. 'They'll see him through, and in no time they'll introduce him to young women of his own class. Young, eligible bachelors aren't ten a penny, and now Neil has walked into 'Rituparna' at such a young age, he'll really be worth having, mark my words.'

If only!

Cora didn't understand her own son, but then she never had.

Dessa had been the making of him and he could neither believe, accept or understand whatever had gone wrong between them.

Those green shimmering early summer days among trees in the park, bursting with bright new tender unfolding leaves; the sound of two pairs of feet ringing as one along the grey paving stones of Twyford Avenue; the feel of the silky sand between their linked fingers; her swaying hips before him as she led the way up those creaking, ancient wooden stairs; all those experiences which linked them, now no more. Nothing. It was not possible. Insights shared, their secret inner souls as one; mutual growth now severed. Eleven sentences had shattered all that mattered to him.

No Dessa. No Gypsy. Nadir.

He parsed and analysed every word of the letter to see if he had missed any nuance.

'Leave you free to start again.' Free? Free to start again? He couldn't bear the thought. How could he ever become another person? She would be in his mind whatever he did. He hadn't carried her with him every day since that parting at Southampton suddenly to wipe her existence from his life.

He re-read the words for the hundredth time. They spoke of accident, error, weakness, shame, but not of love. She hadn't said that she didn't love him anymore. He knew that she couldn't just write off all their years together. They were ingrained in each other like the rings in the trunk of an oak tree. The letter did say she had no choice. She had wanted to abort the child and that hadn't worked, so but for the baby they would be as they were. She wanted to get rid of the baby for his sake. That was a thought. For his sake. He meant more to her than this child. The child was the accident, and he read that she wished it hadn't happened.

If only---

He blamed himself for leaving her. He blamed the distance, the war. Perhaps whoever it was might be—but, no. He couldn't think of that. He couldn't wish someone dead.

His mother's letters were full of invective about Dessa and delight at his 'escape'. She had no idea. Never had. It could all have been so different.

In the early hours of the morning he would lie awake and go over the things they had done together. In the lulls between work, in his solitary evenings he mourned. The future was blank. He spent hours of grief-stricken sadness.

Work was his only antidote, and it was hard work, plus 'the girls' efforts which kept him afloat. They liked nothing better than to have a 'free' young man on their hands.

For them the outlook was simple.

Either you were engaged or you weren't and if you weren't you were fair game. And, come to think of it, Neil was pretty nice-looking, athletic, well-mannered, not some drink-sodden roué, or some idiot totally without a brain in his head. Shy, yes, but that added to his charm, and he had the good record of having been a devoted fiancé. Even some of the older ladies who had previously regarded him nepotally, now let their fingers linger as they passed him his drink. He became 'dear Neil' and found himself needing to pick and choose his invitations. Meanwhile the war went on.

Ever since his broken engagement, Neil had to admit that the people at the club had gone out of their way to be extra helpful and friendly. The news, as news does in small communities, swept through the neighbourhood. He was spared explanations, never left sitting alone in the bar, included in tennis parties and finally, with the special help of Pam, found himself able, after several attempts, to put together a reply to Dessa's letter.

'Darling,' he wrote. He simply could not bring himself to write 'Dear Dessa' in this, his final communication with her.

'Like you, I don't know how to begin or end this letter. Distance has made shrill echoes of all we think and feel. I blame myself for ever having left you and I feel so useless because I was not with you when you needed me most. It seems impossible that our lives must separate.

If there is any good in me, it is because you made it.

Go on being your own self. Neil.'

He couldn't bring himself to mention the child.

Somehow having written brought a degree of closure for him. Of course he worked very conscientiously and successfully managing his tea-garden, which now was the centre of his life, but he also started to throw himself into club activities, such as arranging tournaments, sitting on the Club's financial committee, and even being in the chorus of 'H.M.S.Pinafore'. Rehearsals were fun. Diana was a great pianist. Eulalie sang 'Buttercup' and he started to get extra friendly with Pam who was to become more than a 'sister and a cousin and an aunt'.

The circumstances of his daily life changed materially when Pam asked him over to choose a new pup.

She was older than Neil by nine years. She and her husband had two sons, both back in boarding school in the West country, where Pam's own brother had been educated. She was the daughter of a prosperous Corn merchant and had equal interests in the company with her brother who now ran the firm. Roger, ten years older, and a sometime friend of her brother, had married her when she was only eighteen, pleased to make use of her capital along with her innocent charms. Roger, himself, was a businessman. Initially he had been apprenticed to the tea industry as a tea taster, in Mincing Lane. This somewhat unusual occupation had come about indirectly through his father's family connections with Assam. However, impatient with the job's complexities Roger had given up the apprenticeship and gone out to Calcutta to work for a tea-broker. Dissatisfied with working for somebody else, he took the bold step of setting himself up in the tea business in Jorhat. Six foot three in height and autocratic in manner he was 'in' the Club rather than 'of' it. Pam and he lived on the outskirts of Jorhat itself, and increasingly as the years went by, he went away more and more frequently on business, leaving her to her friends, hobbies and pets. The war, of course, meant that she didn't get to see her boys, who were in the care of their grandmother, so she had too much time on her hands, and her husband never seemed to be around when she needed him.

'Come over and see for yourself. There are five in the litter. They're all adorable. You must choose one to try to get over Gypsy's loss.'

This time Neil chose a dog. He'd had enough of bitches. The new dog was to be Rex. Neil had to wait several weeks for Rex to be old enough to come back to Rituparna with him and it was during this time it happened.

They kissed. They made love. They needed each other. They were very discreet about when and how they met, for in such a small community they had to be careful. Danger added spice to their relationship. When they saw each other publicly they played a pretending game, but always managed, somehow, to catch the other's eye for re-assurance. It was exciting. Pam needed excitement. Neil relaxed in the pleasures of the flesh, and Pam was so kind to him. This was a new experience. Neither of the women in his life to date had been exceptionally kind.

Eulalie, Edith and Dodo enjoyed having their little suspicions.

'It's not as if they're hurting anyone,' said Dodo. 'After all Neil's been through with his ghastly engagement he needs a bit of you- know- what.'

'And Roger deserves some of his own medicine, if you ask me,' confided Eulalie. 'What do you suppose he gets up to when he has to go away so often!'

'Turn a blind eye,' advised Dodo.

'A bit late for that,' added Edith.

'None of our business.' Eulalie winked. 'Be real. It's hardly anything new! If only there were some young women around! Neil's hardly the type for affairs. He wants and needs marriage. He's too young to get himself tangled up for years on end with a married woman ten years older than himself.'

'This beastly war again,' remarked Edith. 'We're shut away up here with no go to nor come from. We could all do with an influx of new blood.'

'I could do with three months back in England.'

'Couldn't we all!'

But the months wore on and on, all round a war-weary globe.

'We have to make the best of it, like everybody else.'

Dodo shrugged 'We do.'

'They are, at anyrate,' added Edith, dilating her nostrils.

NINE

Guy came back unexpectedly while Gwenny was still staying in Dovercourt with me. I fell about his neck with happiness. He had five days leave.

By this stage I was a full eight months pregnant, taut-stomached and large with bulbous nipples, strangely thickened hair and a bloom about me, according to Guy, which made me look fecund and 'utterly desirable'. He looked his spare handsome self but lined and strained, I thought.

'Nothing that a tot of whisky and a good old party wouldn't put right', he said.

A party! We would give a party.

The thought of giving a party was absolutely right. It brought back to me a sense of fun and living life to the full, which had been so lacking in me, during those recent weeks. Gwenny raved at the idea. Perhaps she'd meet someone! She had just started at training college, knew she was pretty good-looking, heard that Ginty would bring his gramophone and the idea of drinks and snacks and an ad hoc invasion of at least ten new people made her feel ecstatic.

'I'll do everything' she said, 'to save you. Cut the sandwiches, wash up, roll up the carpet!'

We invited Mavis to come up for a drink and she was thrilled. We invited Mr. Newman from upstairs, who declined but said he didn't mind the music and mumbled in monosyllables, that he hoped we'd have a good time. Guy bought the grog and got hold of a heap of glasses and we were away! Submariners certainly know how to let down their hair. The drink and smoke got everybody rolling, except me.

Looking back, I guess I was tired before the evening started, having done lots of extra things in preparation. The other problem was I did not ever drink or smoke much and now, never, because of the baby, so the more heated the guests became, the more marooned I felt. Sitting beside me on the couch was Mavis who was thrilled to be sipping port and lemon amidst all the noise. Guy would come up to me dutifully and kiss the top of my head at intervals but I could see increasingly that he and one or two others were getting drunk and occasionally shuffling round the room with a partner. Gwenny was pleased to be so popular. At this moment Guy and she were clasping each other and smiling inanely.

'Lovely girl, your little sister,' Guy was mumbling as they swayed past.

And then it happened. I wish I hadn't seen it but I did.

Guy, who was holding Gwenny very close, slid his hand down between her buttocks and held it there, then, as they mooched round, I watched him as he traced his fingers slowly upwards round her breasts. His eyes were half-shut, and I sensed that he was breathing heavily. She was inertedly relaxed and rubbing the tip of her nose against his cheek.

I could not believe what I was seeing and didn't know what to do. Mavis had already gone, and I had been chatting to another wife, who had been asking about the baby, and saying it was time they went before they all got too drunk to move.

'They're all as bad as each other' she was saying. 'But it's their way of letting off steam. They live on their nerves in those god-forsaken submarines. I think they've had pretty tense operations lately. Time for us to go, I reckon. I'll take Charles off your hands. One less.'

That was when I did a big sister act with Gwenny. She had flopped down on the sofa next to me.

'I saw,' I said.

'Saw what?'

'I'm not stupid,' I said, drawing her aside. 'You're encouraging him.'

She smiled which really made me cross.

'Don't think that's the first time.' she said. 'Blame him, not me. Some men are like that. You should know!'

'And you were encouraging him.'

'He doesn't need much encouragement,' she said.

'You've had too much to drink' I told her. 'And I don't like hearing what you're saying.'

She was trying to make a joke of it. 'I can't help being attractive! Relax! Everybody else's relaxing! We're only dancing!'

'Some dancing!' I felt jealous and left out. 'No clearing up to-night. You get to your bed.'

'Dessa?' She complained

'Yes.' I insisted.

By this time everyone was starting to melt away and Guy was practically asleep in the armchair. I pushed him into bed to sleep it off and crawled onto the edge of the bed beside him, wide awake, disappointed with the whole evening. When I got up before the others, the shambles of the room echoed my very feelings. And I had wanted it to be such a good party. I felt full of resentment.

The next day Gwenny had to return to Portsmouth which I was glad about. She was perfectly nice and happy. Either the alcohol was too much for her and she hadn't remembered, or maybe she didn't want to say anything which might upset me, or perhaps I was old-fashioned and didn't know how young people carried on these days. I felt rather stony-faced. We were all moving rather slowly after the previous night, I with tiredness, Guy, dazed but smiling ineffectually, and Gwenny with strong signs of hangover.

We got her to the station. I wasn't very communicative and she seemed completely oblivious of my impressions of the night before, but kept saying 'great party Dess.'

I was the only one full of rankles.

At the station she hugged me hugely, and said what a nice time she'd had and good luck for---she patted her stomach and winked. Then she swept her arms round Guy with a hug, and said how good it was to have a brother-in law-she really liked. He moved a strand of hair back from across her face. 'Dear girl,' he said.

I tightened my lips.

'Mother's bound to come,' were practically Gwenny's last words. Unlike me, she had moved on in time utterly. She won't let you have that baby on your own. She hasn't been out of Portsmouth since the time she went to Moorfield's to have her eyes done but she'll come, for sure. It'll do her good, a change.'

That evening after supper Guy came over to the sofa and stood looking at me in the lamplight.

'You look beautiful,' he said.

I wasn't to be drawn.

He sat down beside me and took my hand. I turned away.

'Something wrong?'

'I'm not stupid,' I said.

'Would I marry anyone who was?'

I turned to face him.

'That's your schoolteacher face.'

I wouldn't speak.

'Come on.'

'You know well enough.'

'What?'

'I saw.'

'What?'

'You and Gwenny.'

'And?' It was a party! We had fun!'

'I didn't. I was watching you.'

'She's a girl, I just cuddled her up a bit. She's attractive.'

'I don't call that fun! It wasn't fun for me. Do I have to put it into words? She's my sister.'

'And quite delightful. As I would expect. But not so clever.' He put his arm round me. I shrugged it off. My feelings would not shape themselves into words. Instead I clawed his forearms and felt like biting him. All he did was smile.

'More! The tiger in you. I like it.'

I took a deep breath. 'You're never to do anything like that ever again!'

Guy was rubbing the pinch marks and giving me an insinuatingly sexy look.

'Don't smile. I'm serious.'

'So am I.' He looked at me tenderly. 'You care!' was all he said.

My eyes were brimming. 'I don't want you touching other women, especially my sister.'

There was a pause. I could tell that he had felt me stiffen in isolation. He narrowed his eyes, moved closer imperceptibly and took my face in his hands. It was if as a chord had been played, changing mood, tone and key.

He spoke with a strange satisfaction, and what I can only describe as welcome surprise.

'You really do love me. That's wonderful. It's something to have with me always.'

I could tell, he really meant it.

All feelings of rancour were washed away. I thought of the pressures he had to endure. Touch melted the soul's shadow. He surprised me yet again.

Of course it was only a party. I mustn't waste our precious time together. It was stupid. There were only a few days.

We loved those hours in our flat together. The most ordinary things were special. Guy could fix anything. He put up hooks and shelves. He mended Mavis' spare bed. We moved the furniture round. We went shopping. He was always dreadfully extravagant and showered me with colognes and silk shawls. We talked about the baby and he organised a cot and a pram, despite my superstitions.

'It's in case I'm not around at the time. You never know what Keyes has up his sleeve.' That was true. No-one could forecast the ad hoc hit and miss projects the Navy had in mind now they had an ocean-going flotilla of diesel 'D' and 'E' class submarines.

An intensely real and deep affection reinforced our inevitable goodbyes.

Then he was gone.

Everything was empty, tidy and undisturbed.

My job now, was to have the baby.

It's one thing to beget a child and quite another to have one. I had never thought seriously about the birth, before. And I hadn't digested the idea that I would have to be responsible always for what Blake suggested might be a 'fiend', 'struggling' and 'striving.' I had looked after many babies, but had always returned them. I couldn't do that with this one. Was it a fiction or was there a natural umbilical link? I hoped so.

As Gwenny had said, Mother came. No questions. No reproaches. No discussions of marriage or Scotland or Neil, just the baby. Mother knew all there was to know about birth.

I met her at the station with a taxi. There she was, a little egg-shaped woman in a musquash fur coat with a large black fur collar and a pot-shaped hat, carrying a bulging Gladstone bag full of her accouchement accessories. She may not have been literate, but her intelligent eyes behind her pebble-glasses, missed nothing. From Portsmouth to Waterloo, across London to Liverpool Street, thence to Hastings; this was quite a journey for someone used only to cycling up to the garden. I felt utterly moved at the sight of her and as much as I longed to give her an emotional huge embrace, I knew how embarrassed she would be with such overt demonstration. My feelings condensed themselves into a small kiss on the cheek.

We drove back to Dovercourt and, thinking to please her, I asked the taxi-driver to show her the sights of the town, driving along by the smart houses on the promenade, but this held no interest for her whatever. She barely looked out of the window. What she had come for was to see the flat and to work out the strategy for the birth. I had invited Mavis upstairs for a cup of tea to meet her, and in no time they were talking pails, pans, breast-binders and buckets, while I sat by hearing words like 'afterbirth', 'waters breaking' and rubber sheets to protect the mattress. After that was settled, Mavis took Mother round the garden and they were on to de-budding, pruning and murdering snails. In those next days of waiting, Mother won a place in Mavis' heart with her snail-catching device; empty orange peel halves, or better still, grapefruit, and in the morning you could see how many snails you had caught. For some reason snails could get in but never understood how to get out. Like people I thought; caught.

The midwife came round and she and Mother hit it off fine, too. Absolutely no need for a doctor unless something went wrong. That made me blink a bit, but to date my pregnancy had been utterly straightforward, and having mother with me, especially since Guy was off on yet another mission, made me feel safe and excited both at the same time.

'It's surely due any day now,' said mother. 'I can tell because it's dropped.'

She was right. I hadn't really noticed that the shelf under my breasts which caused me occasional heartburn, had moved. Within a few hours I felt a wetness swamp me involuntarily.

'Find some things to do,' mother advised. 'It doesn't all happen at once. And remember it's not called 'labour' for nothing.

I read the newspaper. I found that I wasn't taking in all the things the fuzzy print was saying about the war. I tried knitting but that wouldn't stop me fidgeting either. 'I need to be active to get it going,' I thought. Mother was resting after lunch. 'I'll clean the windows and then the stove.' That should pass the time.

'Things have started' I told mother when she emerged. But she wasn't pleased to hear I had been stretching about.

'Not sensible,' she said. 'Do natural things, walking, not stretching.'

Twenty eight hours later Mo emerged, white, pale, head elongated by face presentation. He took his first faint breaths exhausted by his struggle, as was I. Apparently Doctor Francis had been called in for the final delivery. All my stretching about had caused the baby to turn the wrong way.

A boy.

Extraordinary, this reality of human flesh, this parcel of a new person.

And I had tried to rid myself of him.

I didn't like thinking about that, but could not help the thought crossing my mind.

This child, my child. Ours. I wanted him to grow up splendid and distinctive. I wanted a time-old distinguished name for him, not just an ordinary name, a name that came from Guy's side. Whichever side of the blanket, Guy had descended from the historic Mowbrays. Why not Mowbray for a name? We could call him 'Mo' for short.

News came from the Navy. Once again H.Q. in Harwich had lost all contact with E.9. All that anxiety again. Again. Waiting and waiting for news, but now I had Mo.

Guy was not to see his son until he was more than six weeks old.

TEN

Back in 1916, with no radar, contact from ships at sea mostly depended on pigeons. Something must have gone very wrong with the pigeon post in the early months of the year that Mo was born. What is incredible is how often these birds were utterly dependable, despite gales, enemy fire or freezing conditions. Guy ,who always knew something about everything, and keeping a perfectly straight face, had told me that Julius Caesar would never have conquered Gaul but for his pigeons, and if that didn't impress me, had I ever thought how the Rothschilds had increased their millions? Pigeons again, and being in first at the right time and in the right place to break the news to the world of Wellington's victory at Waterloo.

Waterloo! Who could care two pence for Waterloo? In those anxious weeks the pigeons faltered badly. History doesn't relate what happened to the pigeons bringing news of E9.

A first baby and no father to share him with.

I had joined the ranks of all those wives and mothers, alone, anxious, waiting for news, dreading the terrible telegram. How I could feel for them! I appreciated how lucky I was to have mother with me in those difficult weeks with no news of Guy. Mother made everything seemed routine. She never flapped She never ever said anything about the Navy or the war, and she never made the mistake of avoiding talking normally about him, as if she presumed at any moment that he would come walking right in through the door. She delighted in Mo and cherished him so that his white, stretched little face relaxed miraculously into a normal, sweet baby face. She looked at me blankly when I talked about her return to Portsmouth, and it was obvious that she had absolutely no intention of leaving until Guy arrived back to be with me. She was wonderful and kept me going.

At that time, but for unsightly rolled-out rolls of barbed wire along stretches of the beach at Dovercourt you would hardly have realised there was a war on, unlike Portsmouth where troops, guns and tanks reminded one daily. Seaside, sunshine, shopping and family social chat made it more relaxed, almost like holidays, yet close by was H.M.S. Maidstone, the H.Q. of British North-Sea and Baltic naval operations, and the far waters of that same sea broke over in places as unfamiliar as the Gulf of Finland. Recalling World War one, people think largely of the Western front or Gallipoli, but the need to blockade Germany, along with German military advances against Russia meant that English war policies focused on out of the way places such as Revel and Archangel, and that was where officers like Guy and Ginty were sent. Naturally, we, the wives, knew nothing of British Naval plans and The Navy was often in the dark about the positions of their own ships and crews themselves. As submariner-wives we had to accept the frightening and continuing possibility of our menfolk breathing away their last lingering gasps of oxygen under the ice-cold waters of a sub-arctic sea. Our patriotic efforts were to 'keep the home fires burning' in the hope of 'silver linings'. Understandably we sang sentimental songs; 'Sing for thee, sigh for thee'. We sang marching songs which encouraged us to 'smile, smile, smile', and not to worry. There were 'silver linings,' but it was 'a long way to Tipperary,' and life was like an irregular temperature-chart.

When the men came back into port safely, we celebrated ecstatically. Guy and Ginty had a huge capacity for revelry and they set each other off. We had parties, champagne, feverish lovemaking, and much laughter. They kept us in fits with their unbelievable stories.

Guy always came back between operations laden with gifts for me. He could never quite believe in the reality of his good luck, being alive, having a son, and the marvellousness of a wife and 'family'. I was swamped with flowers, jewellery, silk scarves, a Russian doll, the kind with one inside another and another, 'just like you darling, always pregnant.' True, I was pregnant again, this time with Austen. There were thirteen months between the children, which put paid to mother's advice, that you couldn't get pregnant while breast-feeding.

Guy's 'war' during this time reads like a continuing 'Boy's Own' adventure. E9 and E11 were sent to berth at Revel for two months It was all part of a British plan to obstruct the German' advance on St. Petersburg, and, apparently, the presence of these two submarines unnerved the enemy out of all proportion to their actual strength. Finally, it was directly as a result of this successful ploy that Guy, along with two other officers was promoted to Lieutenant-Commander, a significant promotion, and higher wages.

German Intelligence was at a loss as to what the British were up to. To foil any plans they had sent in two beautiful young women spies to poison key British Naval officers in Revel. The plan went very wrong. Instead of the girls disposing of the men as arranged, they fell in love with their victims.

'What else would you expect?' said Ginty, admiring himself sideways in the mirror.

'We had to play up to them,' said Guy, 'that is, if you wanted us back.'

'I'm not quite sure we do,' Ginty's wife, Yvonne, replied.

She and I were never convinced that there wasn't less truth in the story they wanted us to believe.

'All's fair in love and war, after all,' replied Ginty. 'This was war.' he added.

Whatever the truth, we were never to know, and at least they were back. All we could do was to play very hard to get and make them grovel, which is what we did. In the drink-sodden atmosphere of such goings on in Ravel what were we to think? Pretty extraordinary things had gone on everywhere in the name of the war. Yvonne and I reckoned that our crews had received promotions for sinking far more vodka than enemy shipping. As well as all the other presents, Guy had brought back a little gold-trimmed vodka glass for me, which I still have, although I never drink vodka. Thinking about it now, maybe it was for memories of his own.

The war went on.

Guy's next posting, of all places, was Alexandrovsk, right up in the Arctic Circle. Initially he knew little more than I of what the mission would entail. It was all very hush, hush, and just as well that I had packed up the flat in Dovercourt and moved back with Dad and Mother because Guy was away for months, and Austen's birth was imminent.

A Naval Team had been sent to this outlandish place to set up an armoured unit. Once again the idea was to keep the Germans guessing. It was a bizarre operation which involved getting two small submarines overland under the Germans' very noses. It wasn't as if the submarines however small, wouldn't have been likely to arouse suspicion as their transport was bound to be cumbersome and slow. On reflection, Guy thought that was partly the purpose, for Germany at this time was making harsh peace-terms with Russia, after the failure of the Provisional government and Lenin's return, and the British were doing their best to make capital for themselves by deflecting the Germans' spheres of interest as much as they could.

Making two small submarines invisible and getting them along northern roadways without being caught, was exactly the kind of challenge Guy enjoyed. Strange war-work for a seaman.

It was funny to think that ordinary people like us should be involved in world affairs, but even funnier to have to put into action the ridiculous realities of Whitehall's paper dictates.

Back home all we knew was that Guy and others were away on yet another 'secret mission'. As we were to learn later, the reality of the 'British Presence' in Alexandrovsk boiled down to a mere cluster of log cabins--- exceptionally remote', to be inhabited temporarily by a handful of naval officers and men.

Again, as after the last escapade, we had parties and laughter to celebrate everyone's safe return. This time warmed by gin and whisky, innumerable recollections came to light in the warmth of Yvonne's flat.

'There was nothing. No food, no heating, a few puzzled Russians who couldn't understand us, and miles of snow and ice.' They had had to get random supplies together, 'a crazy mix, but we grabbed everything we could. Jam, reindeer meat, cocoa, salt pork, rabbit, salmon.'

'No shortage of grog.'

Yvonne and I exchanged a look. We were keeping the home fires burning and they were at it again.

'Loved the cold, didn't we, Gint.' Guy and Ginty by this time were sitting on the sitting-room floorboards. There were still seven or eight of us still carousing at two in the morning. I knew the time because I could feel the milk brimming up in my breasts.

'Never once had a hangover. Bloody marvellous,' Ginty relaxed back against the wall laughing.

'Marvellous. The cold,' he expanded his hands, 'just magicked them away.'

Guy was trying to pronounce Russian names. 'Rosta.. cha... ovsky. No. "kovsky" Marvellous chap! Splendid commander! I liked him.'

'And that other chap, can't pronounce his name, either. The Governor. He couldn't have been more grateful. We salvaged all that cargo for him. The bloody ship had gone aground.'

'Gave us something to do. And we did all right out of that, remember?'

'And that's how we won the war?' put in Yvonne.

They couldn't stop laughing. They rambled on.

'The war's not over yet,' I said, 'and it's time we went home. You've had your drinks. The baby needs his.'

I reminded Guy that he might be a war hero, but he was also a dad.

It had been great meeting him at the Town Station on his return from Archangel. He was in high spirits, looking well, handsome and distinguished in his uniform. I felt proud to be his wife. This time his eyes widened with surprised delight to take in the sight of two babies in my arms. Relaxed, laughing, cheerful, he realised that he was now a father twice over. I felt overflowing with love. I was thankful for his safe return, not yet knowing the kind of dangers he'd experienced!

The haphazardness of war intensified the brief splurges of our time together. Guy had the capacity to match and outstrip my sensual needs. He was outrageous, yet understanding, challenging, yet such fun to be with. We made the most of every 'high'.

Just as well, with what was to follow.

ELEVEN

In less than two months we were moving again. The Navy ordered Guy back up to Scotland for finishing touches with Admiral Beatty's secret weapon, the K-class submarine. Once again we had to find lodgings in Rosyth. A number of officer's wives stayed at the Hawse Inn, but for us that was out of the question with one and a half year-old Mo and a small baby. Guy as usual, went ahead and found us a convenient, small furnished house with a garden, but the prospect of travelling all night by train right up to Edinburgh, and then still further across the Firth with two babies was a bit daunting and I was glad that I had accepted Gwenny's offer to come up with me to help, in her holidays. I hadn't forgotten what had happened on her visit to Dovercourt, but that no longer worried me as she had fallen in love quite seriously with a cheeky young man, not in the forces surprisingly, who was working in the Dockyard.

Train travel in the war was tiring at the best of times. Trains were full of soldiers and sailors smelly and tired with kitbags, anxiously rushing off on leave, or more anxiously returning to duty. There wasn't a seat to be had from Portsmouth to London but for two sailors who took pity on us holding a toddler and an infant in arms and bags, bottles and nappies. I think too, that one of them liked the look of Gwenny. Back then there weren't corridors in trains, either, so we were very squashed. Crossing London that evening in a taxi which got held up was an extra worry lest we missed our all-night train, but we made it, only to find one seat between us, so until we got to Rugby, Gwenny had to sit on her suitcase, holding Austen. I felt sorry for the other tired passengers, because Mo cried every time the train jerked, and discreet as I tried to be feeding the baby, I got a mixture of looks, from disapproval to smirks, from others in the compartment. It was good that there were two of us to cope with such an endless, overheated and messy journey. Guy said we looked like a bunch of refugees when he met us.

I was thrilled with the house, which was a little way out of the town with a garden and three bedrooms. I was thrilled even more with the fact that we were a proper family living together, even if only for a matter of months. I had not realised, or even thought that Guy's work would cast shadows on us. Somehow, being right up in Scotland, made me distance myself from the war. How wrong I was. Admiral Beatty had plans to bring the war to us. Guy was to be hardly ever at home, bombarded as he was with preparations for a massive manoeuvre with little time for anything but work.

Admiral Beatty had ordered a posse of distinguished sub-mariners to carry out naval battle plans which were to involve battleships, cruisers destroyers and, especially, the new, untried 'K' class submarines. Guy explained to me that the idea was not only to test out these new vessels in battle conditions, but to stimulate his bored fighting fleet previously locked away at Scapa Flow, to keep them ready for action, should the Germans finally come out of hiding.

'K' submarines were larger than any other submarines yet constructed, and their special feature was their speed as outriders of the Fleet, along with a dual capacity for submerging. To achieve this object they were steam propelled on the surface, with funnels, which had to be lowered and stored when the submarine submerged, after which their propulsion changed to diesel. This was supposed to be a bright and revolutionary idea, the Navy's brain-child of lateral thinking. Such submarines proved to be a daunting challenge for their Captains and Engineers. Meeting up with other wives, who included friends I had made down in Dovercourt, we knew that our menfolk were under much strain. Gatherings in the wardroom were tense, and there was plenty of discussion concerning the possibility of disaster, which had already dogged these craft. We all knew what had happened to K13 in its early trials, stuck in the mud within full view of the shore. Wives and spectators, utterly helpless, had actually witnessed its terrible sinking at the cost of ten sailors' lives. Now this same submarine had been refloated and refurbished as K22, and, understandably, crews were not keen to take her over.

From my point of view, after Gwenny had gone back, I could see that it was a very difficult time for Guy. He had little time for the children or me and I tried to keep them out of his way so he could get some proper sleep. I would hear barely muffled swearing and exclamations as he was dropped off late at night by a group of friends, who, like himself, were much the worse for drink.

He was busy every day, all day, and didn't get home until late most nights. I would sit up for him. Sometimes he needed me and sometimes he didn't. For the first time I wasn't sure how he wanted me to be. I had never had to think that way. We were usually wholly spontaneous with each other.

One night I remember the door slamming. It must have been about half-past ten at night. I could hear him taking off his greatcoat in the hall. He must have been trying to hang it up on the hall-stand several times, and in doing so knocked over the umbrella stand, which clattered to the floor. It sounded too, as though he gave an umbrella a good kick, from all the swearing. He barely looked at me as he came into the living room where I had kept the fire in for him. I could tell he wasn't himself.

Not quite knowing what to do I smiled weakly. He gave me a detached look.

'I bet you could do with something to eat,' I said. There's a sandwich on the kitchen table. Shall I get it?'

No reply.

Just then to make matters worse, upstairs Mo was starting to whimper.

'He's not been very well to-day.'

I had hardly finished making a comment or two before the whimper turned into a full-scale howl. 'I'll bring him down,' I said. Returning five minutes later with Mo in my arms. I noticed that Guy hadn't started to eat anything, but had poured himself a whisky.

I sat on the edge of my chair with Mo leaning in against me, not looking at his father. I cuddled him up and stretched my lips across my teeth in an attempt at another weak smile. Mo was now looking at his father from underneath his eyebrows.

Guy looked at us. 'Give him to me.' The words were said with a hint of aggression. 'These days I hardly know I've got sons. I'll have him,' he said. 'Come to Daddy.' He reached out his arms to Mo, who clung to me.

I stood up to hand him over. I could tell Guy was hurt by Mo's reticence.

'What's wrong then? (said rather brusquely) Don't you want to come to your dad?' He pulled him onto his knee. Mo shrank and tightened.

'A bit of baby-diddy.'

Guy started to jog him on his knee, not very gently. Mo burst into tears and stretched towards me.

'Bloody hell, you don't even know your own father.'

By this time Mo was screaming. Guy virtually threw him at me.

I was protesting and trying to pacify Guy at the same time. 'He's probably been having a nightmare. He does have them sometimes. Careful! I'll put him back to bed. He's half-asleep.'

Guy stormed off to the kitchen. As I took Mo back to bed I heard a plate crash on the kitchen floor

'Come up when you're ready. I'm going to bed,' I called down.

No reply.

Next morning when I woke up there was Guy beside me still sleeping heavily and still in some of his clothes. I woke him gently with a cup of tea.

'You'll be late.'

'Bugger them. Everything's got to be done by yesterday, and it's not possible. It's not safe.'

There was a pause.

'Sorry if I was a bit under the weather last night.' I smiled properly this time, and kissed him.

'You're the expert, remember. Don't let them hurry you.'

He looked very tired and strained. What I didn't know was that in those wardroom gatherings where the alcohol flowed, the crews had already been allotted to their vessels in preparation for Beatty's 'Battle of May Island,' and that Guy was to be the chief Engineer of K14. With the babies and running the house, I had plenty to do and knew very little of the details of what was happening. Whenever he managed to be at home, I didn't ask questions, but just wanted to be there for him, because I could tell from his manner the worrying nature of his responsibilities.

Little did we know that 'Operation E.C. 1' was to have repercussions for us and all those others involved, well beyond any we might have suspected at the time.

The exercise was to take place at night, and for the first (and last) time nine K class submarines were to be use in combination with the Fleet. High levels of skill, nerve and timing were essential to get more than forty warships in a night exercise, through the defences of the

Forth estuary 'in radio silence, with each ship showing only one stern light'. Almost unbelievably, looking back, unforeseen complications arose from the outset. A marauding U-boat, the last thing Admiral Beatty wanted to hear about, was reported as loitering in the very area planned for the exercise. In addition a group of eight armed minesweeping trawlers were already turning into the Forth not having been given any information of the Admiralty's plans. Worse, no thought whatever had been given to possible mechanical failure in such untried craft as the 'K' series, and it was the jamming of the steering of K14 which set in train the fatal sequence of events.

What followed was unbelievable; more like boys playing games with mechanical toys than officers and crews involved in mishap and death. In trying to turn suddenly out of the mainstream to avoid the oncoming trawlers, K14's steering jammed.

K 14's crippled position put it in the path of K22, which had gone off course accidentally and both submarines had collided, largely because these vessels needed larger turning angles than previously realised. This was the start of a series of disastrous collisions. The light destroyer, 'Fearless' rammed K 17, another of the nine 'K' class boats involved in the exercise, causing it to sink in eight minutes, while K6, unavoidably sliced into K4 which went down with all hands, never to be traced.

As I relate these shocking facts I can still scarcely believe that such a disastrous sequence of accidents did, actually, happen. This wasn't war. This was the British Navy, England's Glory, in action: supposedly the most efficient and well-respected navy in the world!

There were still more horrors to come.

The long line of fighting ships steaming towards the North Sea behind this posse of damaged vessels, was wholly ignorant of what lay ahead. Tragically, the escorting destroyers were to sweep over where K 17 had gone down, cutting to pieces and washing away desperate survivors. In little more than an hour and a half the British Navy did more damage to itself in this operation than the Germans ever did to the British fighting fleet in the whole of the war.

The 'K' group of officers, their wives and families who were on hand, which included us, collected together in disbelief. Who was drowned? Who was missing? What search had there been for survivors? Faces were drawn in tragedy and despair. Why had this plan gone so wrong? Who or what was to blame?

As you could expect there was a huge outcry among us all in Rosyth at the time.

Guy was shattered most especially by the unnecessary deaths of his friends and colleagues in the total chaos of the whole exercise. In the weeks previous to the May Island project I couldn't fail to notice how he had been increasingly anxious about the insufficiency of tests carried out. All preparations had had to be rushed to comply with top-brass demands. In addition, the 'K' class, whose complex design had involved so many people, had proved to be an utterly useless white elephant. Guy's own submarine had been very badly damaged with what was left of her bows, well under water. It had taken all his ingenuity to keep her afloat until she could be rescued. She, along with two other submarines and the light-cruiser 'Fearless', had to be towed back into port. The Admiralty did its best to fluff over the whole thing, attributing blame to the management of the vessels concerned, and paying little regard to the machines themselves. All the surviving submariners were as angry as they were powerless. Guy had to appear at the enquiry set up in the following week, before Rear Admiral Goodenough, to give professional evidence as to the reasons for 'K'14's steering jamming. His only possible suggestion was that the vessel's steering mechanisms had been obliged to make a too narrow angled and too-sudden a turn.

The larger question which was ignored, was why, in this planned exercise would a huge submarine suddenly be called upon to make such an unexpected turn in too small a space, and why hadn't the people who planned the whole strategy allowed for this? More questions arose, all conveniently unanswered.

And what about the fate of K22, originally the unlucky K13? Was it mechanical failure or again some unforeseen, mysterious jinx which had made it go off course, causing the initial collision? The Investigations Court sidetracked such considerations, bringing the Enquiry to a quick end by court-martialling one of the submarine officers and severely reprimanding four others. There were very unpleasant shadows of implied blame all round.

Our community in Rosyth bristled with indignation at such unfairness. Guy, Ginty and their friends, distressed and frustrated, drank more as they licked their wounds. Guy, for all his intelligence, professionalism and usual sang-froid became rapidly, thoroughly and increasingly depressed. The Admirals covered up their own incompetence by casting aspersions. Guy's spirits plummeted. Not even Mo's baby talk or Austen's gurgles could help him smile, nor my warmth towards him and offered embraces. He would shrug, and stare into space, becoming increasingly morose and silent, a wholly different person from the Guy who had amusing, ironic answers to everything and stimulated those around him.

I was worried, very worried.

The only good thing which came out of the disaster was that the 'K' class never came up to original expectations and its subs were never used in engaging the enemy. These craft may have had the speed of a destroyer, but their size reduced their manoeuvrability to the 'turning circle of a battle cruiser and the bridge control faculties of a picket boat'.

Meanwhile with Guy things went from bad to worse. Nor was he the only officer shaken severely by this enterprise. Several declined to serve in those submarines ever again.

Guy was asked to supervise the de-commissioning of 'K' 14. This meant that we, as a family, remained in our little house up in Scotland for some months. Guy threw himself into his work systematically, but it became quite evident after some weeks that his depression and his drinking problems were getting worse. Brian, the naval doctor, who was his friend and very understanding, suggested that a spell in a sanatorium would get him on his feet again. He needed space, rest and professional drying out.

'Sanatorium? That's another name for a loony-bin.' He refused to entertain the idea. His answer? Another drink.

'Rubbish,' I told him. There was nothing wrong with him that stopping drinking wouldn't fix. And why did he drink and why did the others drink? Pressure, anxiety, the war. And if that was the reason those who caused the war ought to be the ones to put things right. Brian wouldn't have suggested it for any other reason beyond the fact that the Navy wanted him back on active service again. At the moment he wasn't fit.

'You're a well-thought-of, highly experienced officer, in need of care,' Brian told him. All those things which have happened take their toll'. The navy needed his expertise. It wasn't as if he was on his own, he went on. 'War is less than human and there's a limit to what humans can bear.' A sanatorium would put him back on his feet. What he was telling him was an order, not a choice. A few weeks and he'd be 'back to his old self'.

Finally he agreed.

Arrangements were made for him to go to Wellington Lodge in Surrey, a hospital which dealt with the effects of war trauma on members of the armed forces.

It was pointless for me to be in Scotland and for Guy to be down south, so once again I packed up house with the help of friends and moved in with Mother and Father. The train line from Portsmouth to London went directly through Godalming, so it was comparatively easy for me to get to see Guy. I wasn't allowed to visit him initially, but after some weeks I could go on Sundays.

It was so sad to see so many maimed men. Compared to most, outwardly, Guy wasn't in bad shape. Apart from the ones shut away from the world in the wards, the ones around the hospital ground, shocking enough to see, were in wheelchairs, or misshapen, or in bandages and plasters. Some wandered alone, staring and not speaking. One could only guess with horror what they had endured.

Guy never said much to me about the treatment he received. I presume he co-operated to get out of hospital as soon as possible. Surrounded by so many shells of men, I think he considered himself lucky. Eventually he was passed fit and discharged just about the time when it seemed the war would be over. I was utterly thankful to think that he had survived. I went up to Godalming to bring him home.

Home?

We didn't have a home. All the time Guy was in hospital I was staying with Mother and Dad (Mother wouldn't allow anyone to call her anything but 'mother' but Dad was different). It was at this time that Dad came to our rescue. Malins Road was full to capacity, with Gwenny, Morris, my two children and me and now there was Guy.

'Time you two had a house of your own,' he said, and he put up a large deposit for us on a house in Inhurst Road, near Alexandra Park and close to sister Maud. It was of great help to us as a family and the kindest thing he could ever have done.

When Guy came out of hospital our new house was just the fillip he needed. He could put up shelves, make cupboards and organise the garden. We had some months of much needed 'normal' family life, which we both valued after our recent upheavals. Our time in Inhurst Road helped Guy to put the worst behind him and allowed him to start thinking about ordinary living, rather than war. Besides, on his leaving hospital, the Navy had made it clear that he could be very useful in helping train new submarine engineers.

Yet something had changed, something I sensed.

For the first time in my relationship with Guy, I realised that I had to be the strong one of the family. Although he had always been the one who had made all the decisions and had been so amusing, sweeping and debonair, he was now very much in need of back-up and the stability which I could give him. The pressures of the war seemed to have changed the balance of our relationship, as I guessed it had done for many others.

In the November of 1918 the Armistice was signed, to great celebrations, waving of flags, dancing in the streets and lighting of bonfires. The war was over! We all had to take stock of four decimating terrible years but at least now it was peace-time. No need for warfare of any kind!

Or so we thought.

Guy was just settling into a more stable life with a new lecturing job at the submarine training depot, Lucia, in Portsmouth when yet another challenge came. The Navy co-opted him for active-service.

We wondered what this meant. Active service implied war-service and the war was over. The year was 1919. Both operation and destination, top secret.

Guy came to life overnight. Such mystery added spice to life. He had under three weeks in which to prepare himself. He and his naval friends had no idea where they were being sent or what was their mission. Vladivostock? Egypt? They joked about it.

I was pregnant again and he was off again.

What was new!

The only consolation for me was that he seemed very much like his old self, again, challenging, humorous and ready for adventure, which he loved.

TWELVE

The Caspian Sea? Where was that? I had to look it up in an atlas. To me it was a very unfamiliar area of what was in 1919, a racial mix of Armenians, Azerbaijanis, Tartars, Cossacks and Turkestanis, bare, brown dry mountains yet, apparently, also, places beautiful with waterfalls, and green fertile valleys plentiful with orchards and corn.

To think that this was where Guy had been sent and we thought the war was over! At the time neither he nor we had the faintest idea where he was or why, and we weren't to know for weeks.

I was in our new house with two small children and after the time in Scotland very glad to be back among family and old friends particularly since at this time Mo became extremely ill with measles. Really ill. Doctor Maybury came to see him every day because his temperature was so high and he was delirious. I took him into my bed, kept the curtains shut because he couldn't bear light in his eyes; I rolled him in a piece of old blanket to stop him shivering, and I kept a fire burning in the bedroom night and day. We 'very nearly lost him' Doctor Maybury said.

Mother came round to stay because I was so worried. Poor Mo was as weak as a bee wilting in winter. When he was over the worst he could barely walk and it took weeks for him to be himself again. The virus weakened his eyesight and he had to have glasses at a very early age. With his spectacles and peering always into books he looked like a little old professor. Maud, thankfully had taken Austen to stay with her. He had been running around driving us all mad. Even though he was to catch measles later, he got it so mildly he was hardly ill at all. They were different boys in every way.

Mo and I were very close. It wasn't until I had other children I realised how much he thought like an adult. He was constantly surprising me. I was a teacher by trade and had been in contact with children of all ages all my life, but he still often astonished me. From about the age of two and a half he was fascinated with symbols and numbers. Not numbers as in counting on your fingers, or as in 'seven swans-a-swimming', but the actual numerals themselves. He would sit quietly for ages with a book he couldn't possibly read. Eventually I couldn't help but wonder what he was doing, so I watched him out of the corner of my eye. At first I thought he was just flipping the pages but then I discovered that he was carefully working out the number of the middle page, this, with books of many pages. This fascination with symbols took him into words and I noticed when he sat on a stool by me reading stories, he was as interested in the letters upside down as the right way up. He was reading properly when well under four and never had to be taught like most children. Of course he wanted help with difficult words but his reading and capacity to express himself was unusual for his age. Austen, in contrast had little interest in numbers and words at all. He liked stories but he zoomed about with toys and threw himself around rarely concentrating on any one thing for any length of time. Mo was always thinking and asking questions like 'why did we read from left to right', or 'where, did a line begin or end?' I couldn't always give him satisfactory answers. Austen's questions were wholly down to earth. When was it his turn? How many biscuits? Could we go to the swings? They were like the heads and tails of a coin.

At last we heard from Guy; a postcard for the children from the last ever thought of, of all places, Bagdhad, 'letter following'. Imagine our surprise!

Bagdhad! For me the name conjured up sultans and harems and fabulous birds like rocs, and princesses like Scheherazade and the 'Thousand and One nights'. What was the British Navy doing there? Where was the sea? The war was over. What was going on? Detailed peace-talks were in train at Versailles. Why send sailors to Baghdad?

My family and I had never given a thought to the wheels within wheels of the British Secret Service. The mood among us and our friends as we thought about the war, was that England was creating a new and fairer world, a world which somehow would make some sense of all the deaths and sacrifices. Yet here was Britain, Great Britain, keeping a wily eye on the oil wells of Baku, and actively suspicious of any revolutionaries who might threaten Northern India.

Politics.

Machinations.

They made nonsense of all those high-flown ideas we ordinary people thought we had been fighting for.

Certainly India was highly important to us, it was still Queen Victoria's 'Jewel in the Crown,' but why did that mean we had to be involved with Communists who had murdered Tsar Nicholas II, his wife, son and four daughters? The Tsar was first cousin to our King, certainly. They actually looked alike. But what did the Russian revolution have to do with us now the war was over? And what was the government doing sending Naval personnel to Baghdad? Why get involved in somebody else's war?

As we were to learn later Guy and his fellow officers were part of a British Cabinet plan to maintain control of the Caspian Sea, supposedly to prevent Britain's whole Eastern Empire from 'rocking'. The force was to establish a flotilla of small armed ships on the Caspian Sea to keep out the Communists. Already back in 1918, primarily with oil in mind, a 'Dunsterforce' had been sent out to Baku. No-one had had any idea of what had been going on, least of all the Navy. It had consisted of a convoy of 41 Model T Ford cars, later augmented by infantry and guns. This group had mananged to survive the local perpetually-warring parties and to establish naval bases at Enzeli and Krasnovodsk. Now the Navy was involved also and Guy's job, along with a handful of other naval personnel, was to keep the sea free from 'forces hostile to the British'.

This proved to be a very challenging, ad hoc commission. Guy's team was ill-equipped, poorly advised and had to depend on its wits. Guy never talked about confrontations with the enemy. He always underplayed his role, reducing feats of daring to 'practical common sense'. It was while serving on H.M.S. Emile Nobel, in May/June 1919 that Guy added a bar to his D.S.C. awarded for 'valuable services rendered' and 'exceptional ability in executing repairs during and after action with the enemy'. Once again he had faced personal danger with fearlessness and calm, and was responsible for the rescue of his crew.

Guy! My husband! A hero, twice over. I felt fear, pride and relief, equally.

His homecoming that October was euphoric. Mo and Austen made flags to wave as their father arrived back at the Town Station. I was holding our new baby son, Gregory, in my arms. Gwenny and Bill, Father, and even Mother, turned out to meet him. He, for his part brought parcels and presents for us all.

Looking back, those post 1918 months were days of hyperbole, but after such a sequence of extraordinary events Guy couldn't go on living at that level of excitement. He, especially, had to draw breath and return to what was designated 'normal' life. This proved especially hard for us and for many of those other war-scarred families at that time.

As I see now, this was the point when Guy's life started to lack lustre and he went from the heights to the depths. At the time it was hard to realise that the random silences and absences weren't just a teething period of adjustment to his new peacetime job.

After a brief posting at Devonport instructing young sailors in submarine engineering, he had been transferred to H.M.S. Victory in Portsmouth, doing similar work, which was easy for him; too easy perhaps. The bombshell came when he was asked to leave the Navy in 1921.

He took the news with little comment, but that didn't mean that he wasn't devastated. I was the one furious, full of protest, fulminating against the Navy which he had served all his life not merely with exemplariness but valour. How could they do this to him? To us?

I never asked exactly what happened, but Ginty's wife Yvonne filled in details. Apparently Guy had little time for this senior officer who was one of the few who had never liked Guy's dash and devil-may care, not to mention his cleverness. Even though Guy rarely bitched about the people he had to work with, apart from an occasional mutter or raising of the eyebrows, I did know that he had little respect for his boss, and had heard him swear when he realised that this particular officer had been appointed to senior command at the 'Victory'. He had been part of the Firth-fiasco team and Guy had made it all too clear what he had thought about that.

Yvonne had looked at me straight. I knew I wasn't going to like what was to follow. 'Dess,' she said, 'You have to know.'

I think I knew what she was going to say before she said it.

'Guy's started drinking again. Ginty's tried to stop him.'

My heart sank. If he was back into that nothing could surprise me. The future was bleak. My look was enough for Yvonne.

'You mean you didn't know?'

I nodded. I couldn't believe it. That was worse news than the dismissal.

'You need hardly tell me more.' I could imagine what had happened. I shut my eyes and I could see it all.

One day they had an almighty and all-too public row, which was to seal our fate. Guy's war-record saved him from total disgrace but he had no option but to leave the Navy at the age of thirty three. There were general cuts at this time to all the armed forces, so our position was not as embarrassing as it might have been. However, we had three sons, he had no job, and we were caught in the huge economic depression following the war. What was the future for us going to be?

Until then, money had never been a problem. Now it was. Guy had been everybody's darling in the Navy. His expertise, his intelligence, bravery, dry humour, made him a favourite and now he had to find a totally new way of life in the atmosphere of closure and economic down turn after the war. People were out of work. Gwenny's Bill's job in the Dockyard had come to an end. Qualified as he was, he mended bicycles, soled shoes and emptied old shells from the war on waste ground because there were no jobs. They couldn't get married because he hadn't a career and, she, as a married woman would lose her teaching post if they did.

Guy had been given an invalid pension, but that wasn't enough for us all, the mortgage and, double all of those, his drinking habit.

I sigh when I think about it.

The war had made him live unnaturally on highs and excitements, and even more on suspense and fear. Ordinary life didn't suit him at all. Our lives together, to date, had been all whirlwind and now we had to fill our time with babies, children, mealtimes, bedtimes, the park, and banal things such as shopping. I was used to family routines, but he could not cope with his own involuntary levels of dissatisfaction and ennui.

His answer? I should have guessed. Alcohol.

You can imagine how I felt and how, now, his drinking had ransomed us all. He had to put an end to it. He was too young; we were both far too young not to consider a future. And there were the children. Their lives.

He had to stop drinking. He had done it once. He could do it again.

I could feel myself getting increasingly shrewish with worry. Not surprisingly his dismissal made his drinking habits worse. We needed money. It made me furious to think how his alcohol drained away our already inadequate resources. I couldn't get work, besides there were the children to be looked after. It seemed I could no longer rely on him for anything.

We had rows.

I cajoled.

I reasoned.

All useless.

I wanted a normal husband, not one I had to share with a haunting, destructive, black beast.

As is the way with alcoholics, you never see them drink. They can look you straight in the eye and swear they haven't touched a drop, when you can smell it on their breath. Somehow all those wardroom gatherings, the bonhomie, the living on the nerves, the weird expeditions overseas, had built up into this. The time spent in the Sanatorium had made not one iota of difference. He had to listen to reason, even though I realised the problem had nothing to do with 'should' and 'ought'.

'You have done it once. You have to do it again. You have to do it for us. We need you. We love you. You're only thirty three.'

I was at my wits end. Who or what could help us?

Dad came to the rescue again. What we would have done without Dad at that time, I cannot think.

Guy had never known his own father, and had great respect for mine. I was far too emotional to be of any help, but Dad was relaxed, determined and positive. It was Dad who got Guy going again. It was Dad's idea that he should study for the Institute of Mechanical Engineers' exam. It was Dad who paid the mortgage. It was Dad who got him off the drink for the second time. He was no longer in the Dockyard so now he made Guy's rehabilitation his goal in life. It worked.

Guy got a job at the Portsmouth Technical College teaching what he knew so well. At last I believed we were starting to lead a pretty happy ordinary family life, despite Guy's having frightful nightmares sometimes. When he tossed and agonised in his sleep I would hold him in my arms and calm him. We would make love. He would whisper great tendernesses to me. He was always greedy for sex and would explore every permutation and fingertip of lovemaking with a mixture of delicacy and savagery. I could rarely deny him, nor wanted to. I think it made him feel alive and forget himself.

Not surprisingly I found I was pregnant again. I was to have a fourth boy in the following year.

'We'll call him Henry after your father. He has been so good to us.' They were Guy's words. He knew how Dad had worked to bring him back to us.

Four boys: Mowbray, Austen, Gregory, Henry. And still dear Daisy couldn't get pregnant. The ironies!

I thought back to those early teaching days, my room in West Meon, my plans for the future. I remembered all those images of India and of course, Neil. That had been so organised, controlled, arranged, and now this.

What had taken me over? I had never even considered pregnancy let alone the possibility of having children, and look where that had landed me! What sort of life? I hadn't wanted to suffer all that mother had endured with endless pregnancies and children. I had wanted a life of my own. I had thought I was different, special, and now I was the same as everybody else. A family of four! That was something you could not walk away from. It was something I had never supposed would happen to me. How had I been so stupid! Cabined, cribbed, confined, bound, and.... was this everything that my one life was to be about? On top of it all, Guy's drinking? The worry, the promises.

1926 had been a rough year for everybody. The General Strike did not just affect the miners but the railways, the canals, and other industries. Socialism and trade-union power flared into action as inflated wartime wages gave way to pay cuts, causing unemployment and poverty.

Once again I was aware of Guy's unease and boredom and wondering where it might lead this time. After the last bout, it always worried me that he might start drinking again if he wasn't sufficiently interested in what he was doing. He always seemed to be needing excitement, a new challenge, a new outlet. I could sense him feeling, looking. His eyes darted about quickly. He needed to be on the move.

It was at this time that he spotted an advertisement for an 'innovative engineer'.

'Great,' I said, 'where?'

'Africa.'

I thought he was joking, and laughed.

He stared at me perfectly seriously. 'I mean it. Yes, Africa. Why not?'

'Why?'

I was taken aback. 'Well!' I was ironing at the time. 'Aren't we all right here? The house, the kids... I mean Africa!'

'Could be a bit of fun,' was how he put it.

'What sort of fun, exactly?' The last thing I wanted was upheaval.

'The job.'

I shrugged. 'Maybe for you, not for me.'

'No harm in finding out about it.'

'But Africa! Who wants to go to Africa?'

'They want an innovative engineer.'

'I suppose you think it sounds like you,' I said, resuming the ironing.

'I'll write off and find out about it.'

I didn't give the suggestion any serious thought, but he wrote off straight away and brightened considerably at the idea of challenge and change. Anywhere but where we were. Places off the map obviously intrigued him. Working at the Portsmouth Tech had answered his desperate needs temporarily when he had come out of the Navy, but the job was not exciting enough for him. He had burst out with exclamation when he read out the 'Ad'. It alone had sparked off energy in him. He kept talking about it.

'Imagine, Dess, Africa!'

'I am imagining it and don't like the idea much with three boys and a baby. I like where we are.'

'Don't be so dull, Dess. That's not like you.'

The 'ad' had put him into a buoyant mood.

'Where in Africa?'

'South Africa.'

'That's where Bill's sister worked in a convent; a missionary station. She died there with some awful fever. Not my choice.'

'Funny you should say that. This job is to set up a mission station. They need an engineer.'

I was still not taking the idea seriously. 'An engineer? I thought mission stations were to spread the Word. Whatever help would you be?'

'Water. They have to have provisions for water.'

'And what do you know about that?'

'Enough. I like the idea. It would be a challenge.'

'Easier for you than for me.' I went on. 'I don't much fancy darkest Africa with a tiny baby. You can't be serious. In any case, what about schools for Mo and Austen? Mo's about to sit the scholarship for the grammar school. We're settled here.'

'I'm not.'

'But I am, and so are the children.'

I dismissed the idea completely. It was just escapism. The last thing I wanted at this stage with a new baby was Africa! I was comfortably settled in our new house with all the latest conveniences such as electricity. We had something like a proper family life. Guy was doing well off the drink. Surely this was just a flight of fancy, although I had an uncomfortable feeling that he was seriously attracted to the idea. He started to get sparky, cheeky, more like his old self. He needed to be moving around unexpectedly to unexpected places and what seemed peaceful to me seemed undemanding and lifeless to him.

He persisted.

'It won't hurt to find out about it. Be fair. It sounds more adventurous than trailing down in the tram every day to the Tech.'

'I thought you said it was a Missionary.'

'It is.'

'Don't make me laugh. You haven't been to church in years!'

'Time I began!' He was smiling.

'We're hardly missionary types.'

'They're not advertising for missionaries. They're advertising for an engineer. That's what I am. They want water brought to their new settlement.'

'All right for you but what about me? I'm not religious. I don't want to be in the middle of nowhere communing with God, or having to be with the sort of people who convert the heathen.'

He smiled again. 'A good experience for them, and you,' he added. 'They can practice on you for a start. Besides, don't get too excited. I've already written off for information and details.'

The letter, apparently, had been addressed to 'The Very Reverend Father Gabriel, Society of Mark the Evangelist.'

Guy? Me? Religion? It was my turn to smile. 'You're not serious,' I said.

'Not exactly tailor-made for us, I agree,' he had answered. 'But perhaps that's just what's been missing in our lives. Who can tell?'

This Society of Brothers was extending their Mission to the Transkei. They needed a competent Engineer to fix up the entire water arrangements for the settlement. When the information came back to us I could see that Guy was very interested.

'See this, Dess.' He read it out. 'Furnished accommodation, servants. How do you like the sound of that?' He paused, 'and a large salary compared to the City Tech! And that's not the end. "Family passages all paid. Paid leave every three years" and, guess what! They would like to interview me on a short-list for the job.'

I didn't know what to think. The whole idea seemed unreal. Besides, I didn't have to get too worried. He hadn't yet been offered the job. On the other hand, I knew full well that he could put on an impressive manner, if he needed to.

He got it, of course.

Deep inside I had the feeling that he would. I knew that whatever else, he was a colourful, articulate, intelligent engineer, logical, and able to convince. Also he had the advantage of being a war hero. That didn't count for nothing.

My family took the idea even less seriously than I had. Africa, for a start; who would ever want to live in Africa? In addition a mission station was comic in the extreme. Guy and Dessa, religious? Since when? We didn't say grace before meals. We didn't say our prayers at night. Mother had only ever packed us off to Sunday school to get some peace in the afternoon. We knew our Bible stories and that was about it. Maud, who had always resented Mother spoiling me at her expense, couldn't resist a crack about her having let me have a carriage and a fancy white dress for my confirmation. 'Brides of Christ' she said.

Though tempted by the salary, and even allowing for the religious complication, I was still not wholly attracted by the overwhelming and unavoidable ramifications involved in transporting all of us to such a dark continent. I was worried particularly about the children's schooling. I hedged. I would only consider going on certain conditions. Before Guy accepted the job I made him make special enquiries about the boys' education. Father Gabriel replied saying that the society would pay half the boarding fees for them at St Paul's School in Grahamstown. That, Guy's own enthusiasm, and the promise of a car, made we give way, finally, to what seemed so important to him.

The job started in the November of 1927. Henry had been born in late August, and the idea was that Guy should go out on his own to get into the swing of things and I would come over just before Christmas when I had got into a routine with the new baby. This would be better for the boys by not interrupting their school year. Also I needed the energy to prepare myself for such a change.

Africa.

When I was young the idea of travel was very exciting. One of the reasons I had been interested in Neil was all the things he had told me about India. Naively I had loved the idea of The Empire and what seemed to me the attractiveness of being important white people 'abroad' and I, too, wanted to be part of a 'Club' and its upper class snobbery, a means of 'going up in the world'. However, anything I had heard about the Transkei and a Mission station on the bare fringe of civilisation bore little relationship to such a life, and as much as I wanted to keep Guy challenged I had my own misgivings in setting up house miles from anywhere, and among strange people. Such challenges did need the passion of a religious 'calling' which neither of us had. Was Guy's craving for adventure enough of a substitute? I didn't know. All I knew was that the idea had visible effects on his spirits, and ultimately I felt I could not refuse.

A big family party saw Guy off on 'The Harlech Castle' to Capetown, thence to Port Elizabeth. For once Guy could be a guest on a ship, with no responsibilities, so he was wholly free to have a good time. As we waved him off, it crossed my mind what sort of a good time that might be, but he swore that no drink would pass his lips.

'I go to prepare a place for you', he had quoted laughingly as we kissed goodbye. That was his idea of a joke. Unfortunately I had heard those words years before.

'Don't tempt Providence,' I had replied.

1927

ONE

W hile 'The Harlech Castle' was cutting across the Cowes Roads, the turgid waters of the Thames were churning to a grey-brown white as 'The Eastern Aurora' revved her engines en route for Calcutta.

Celia had no family to wave her goodbye. She had been robbed of her young husband in 1917, and her father, Mervyn, had died back in '22. She wasn't one prepared to live permanently in the past and responded finally to the urgings of spry old Ada, now living happily in a small seafront flat in Southsea, which caused her, finally, to break off her liaison with a shilly-shallying married man, to seek her fortune on the other side of the globe .

Another World-war one Widow.

Adrian had gone down on a Trans-Atlantic convoy, all souls sent to the bottom by a marauding U-Boat. Of course she had grieved, she had grieved bitterly, but she was a practical girl who got on with life, and the last thing she wanted was to get landed in widow-ridden Southsea.

London was the place for her, and with her aplomb and elegance, she soon found herself a job as manageress of a prosperous boutique hotel. She rented a one- bedroom flat in Gloucester Road round the corner, and lived it up with a smart set until getting entangled with Robert. Their affair dragged on. Marriageable men were hard to find, younger girls were making their mark, and by the time she was the wrong side of thirty three, Celia, along with her observant mother, felt she needed refreshment.

'Darling you need a change, a holiday, a real change. Not just France and Italy Why not a little 'recherché' into your past? India, Assam? There are still people there who know you. They'll give you a great time. It's just what you need.'

'I've got too good a job here.'

'Yes, but, darling, just take six months off. Have a real change. You haven't been back since you were fifteen. The tea-gardens are absolutely beautiful, remember? All those rounded terraces of an amazing green. And a marvellous social life. Besides you never know what's on the cards.'

This was appealing and Celia started to take a hard look at her present life. Robert's attentions were lacking in lustre. He could never make up his mind to break with his wife and the last thing Celia saw herself as was a convenience.

The next time Celia 'popped down' to see her mother, Ada had a surprise for her.

'Of all things! Guess what, darling! An invitation from dear Dodo and Angus! To Rituparna where you grew up! They want you to come out. "Come out and stay," they say. See, read it for yourself! They need livening up, "fresh blood," is how she puts, it.'

Celia had gone down to Southsea for the week-end because she was utterly fed-up with Robert. She'd just had yet another row with him. He would not leave his wife. He was making a total convenience of her. Always on about the children. 'And what about me?' she had said to him icily.

'You don't understand. You haven't got any children.'

That was it. Children. Always the children. Thank goodness she didn't have any.

Celia decided she couldn't bear him to come up with that same excuse again. When she had gone down to see her mother, and the invitation had come up, she wasn't prepared to shilly-shally any longer.

'I'm off,' she told Robert. 'You had better spend your spare time looking after your precious children.'

She made arrangements about her job, she sub-let her flat, and she booked on 'The Eastern Aurora' first class, (Port Out Starboard Home) blowing a small legacy her father had left her. If she was to have a holiday, she'd have a good one.

In the Granada Hotel in Calcutta Celia turned on the new tap in the new en-suite bathroom. Like a dyspeptic frog it gurked foetid air at her with no sign of water. She rang the bell. A 'boy' of at least twenty-five appeared to whom she attempted to explain the problem. Ten minutes later two boys arrived with ancient enamel water cans marked hot and cold, both of which were cold, followed by a third bearing a breakfast tray. Yes, she was back in India. How many years? More than fifteen years ago, and a war. The street smells, the crowded streets, the families asleep on the pavements, the cows, the beggars, it was all coming back to her. She sipped her tea as she looked out of her balcony window. Traffic, cars, lorrics,—they were new— held up behind carts, were winding slowly round a circle of tired vegetation and forking away into the distance, along a rather grand, wide street, with large, pillared buildings on one side and a park on the other.

She stretched out on her bed to enjoy a moment of stillness. India! She was there, finally! The shipboard life had been a bit of a lark and already she was feeling much more like her old self. Her mother had been absolutely right! Her blood was up for adventure. Nothing venture, nothing win!

She was enjoying relaxing, looking around. The smells and the sights brought it all back!

She found herself watching a rather large insect on the ceiling. On board ship there hadn't been any insects, only the phosphorescent glitter of surface sea-life in the darkness and the lilting cushioning of the sea itself. Now the land. Back on land.

The insect wasn't easily definable. Not a beetle, nor a spider nor a daddy long-legs. She closed her eyes for a second. When she opened them again it had gone. There were no mouldings nor cracks in the high newly painted ceiling where it could be hiding. She wasn't afraid of insects but she wanted to know where it was. Not knowing disturbed her. She had to locate it.

Her mind wandered to and fro again.

Adjusting to where she now was, took her back to when she had left India with her parents, to start schooling at 'Medhurst' in Godalming. Ada and Mervyn had organised their furlough especially to set her up in a small girls' boarding school and they had all stayed here in Calcutta together, en route for England.

How excited she had been! At last Civilisation! Shipboard life! London! Escape! That was what it had seemed to her schoolgirl self. Now, after all the upheavals of the war she was equally glad to be back.

The heat here reminded her of how cold she had found it in her Spartan boarding school. That had been the first real culture shock, an ice-cold dormitory with fourteen iron beds and green linen bedspreads. How could she forget that sparse Victorian Gothic house, with its Janus-like cross over the front porch! Not much love and kindness there! Her cross, that was a fact. Still, she had commonsense. She had get-up and-go, enough to take stock of what impressed the Misses Jacksons. She determined to subscribe to whatever they wanted. That was the way to handle people! The school was privately owned by them and they seemed to spend more time playing Mahjong in their private apartment than actual teaching. Both were large ladies, who, between them covered most of the syllabus, save for a resident 'mademoiselle' and a visiting piano and singing teacher. As for the domestic arrangements, they were allowed one bath per week, cod-liver oil for health, and very nasty food. She could never forget the rumblings and crankings of the food trolley as it was winched up grindingly from the cockroach-infected kitchen in the basement to the dining room, a dark brown panelled area which matched exactly with the colour of the tepid bowls of stew. And the smell, stale, like underarm sweat! And beetroot, the cheapest vegetable in the market; how she hated beetroot! All too often they had beetroot sandwiches with no butter even, for high-tea. The only decent meal was the midday Sunday dinner, when visitors came. Before she joined the ranks of the abandoned children of parents employed in the 'Colonies', she was excited at the prospect of living back in England, but her schooldays had not proved nearly as wide ranging and exciting as she had hoped. She lay back on the pillows, thinking. She might not have enjoyed her life much at the time, but her experiences at 'Medhurst' had been a very good preparation for life. There she had learned to say one thing and think another. She said what people wanted to hear, fulsomely and with charm, and it had got her on in school and in life. It had made her tough, or she wouldn't be here, now, with every intention of carving out a new life for herself in Assam.

It was at this point that she realised that she was still staring at the insect. It was on the blind. She would get it! She was usually a pretty good shot. Motionless, except for a snaking hand feeling for her high-heeled shoe under the bed, she prepared for the kill. Just as she was about to strike, it sprouted wings and glided insultingly out of her reach. She threw her shoe at the wall.

Better get up.

That evening at eight o'clock the train left for Tezpur, thence for Jorhat.

Celia felt ready for anything.

She had every intention of having a great holiday.

Meanwhile in her bungalow among the tea gardens Edith Rutherford was in the middle of giving a birthday lunch party for Dodo. Just a small affair with Betty, Verity and Eulalie. They had already drunk a toast, and were at the coffee stage in the drawing room nibbling on rather stale Fortnum and Mason sugared violets.

'She's arriving next week.'

'A new face. That'll liven us up a bit.'

'If she's anything like her mother---'

'I liked Ada. She had a sense of humour.'

'More than could be said for her friend Cora.'

Smiles criss-crossed at this remark.

Edith continued, squeezing together her shoulders and putting her head on one side. 'Very tight-lipped, always. She really was of the old school. Dudley had to put up with a lot.'

'He was too nice to notice,' put in Verity.

'Celia's a widow, poor girl.'

'Another one,' Betty added.

'She lost her husband in the Navy. Sad. They had only been married a couple of years.'

'The same as Stephanie, Gordon's niece.'

'We don't want another one like her.' Eulalie settled back in her chair, stretched her legs in front of her looking at her pretty, snakeskin shoes. 'They all come out looking for husbands.'

'Stephanie was lucky to get one in the first place' Edith put in. 'She was rather painful, to say the least. She got on my nerves. Always so apologetic.'

'I don't think you'll find Celia's the least bit apologetic, not if I remember rightly. We stayed with Ada and Mervyn when we were last over. She's very attractive. I liked her. She's full of 'go'. That's why I've invited her.' added Dodo.

'Who have we got around?' questioned Betty. 'That nice trainee, Stephen is far too young. Celia's not exactly in the first flush.'

'There's always Neil.'

The girls exchanged looks.

'Yes and no.' Betty shrugged.

'Pam of course.'

'Pam's ten years older. Besides, she's already had a good run! At least Celia and he are the same age. Neil really does need a wife of his own,' Dodo pronounced. 'Be realistic! Running a large garden as he does single handed is tough. He needs marrying off. Remember all that trouble he had with that girl he was smitten with, back in England, who did the dirt on him? Cora hated her.'

Eulalie smiled.

'No time like the present! We'll bring them together! That'll be a bit of fun! I'll give a special dinner party. 'A la recherché and all that! We'll see what happens.' She crossed her ankles and looked round at her friends, who were equally delighted at the prospect.

'You see I was right' said Dodo. 'It will liven us up a bit.'

A virtual guard of honour of scarlet and yellow canna lilies stood to attention at the prospect, as the cars revved down the drive.

TWO

C elia stretched herself lazily on Neil's large bed, tracing his naked flesh with the backs of her fingers. She looked at him through half-closed eyes. 'I am having a good holiday,' she said.

He didn't reply with words, but leant up on his elbow to look at her.

She was pretty and knew it.

Fair hair shaped into the nape of her neck, skin soft and scented; what man wouldn't take her to his bed, given the chance, and she had given Neil every chance.

It had been so easy. She had driven up in Dodo's car to take photographs more than once.

'Mother insisted. She bought me a camera specially. I've taken heaps of 'Rituparna.' Sad that Aunt Cora and Uncle Dudley are no more to see what you've done with everything. The garden's absolutely lovely.'

'Dad's basic layout, not mine.'

She propped herself up on the pillows, half covering herself artistically with the sheet, and looking round the large room.

'Too much furniture.'

'Mother's.'

She brushed his nose with her forefinger. 'Needs a woman's touch.'

Neil sat up beside her, putting his arm round her shoulders languidly.

'I'm open to suggestions.'

She nestled against him. 'Well if it were mine...'

What she was thinking was 'I've stalked him into his chamber.' What next?'

Ever since Eulalie had given the dinner party, Celia's social success was secured and sequential. Preceded by French perfume her silken legs descended prettily from the cars of whoever was driving her around. The whiteness and pinkness of her porcelain elegance brought London's Chelsea to Jorhat.

Eulalie's party had been a highlight for everyone. Its special fun was to witness Neil's surprise in seeing Celia, and vice versa. Atypically, he arrived late, to find some dozen of his friends well into their second drink chatting loudly in a bunch together in the sitting room.

'You should have seen his face!' Violet told Betty who had been disappointed at not being able to go to the party at the last minute. 'He stopped in his tracks and went bright red, and said something that sounded terribly like 'Jesus!' Celia, cool as a cucumber, went straight up to him and kissed him on both cheeks and said 'Neil Langford! Why, you're better looking than ever!'

After that the evening really took off. Everyone talked about Ada and Cora, dear Dudley and Mervyn, and the awful 'flu after the War and how glad they'd all be if they'd known how those two would meet up after all those years at Bob's and Eulalie's! Celia explained how fed-up she was with London and needed a holiday and wanted to see all those places she'd known as a child. Her mother had bought her a special new camera, with instructions to take photographs of everything, just everything, so as to remind her. Neil could hardly refuse her coming to 'Tinkharia' 'and,' Dodo wrote to Ada, 'as you well know they haven't looked back since!'

Neil was not the only one showing interest in Celia. She only had to appear at the club and John or Quentin would buy her a drink or old Gordon would chat her up. She fitted in wonderfully. 'It's as if it were "meant" Edith and Beatrice were heard to remark, 'He'd be very silly at his age (referring to Neil) not to pop the question.'

Pam was really the only one who was likely to mind, but then it was lucky that she and Roger hadn't yet got back from England. 'Fate,' said Betty, who had been reading Celia's horoscope. According to Jupiter's rising in the heavens towards the Pleiades, this was the most propitious time for Scorpios to acknowledge compatability with old friends. 'There you have it!' She smiled triumphantly. 'Not that I believe in that sort of thing, but,' she arched her eyebrows, 'what is there to stop them!'

On Neil's verandah, Celia and he were sipping long iced whiskies and lime.

'This could set tongues wagging,' she said, looking at him knowingly from under her lashes.' He shrugged and smiled.

'So?'

He took stock of her.

She was smart in white and grey linen. Her oval, little-girl face was very attractive. She had plenty of personality, enough for herself and himself put together. Perhaps he really should consider marriage, if she would have him. Pam wasn't really an obligation. She was a good friend, but she did have a husband and two boys and they'd always had a tacit agreement that divorce was out of the question. Beside, on a practical level, Roger had been exploring new business prospect in London ever since the boys had found jobs back in England, so the chances were that they wouldn't be around in Jorhat for much longer.

'Funny, isn't it.' Celia tossed her head sideways a little. 'I sense that people are throwing us together on the one hand and longing for scandal on the other.'

They were sitting on rattan chairs with a low table between them, overlooking Neil's delightful garden, with its rich background of velvety ridges of row upon row of tea-bushes curving into the distance.

Neil raised one eyebrow and laughed.

He wasn't really much of a laugher, yet here he was laughing! Perhaps it was just the whisky, but no, it was more than that. Watching Celia at work on him did make him laugh. He laughed silently to see her way of negotiating herself into his life.

What was it she had she asked him, all so innocently? Yes. About his parents' house after Dudley's death, a couple of years after his mother's; how she remembered coming there with her mother and Mervyn, how, later, they had all taken a box to the King's theatre for Cora's birthday. 'Had he sold it? The house. It was a rather handsome house' she remembered. Must have been worth a good bit, with all that land, and in such a good position! Her mother, too, had sold their place for a really good price after Mervyn had died, and she had bought just the sort of little flat she wanted looking right across the sea, so that sometimes, at high tide it looked as if the Isle-of-Wight ferry was aiming straight for her sitting room!

She was doing her best to remember the past. Hadn't he thought about being a teacher at one stage, or was it a lawyer? She seemed to remember his working as a sports Master at some Prep school. Did he remember Southsea? And why hadn't he ever been back? What did he do and where did he go on his leave if he didn't go back to England? She knew he had had quite a serious affair with a girl in the past, what was her name? A funny sort of name. Yes. Dessa wasn't it? A teacher, wasn't she? She had met the sister, too. Her husband had been a friend of Adrian's in the Navy; they had met at a party. She remembered it because the hostess was a famous dancer and had danced a fantastic tango with one of the naval officers.

She looked sad. 'The war.' That party had reminded her of the war, and Adrian.

She sighed, pausing as she remembered. Her face had softened. 'We only had two years together.'

Neil had nodded.

'Marvellous years. It couldn't have gone on like that. We never had the banal side of marriage, children, routine. We lived for the moment. Since then, well, the odd affair, nothing serious. A bit of gadding about, in London, but now it was time to think of the future. Life had to go on.'

Vikram appeared and refreshed their glasses. They both drank deep.

Stretching her elegant legs, and crossing them neatly at the ankles, Celia changed her tone.

'You know, Neil, you must take me seriously.'

Neil smiled.

'No, seriously, I mean it.'

'I do,' Neil smiled again.

'You're a bit impossible. You seem to be here and yet you're not.'

At this point Titus, Neil's dog, rose up from beneath Neil's feet, stretching himself and waiting for a pat. Neil was glad of the interruption.

'You see, I think you like your dog more than me.'

Without speaking Neil fixed his eyes on her and smiled amusedly.

'You don't even reply.'

She gave him a barbed, quizzical look.

'You see, you do! You don't even deny it. You're impossible.'

'I agree.' He went on stroking Titus.

'And so it goes on. It's not even as if ...' she paused, looked at him and then looked away. 'I can't stay out here on holiday forever.'

She brushed an invisible thread from her skirt as she cast her eyes downwards.

Titus was lying full length at Neil's feet, his face on his front paws, his eyes fixed on Celia

Two against one, she thought.

Neil didn't move. Only his lips. Celia had almost to hold her breath to hear what he was saying.

'I'm not sure I have enough to offer you, and... would it work? Us, I mean.'

'If you wanted to make it work it would.'

'I might bore you to death in weeks. I bore myself.'

'Then don't make a habit of it. If you make habits you can also break them.' She paused. 'People, I won't say who, are already asking me when I'm going back. It's getting a bit embarrassing.'

Neil was looking at and through Celia; her whiteness, her shapely figure, her prettiness. This was a more humane and much less sweeping Celia than the one he remembered sitting alongside Aunt Ada, on his mother's sofa in the morning room at St. Ronan's Road. In those days they had presented a twin look as fierce as the double-barrels of a gun. But marriage, death, loss, and the no-man's land of the aftermath of war, had softened her, and if he asked her to be his wife, he would be the envy of many of his friends.

He felt like a shopper in a sale, turning over an undoubtable bargain, but a bargain was only a bargain if you really wanted it.

And why shouldn't he want it? What else was there? Could they really mean something to each other? The girls had been trying to marry him off for years. They were almost getting to the point of calling him 'poor Neil,' he reflected. There had been that embarrassing time with Stephanie. But Celia was different. Celia was something of a catch. How delighted Cora would be to think that at last, her boy was to marry not just someone of his 'own class', but her best friend's stunning daughter!

Celia stopped leaning back and looking at the view. She drew up her legs and clasped her hands together. Neil sensed it was now or never.

He stretched out his hands across the table towards her, palms upward.

'Celia,' he said. 'Marry me.'

There, he had done it.

She regarded him squarely in silence, for what felt like a very long time.

Trying to suppress a little smile, 'Say please,' she said.

THREE

Travel!

Back in 1927 to go to Lulworth Cove camping was a big adventure, and going to the Isle of Wight on a ferry-boat, a thrill. Imagine then, the excitement of packing up house to board 'The Queen Adelaide' for Capetown and Port Elizabeth in Africa!

Lounging in Mediterranean sunshine, light-years later with few responsibilities, on board yet another liner, how could I ever forget the upheaval!

A baby, nappies! No easy task aboard ship! And milk was a problem. In earlier days, wealthy families even took their own cow on board with them for the sake of the children. Lucky I was breast-feeding. That at least wasn't a problem.

Guy's letters had given me some indication of what was provided for us in the way of family household goods, but I still had my list of 'musts', more to bolster my own confidence in a strange land. On reflection I don't think I ever used any of the bottles of Sloane's liniment I took with me, but mother always 'swore by it' and to be without it in the middle of nowhere filled me with panic. My 'vital' list included cod-liver oil, cough-mixture, hairpins, hair-tongs a magnifying glass, special kitchen knife and tweezers. Out in the wilds who would know what might happen with three children and a baby?

What to pack? What not to pack? Mo and Austen insisted on taking their own treasures, and Guy had specially asked me to bring trivial things like scissors and a decent shaving brush. High on my bed lay a heterogeneous, unattractive pile of essentials, none of which could be left behind and no space to pack them.

Before Guy had left we decided to sell most of the contents of our new house and let it unfurnished. We had no idea how long this new job might last. Initially it was a three-year contract, but open-ended enough for changes, whatever they might be. We had no idea how long we would be away. How long does it take to build dams and channel water? Guy had studied the geology of the area but he could make no definite plans until he had reconnoitred in person. That was his worry. Mine was getting the family there and adjusting to a very different, new life. It was both stirring and scary; in a way we were pioneers going into a strange world.

The children were irrepressible. Even the silent, resourceful Mo, who usually maintained a degree of superciliousness, was agog. Gug, (Gregory) spent his time constantly jumping up and down, wetting his bed and never concentrating. He nearly left behind his 'smell', an essential, precious, ragged piece of flannel which he carried around with him from when he was a baby. Austen, meanwhile, made a tear-off calendar of all the days until he would see his father, and drove us mad reading out facts about Africa from an encyclopaedia. Did we know it was the second largest continent? Did we know that hyenas would devour anything, including babies? Did we know that there were cat-snakes that lived in trees or that we could have a mongoose for a pet?

Yes, yes, no, no. We stopped hearing.

At last all our belongings were in cabin-trunks and suitcases and finally had been taken off by the carrier. I remember sinking back with relief and exhaustion. Nothing I could do about anything now.

Bill took us to the Docks in his new car. He and Gwenny had been married by this stage and were living in Southampton. They came to Portsmouth especially to pick us all up. There were hugs, shouts and waving from two boys in the dickey seat, me in the front with Bill, and Gwenny in the back with the baby. We were off!

It is a strange moment when a large sea-vessel casts off. For the next weeks you are in a new world, a kind of limbo. You can't do the usual daily tasks. Like being in hospital you settle into regime with its own built-in rules and sense of lastingly-temporary friendships.

Our time on the ship was magic.

I only have to look now between this ship's white rails to recapture the excitements of that journey.

We had time. We had each other and the ocean encircled us. There was the fun of swimming in a boat which was itself swimming. There were always things for everyone to do, quoits, a fancy dress-party, deck golf. The boys loved it. I had time too, to think, to think about the implications of being part of a mission station, something I would never ever even have dreamed of. I remembered those stories I used to tell my class in West Meon, 'Joseph and the coat of many colours,' 'Moses in the bulrushes,' they were good stories, but we were hardly the sort of people who were fired with bringing Christianity to native Africans. Literacy, yes I could help with that, but I was totally inadequate if it were to come to intense prayer and conversions. Mo knew how I felt, and he felt pretty sceptical himself. I warned him that he would have to watch what he said when he got to his new school in Grahamstown, which was a religious foundation with regular chapel services, 'grace' before meals and divinity lessons. I reminded him that he and Austen were going there as boarders, largely by the courtesy of the Brothers who had been so helpful to us and that it was all part of the deal.

'Isn't it immoral for us suddenly to become religious?' he asked.

What he said echoed what I had felt all along.

'I'm not suggesting we should,' I told him, 'but they are doing a lot to make it possible for us to come here so the least we can do is to keep an open mind.'

'You and Dad have never bothered much about religion,' he countered, 'until now.'

'Then perhaps it's time we did,' was my reply. 'The Brothers are very good, humane, people and we should be ready to learn from them.'

Despite not being 'religious' I felt this and thought that at least I should start to take seriously what they considered essential to the meaning and purpose of life. From the start I had been amazed how readily Guy, of all people, had been prepared to take on such a mantle, but that was before I knew how essential this job was for him and us. Only later was I to know how imperative it was for him to get a job. The authorities at the Technological Institute had threatened him with termination of his appointment at the end of the current term, for reasons I could only guess. With those considerations, working on a mission station was a means of saving us, we had no choice but to seize the opportunity.

Drink? Women? Insubordination?

Guy was capable of all three.

Whatever had given rise to this African adventure and whatever the future held did not wreck the exciting time we had on board. We all loved it.

No-one felt the least bit sea-sick in the Bay of Biscay unlike some of the unlucky white-faced passengers. The horizon beckoned, the sea was alive with flying fish and dolphins, reflecting every changing mood of the sweep of the sky. Mo would sit with me sometimes, awed with such powerful beauty. Austen was more interested in the ship itself and the time changes as we journeyed. Gug, in the children's room crayoned his way to Africa, making endless paper hats. The two weeks aboard were packed with a sense of wonder and timelessness.

None of us ever forgot the morning when we sailed into Cape Town harbour, with the sight of table Mountain emerging from the clouds. We were not to disembark here, however. Guy was to meet us in his new car at Port Elizabeth.

In those days that city had no dock and you can imagine the children's delight when we and our cabin luggage had to be got into a crane basket and winched into a tender to take us ashore!

Daddy! Daddy! Guy!

Hubbub, chatter embraces! Much excitement at our re-union! Guy looked thin but sun-tanned and well. All the inventing, adapting and pioneering was just what he needed to keep his mind alive and electric.

We were together again! Henry had grown out of all recognition. Gug jumped up and down for dad to give him a piggy-back. Austen kept asking questions about the car. Mo's natural aloofness vanished as he openly welcomed his father's arm around his shoulders. Guy held me close and whispered quietly how much he needed me, and how he had missed me.

It took the best part of four days to drive to the mission station which was past the settlement of Tsolo and over the River Umzimvubu. We stopped at Grahamstown on the way to introduce the boys to their new school, where we met the headmaster and looked round the boarding house where they would live. Once we had all settled into our new quarters Guy would bring them back to start the new year, after which they could get to us by train even though the journey took a full two nights. Austen was to be in the top class of the prep department and Mo in the second year of the senior school as his academic reports showed him to be well-ahead with his work. Having fixed them up with their school needs, and familiarised them with where they would be living, we set out on the last part of our journey to the Transkei.

Rising hills form a sharp background continuously to this coastal strip of rough plain and scrubby land which borders the fringe of the

Indian Ocean. This was the traditional land of the Xhosa, the people to whom The Brothers were to bring the word of God. Accustomed to the hedged green fields of England and the beautiful New Forest, I felt like an alien and wondered what strange, unknown experiences lay ahead in this unaccustomed land. With a young baby in my arms I was feeling less and less like the pioneer I had agreed to be. I had to keep telling myself that what we were doing was adventurous, that it was for Guy, that we wouldn't take long to get into this new life. Seeing his healthy face had to be worth dragging us all out to such distant parts, nevertheless I had grown to be more cautious and worries grew with every mile.

He dismissed my hesitance with the problems of religious commitment with a wave of his hand.

'You'll love everybody, darling, they are great people. Not at all painful and churchy. You'll find them really good friends. They've been marvellous to me, I tell you.' He put his hand on my knee and smiled.

'Relax, you're tired.' He could see that I was looking pretty worn with travelling, the dust, feeding the baby and stopping the boys arguing. 'It's hardly the town-hall square, but our house is very adequate, and there are basic facilities for all we need. The buildings are all set round a simple wooden church. The Brothers share a house on one side. On the other is the school which doubles as a general meeting hall, and on the far side that's us, and next to it the house which the three deaconesses share. Between them, they, "the girls", I call them, look after the school and the surgery. On the opposite side is the hospital building. Two of the deaconesses, Sister Naomi and Sister Rachel are fully trained nurses which is...' he paused, gave me a look and chose his word with a smile, 're-assuring.'

He was just like his old, jaunty self.

'I've told them what a good teacher you are! You'll have lots of help in the house, remember, so you won't be bogged down with the baby all the time. You'll be able to help out in the school. They'll be glad of that.'

His confidence made me feel better. The children, too had been settling down and were wholly pre-occupied with the car. We'd never owned a car before, and Gwenny and Bill were the only ones with a car in the family. Guy loved driving, and he let Mo and Austen steer along the empty stretches of road, of which there were many. Mileage and petrol had to be worked out carefully; always a spare can for emergencies. For once I was really glad to be married to an engineer!

We drove along miles and miles of nothing, or so it seemed to me. We stopped for a night which enabled us to wash the baby and ourselves. We were getting closer to the Mission itself and increasingly I was feeling a mixture of apprehension and excitement.

'I'm building two dams, at the moment,' Guy explained. 'And I'm having to work out rainfall and the availability of river water which is pretty low at this time of year. I'm laying pipes into a central tank in the settlement itself. I spent a lot of time trying to find a natural bore without any luck, but that's all part of the deal.'

We crossed the river.

'Soon there, now, kids,' he called out to the back of the car.

'I can see it! Look!' Mo, breaking his own unwritten rules, allowed himself to be spontaneously excited. He was pointing energetically to a line of flat buildings emerging from the dusty bushland. Gug was pointing, copying him, bouncing up and down.

'I saw it first,' said Austen. 'I did! We're there, we're there, we're there!'

'Doesn't look much' said Mo.

'What did you expect in the middle of nowhere?' said Guy. A month or two back there was nothing here at all. It's amazing what's happened in such a short time. We've all worked very hard.'

A number of black people, women, children, men were crowding together to meet us. They had been quick to spot the cloud of dust in the distance. Guy and I waved, the children all waved, the Sisters and Brothers appeared, waving. We were big news!

This bare, stark place was to be our new home.

FOUR

I have two photographs left of our time at the mission station. There is a picture of Guy with Gug on his shoulders, giggling with delight, alongside him, Sala, our nanny, holding a bonny-looking Henry of about eight months. It is taken from outside the front of our house, showing a step up to a covered porchway, with the living room window on the left and the small window of one of the bedrooms on the right. The second photo is of Guy and of me, pregnant again, though not obviously so, with the curly headed Mo and Austen. They were back home for the holidays. The camera has caught Mo standing by his father, looking up at him, while Austen is between Guy and me, screwing up his eyes a bit in the sun. Guy stands very upright, smiling slightly, but rather drawn in the face and thin, a typical Englishman in the colonies, while, though I say it myself, I am looking rather well and smiling broadly, wearing a headband and a flowery sort of dress.

I was still happy.

I had never tried pioneering before, but found, like teaching, it suited me absolutely. With Gug at school for at least half of every day and an uncomplicated baby looked after by Sala an intelligent, clean, reliable black seventeen year-old African girl, I had the time, and was pleased to be, a real help in the school myself. The little and not so little black children were a delight to teach, keen to learn, smiling, well-behaved, with a sense of humour all their own. The Sisters too, were really grateful for any help I could give for it meant that we could have smaller groups, and, as any teacher knows, that's half the battle in putting over ideas and getting a response. I often thought back to those classes of forty two children at Church Street School in urban Portsmouth, and of the poverty of one or two families who sewed their children into brown paper for the winter, and decided that the life and the air and the grateful simple happiness of these country, tribal African children was in many ways preferable.

Brother Edward was in charge of the settlement which had only been going for less than two years. Having organised the land and the basic building, he had come over to England to the central St. Mark's mission in Cambridge, and along with the Very Reverend Brother Gabriel had interviewed applicants for the engineer's post, subsequently given to Guy. He, too, had been responsible for bringing over Sister Naomi and Marian Parkinson. Marian hadn't yet been ordained in holy orders as had Sister Naomi and Sister Rachel, since she wanted first to try out the work before committing herself. Like me, she was a trained teacher and although eight years older, we became good friends. Sister Rachel was an extraordinary woman, strong and humorous. She was a tower of strength and we all depended on her. She had worked on the Western Front in every nursing capacity possible in the War and was as unflappable as she was jolly. Being in Africa with the lively, hardworking Xhosa families was pure holiday, she reckoned.

As a group of people all of us on the station worked well together, even though, or maybe because, we were very different. Brother

Edward was thorough, organised and practical in contrast to Brother Dominic who was firm, spiritual, kind and tireless. Brother Geoffrey was the youngest of the three, and like Sister Rachel, had taken up Orders after experiencing the senselessness of war. In our isolated outpost, relationships and teamwork were very important for the successful running of the Station.

The deepest available reaches of the river were about half a mile away. The nearest Xhosa village lay on the far bank and the Africans had flocks of sheep and goats in nearby grassland, going into the foothills, depending on available feed. Such livestock brought with it the problem of predators, hyenas in particular. The Sisters had their own heavily guarded hen house, and if we heard hyenas at night which we sometimes did. Brother Geoffrey and Guy would go out with their rifles to frighten them away, for hyenas were known to savage anything, dead or alive. Their howling did scare me a bit and made me realise just how isolated we were. I always took special care of the baby making sure he could never crawl off. Guy kept a revolver in the cupboard by our bed for emergencies and showed me how to use it.

Guy had thrown himself wholeheartedly into his work, so essential to the settlement. His original thinking and quick understanding of the seasonal droughts and rainfall patterns, caused him to come up with a range of practical and economical solutions. The Brothers were delighted with him. Labour was no problem and the two large dams already under construction by the time we arrived, were to be in working order when the spring rains came.

I liked our house, primitive though it was. I had been prepared for basics, and I enjoyed arranging our bits and pieces to make this new place as attractive and homely as possible. My sewing machine proved to be worth every ounce of its heavy weight, and I made curtains and covers, liking nothing better than to have surprises for Guy when he came home. Having a cook (Martha) three times a week, and a cleaner, (Patience) was great and I had more time to do the things I liked. The paraffin burners made life a bit like being back with the Macdonalds at West Meon. We had paraffin lamps, too, of course. There was a wood range in the outhouse with a bread and roasting oven, and my early training from mother in her own old-fashioned kitchen proved invaluable. Gug, Henry and I soon settled in and made friends with everyone who came to the mission.

Central to our whole settlement was the church, and we attended services on a regular basis. Sister Naomi played the harmonium and I joined her choir along with numbers of blacks who loved singing and who sang with unforgettable joy and fervour. Once again I was reminded of West Meon all those years ago before the war. I smiled as I remembered that long-faced serious young curate. Religion here wasn't serious at all, rather a lively lifeblood.

And Guy and I had each other.

After those months apart and in such new circumstances our lovemaking was a necessary reinforcement to our lives. Our world was in each other in our bed and in our passionate nakedness. I, as I thought, gave him all the excitements he needed in full imaginative measure, and he would smile at 'the lineaments of gratified desire' which he gave me. His arm gently across me, his cheek close to mine, he would say memorable things to me amid our fragments of whispering.

'You punctuate me, Dess. You make sense of my consciousness.'

I smiled at his shaping of words.

'Is that a compliment? An exclamation mark or a full stop?'

His turn to smile.

He loved the baby who chuckled at his touch. Gug would wait for him to come in the door to assail his leg, both arms clasped round it waiting for throw-ups and piggy backs. Looking back, it was only when the immediacy of the project started to wind down in pace with the slowness of execution of his plans, that he began to suffer from frustration. That, and one day there was a big row.

Two big rows, actually.

A fight had broken out between some of the pipe laying team which resulted in bad damage to the pipe itself and necessitated major replacement just at the time when the river was in spate. Guy was furious. Usually cool in emergencies he started to shout and dragged two of the workers up to Father Edward's office to sack them. Bad went to worse when it was discovered that the necessary materials needed for repair were missing from the depot. It transpired that there had been thefts. This spoiled the atmosphere of the Settlement, and the casting of suspicion caused strains between Guy, Brother Edward and Brother Geoffrey, who, previously, had always trusted their workers fully.

It was at this time that my instincts told me that Guy had started drinking again.

Drinking. How could he drink?

I had to smile to myself. The only alcohol on the settlement was communion wine, which in Guy's own words was as 'potent as pig-piss.' Besides, I felt sure he would never subvert the Mission and all it was working towards ever to let himself down by drinking again.

It wasn't that he didn't do his usual day's work, it was more like a change of key in how he seemed. It was as if he was dissociating himself from me and the children. I couldn't exactly put my finger on anything, but I felt it.

One day he had to drive into Tsolo. This didn't happen very often and usually I would go with him to get supplies from the store, but on this particular day, with much excitement, my class was having the dress-rehearsal for their play, and so I asked Sala to go with Guy instead.

That night he got abysmally drunk.

I hadn't seen him drink, but he had disappeared after supper up to the depot.

When he returned at about half-past nine, the children were in bed, and the whole settlement dark. I sat under my lamp in the sitting room, mending.

He came back, slumped in a chair, staring into space.

The alcohol changed not merely him but the entire atmosphere of the room.

It was much more than the smell.

I put down my sewing.

He didn't speak.

I didn't know what to do for the best.

I picked up my sewing again.

'Can't you even speak?' he said.

I couldn't. The enormity was too much.

'Fucking, bloody God.'

I pretended to fasten off my cotton.

'Bloody God!'

Silence.

'Talk, woman! This god-forsaken place is buggered.'

I didn't speak.

'God's an atheist! Howzzat!'

I still didn't speak.

My silence proved the gambit to his letting out a stream of uncontrollable filthy language, and kicking over the small table. He was beyond himself, past comfort, past sympathy and eventually past anger. Wrung out he collapsed back in the chair. Somehow I got him into bed.

Next morning he had, even for him, a tremendous hangover. I sent a message to Father Edward that he wasn't well and another to Sister Rachel that there was no need for her to come round.

He slept it off.

That evening he was all apologies. With tears in his eyes he promised never, ever, to drink again. He meant it. He knew exactly what disaster it would spell for us, the family, the Brothers and the trust we all had in him. He made me come down to the depot where he unearthed a second bottle of grog which he had hidden away, and gave it to me, in earnest of his intentions.

My heart was heavy. I could forsee collapse, broken trust, misery for us all.

Maybe you can guess what happened. Well partly.

Love was not enough.

I had always thought that love had total power, no beginning and no ending.

I was wrong.

I could hear Father Dominic's quiet, tranquil voice reading Corinthians 23. 'And now abideth Faith, Hope, Charity, these three; but the greatest of these is Charity.'

Love.

Charity meant the most enduring sort of love, agape, this mixture of caring, romantic love, but as well there were the incomprehensible swellings of erotic love. Mistakenly I thought that the healing power of love could conquer all things, a true-faith healing, that Guy, feeling and knowing how much I loved him in sickness and in health could gain enough strength to hold himself together for all our sakes.

Wrong.

I was to be overwhelmed by helplessness, I, a person who automatically put all my mind and effort to helping solve problems, a person to whom other people came to help solve their problems. I can tell you from experience that such helplessness leaves you gutted, empty, desiccated and desolate.

Whatever his stache of liquor, or whatever sort of alcohol he was resorting to, and I even suspected methylated spirits at one point, I had no idea. After that one occasion he never came home hopelessly drunk. All I can say now, is that there were growing, invisible barriers between us.

It was quite another set of circumstances which was to bring matters to a head, however.

Only some weeks earlier, I had discovered, not surprisingly, that I was pregnant. A fifth child! This had been the time of that happy photo.

Our sharing of this news, fortunately, had taken place more than a month before that terrible night when Guy had come home totally drunk. The realisation of another child, I felt sure, reinforced our togetherness, here in this wild land. Our lovemaking was utterly special for both of us; dramatic, satisfying wonderful, as I thought. I never dreamed other than that he loved me intensely, and I had never asked questions about all those gaps in our lives when he had been sent off to Archangel or Scotland or the Caspian Sea. We sub-mariner wives understood the stress levels our husbands endured, and would joke, or raise an eyebrow rather than nag and bitch about a spot of sex here and there attributing the chance of such opportunities to the fallout of war. In the same way we had accepted the intense drinking habits. As a Service they were dare-devils: that was part of the appeal.

That said, I need to tell you what happened on September 20th 1928.

I had gone to school as usual that morning, taking Gug with me. As usual I was having a happy time with my group of children making paper houses out of sixteen squares, when Marion told me that Gug had vomited badly, and she thought I ought to take him home.

I opened the door to our house and was walking to the kitchen with him to wash his face when I heard a noise. I called out for Sala. To my surprise Guy emerged from the boys' room into the passage.

'Didn't know you were home,' I said, What's up?'

'Forgot my notes and slide-rule.'

'Well you won't find them in there,' I said innocently, 'You've left them by our bed.'

At that point I had to go to the chest of drawers in Mo's and Austen's room to get Gug some clean clothes. To my utter surprise, there was Sala behind the door hurriedly getting into her dress.

I got it in a flash. Not all of it, not the worst bit, but, yes, Guy had been in there with her, and from her barely controlled confusion I could guess what had been going on. For a second I stood frozen like a pillar, holding my breath.

Then I exploded.

'You silly girl, you stupid silly girl.' My voice spelled out the syllables each one a bullet of disbelief.

Instead of her looking ashamed and embarrassed, to my surprise and fury she looked at me boldly.

Her look was what made me lose all control. I could feel my eyes stiffening with intensity.

'Exactly what have you been up to!'

Again the defiance, and worse, a slight smile.

'Mister Guy love me. He give me baby.'

She tilted her chin upwards and held her head high.

I slapped her face.

She did not flinch.

I turned. Guy was standing in the passage. He saw me hit Sala. I was shouting.

'Leave! Now! Go! Pack your things and go! Get out of this house!'

I swung back to Guy. I was raging.

'How long has this been going on?'

I swept into our bedroom. He followed me.

'We need to sort out a thing or two!'

I turned on him. I clenched my hands in horror and fury across my mouth.

'A black woman! You! She's only a girl! What's wrong with you!'

I hit him with all my might, his face, his head. 'You shit, you bastard, how could you do this? Don't blame the drink, what's rotten is you!' I was heaving, beside myself.

'All this time! How long has this been going on? Are you out of your mind?' I threw myself on the bed, angry, sobbing, tearing at the blanket. He stood silent, at the far end.

I dragged myself up, held my head erect, and stared at him. I felt white with rage, disappointment, hurt, disgust. I was powerless.

'She's going to have a baby? I don't believe it. When is she going to have a baby? How long has this been going on?'

With a woman's instinct, I knew that Sala's self-possession was the result of her youthful pride in Guy's wanting her. He knew all right.

'I suppose you know how well this will go down with The Mission! Some mission! What sort of apostle are you! Prophet of Doom more like. Our doom.'

I was holding my head in my hands.

'You know what this means, don't you. It's the end of us. The end of our family. Couldn't you ever think of someone other than yourself? The boys? Their lives? Everything's ruined for us all!'

At that point I remember seeing poor little Gug, standing white, in the doorway, his little face distressed and questioning, as he looked at us from one to the other.

Guy moved without a word, stroked Gug's head and gave him a kiss. Then he left the room.

There was a ghastly silence. Gug watched his father leave the house, then ran, sobbing, into my arms. After that he always stuttered.

FIVE

I was hastening over to the depot when I heard the shot.
Too late.

In my heart I knew that with his experience of weaponry he wouldn't have made a mistake.

The double door was slightly ajar.

There he lay, face downwards, spread-eagled and bleeding.

Rolled tipsily on its side was an oil drum.

My hand covered my mouth involuntarily.

I was closing my eyes and biting my lip. Anything not to look.

My insides knotted.

I couldn't move.

His name was echoing continuously in my brain.

I ran to him.

I saw the mashed back of his head. He had blown out his brains.

I had to think quickly. Others would have heard the shot. I had to have a story, a feasible story. Not suicide. Suicide was an unpardonable offence. This was a religious settlement. God determined when you were born and when you died.

Beside him was his rifle.

Yes! That was it. He was cleaning his rifle. He had been outside the back, sitting on the oil drum, oiling his rifle.

Oil! A rag! I had to produce his oil can and a rag. He had been out only the other night after hyenas. His rifle needed a clean.

Already I could hear noises of people coming. I had to be able to produce evidence. No time to look now. I could say that's what he said he was going to do when he went out. He had come home not only for his notes and slide rule but also for a rag. His oil can was in his office. I had to make sure I got hold of it.

I knelt beside him in disbelief.

I couldn't look at his shattered face.

Some workers were coming into the compound their running slowed to a halt as they realised what had happened.

Brother Geoffrey and Brother Dominic came up behind me, and were kneeling down in horror. 'A stretcher. Fetch a stretcher from the Hospital,' Brother Geoffrey directed. 'Tell Sister Rachel there's been an accident.'

That's it, I thought, an accident. Of course there's been an accident.

Brother Dominic had put his arms round me, and turned my head away from the sight of Guy. The only emotion I was feeling was anxiety lest anyone should realise that he had done this to himself.

There was a hubbub of voices. The men liked Guy. Their native babble was interrupted with bits of pidgin, 'good boss man, Mister Hall, he dead, he very bad, he bleedin.'

'Get back, get back. Stand back. Make room for the stretcher.'

Brother Geoffrey was taking over. He and Guy were good friends. Of the Brothers they were the closest. They had both been in the war. Brother Geoffrey had been at Gallipoli and had joined the Society after the war was over.

By this time Sister Rachel was on the scene with two stretcher bearers. All she could say was 'Jesus.' She knelt down to look more closely at Guy, and shook her head gently in grief. The boys turned him over carefully and there was a gasp of horror among us all when we saw the mess of his face. He was rolled onto the stretcher and covered with a piece of sheet.

'Take him to my surgery in the hospital', Sister Rachel said. 'And bring Dessa,' she said to Brother Dominic.

Life and death in half-an hour.

Our dreadful row.

What had I done?

Sala, Gug, the baby, Guy. The end of Guy.

And, two new, unborn babies.

I closed my eyes. No time to think about that now.

I had to keep thinking about an oil can and a rag.

No Guy. No husband. No father. No money and a baby to be born in February.

What could I do?

Guy's suicide may have been a coup de grace for him, but it was anything but a coup de grace for me.

All these realisations came to me in a flash.

I could understand why he had taken his own life. He knew he had made a mess of too many things, this last, the worst.

It was sad, sad, sad, so very sad, and it hadn't needed to happen.

He hadn't realised that we could have got through this somehow, together.

Too proud.

An intrepid hero in face of death, it was life he could not face.

What irony.

His way of coping had been drink. Someone of his sensitivity had to close down all the nerve endings with drink. He wasn't alone in this.

There were many alcoholics in Wellington Lodge. There were officers from both army and navy with all manner of psychiatric disturbances triggered by the outrages of war. Depression and nervous breakdown were unmanly, inadmissible realities. Alcoholism, too often was the cover. Then, it wasn't reckoned a disease, but a sign of total weakness and moral failure. Guy was brave, clever and witty, but in his own eyes and in the eyes of his contemporaries, his uncontrolled drinking was as contemptible as he was unredeemable.

And now, suicide.

That was totally inadmissible.

A Coroner would judge Guy as a man who took his life while of unsound mind. He would condemn him. What justice there?

He would be regarded as an outcast of society, along with us, his family.

All this went through my mind in less than a second.

It has always struck me how, in moments of crisis, the mind sees everything, simultaneously and crystal clear.

Whatever else I did, I had to I had to stand up in court and swear that Guy's death was an accident. I had no alternative.

'Yes. He said where he was going. He said what he was going to do before he left the house. He asked me for a piece of rag which I gave him. He kept an oil-can in his office.'

'Was this found by the body?'

'Yes, I found it'

I looked down, bit my lip, and covered my mouth with my hand. I wasn't acting. It was a wholly involuntary action. In that second I wasn't covering up a lie, but seeing Guy's scarcely recognisable, bloodied face. The courtroom, the memory of Guy's shattered head, made me feel faint, but I had to stick to my story at all costs.

The coroner's voice was echoing in my head.

'I realise that this is very painful and difficult for you, Mrs. Hall,' the Coroner said, 'but the Court has to ask you these questions as you were the first on the scene.'

'I understand,' I replied.

'And this is your husband's oil can? And this the rag?'

I nodded.

'Had your husband any reasons that the Court should know, which might make him want to take his own life?'

I breathed an inward sigh of relief. This was the opportunity for me to play my trump card.

By this time I had regained my equilibrium. I looked straight at the Coroner and spoke quietly.

'Quite the contrary, Sir,' I replied, 'I am four months pregnant.' A hush swept round the room.

'My husband was a devoted, family man. With a fifth child coming he had every reason to stay alive. We were hoping this one might be a girl.'

I felt the tensions ease. No-one knew about my pregnancy except of course, Guy and Sala, and she had disappeared since that fated morning. The Brothers, Sister Rachel and Marian were all in court and none of them had any idea that I was expecting another baby. I still remember the shock on their faces, and this seemed to make very good sense to them that Guy's death had been a terrible and unforeseen disaster.

The verdict was accidental death.

This meant that Guy's name was cleared. This meant that I was a bona fide widow, that my children were orphans in need of help and care. This meant that I could get financial assistance from the Navy, help with school-fees for the boys, and this meant that Guy's image as a war-hero was untarnished. Maybe he didn't wholly deserve this but I did. As it was I had more than enough to do.

First there had to be the funeral. I decided not to bring the boys all the way back from St. Paul's in Grahamstown. The day that Guy died, Father Edward had sent a wire to their headmaster with the news of the accident and of course I wrote them a long letter explaining how we would soon get together as a family once the funeral was over to discuss the future. Apparently, as I learned later, the head had been very helpful and had taken them for a walk into the hills with a picnic. They had sat together reading Psalm 121 and even Mo was moved by the occasion. Years later, Austen, especially was to remember this kindness.

Back at the mission Marian was very helpful and supportive. She knew that Sala had walked out suddenly just at a terrible time, and she never asked questions or probed in any way. She came over to sleep in the house with me for company, for more than a fortnight and Martha took on the baby during those very difficult days. I had so much to face that I did not grieve deeply until weeks later. Preparing myself for the inquest had sapped all my emotion. An ill wind as it were, in a strange way.

Next, I had to leave the Mission.

From The Society of St. Mark's point of view, they would have to engage another engineer to complete Guy's work, so essential to the running of the station. Even though I had done a lot to help the Brothers with the school, voluntarily, they could not afford to pay me as a teacher, or let me go on living in the house, which I well understood. Without a lot of time I had to think what to do and where to go. Father Edward made the suggestion that I could get a job in Grahamstown where they were always glad of teachers, and since the Navy would help with fees, the two boys could stay on at the school where they had newly settled in.

Something inside told me that this wasn't an arrangement I could sustain. I had a lot to consider, not least having a new baby. Money would be very tight, and I would have to manage the four boys single-handed in a strange place and in an unfamiliar land.

I was tough, but not that tough. For the first time in my life I really needed the support of people close to me.

What helped me make up my mind was a letter from Gwenny. It was spontaneous, heartfelt and warm; just what I needed at the time.

'Come home,' she wrote, 'come home at once. Come to stay with us to have the baby and to sort yourself out. There are three bedrooms, and plenty of floor space. Our house in Southampton is waiting for you. Morris is here in Southampton as well, working in the same office as Bill, so you'll have two spare men to give a hand with the boys. We have a car and can get you to Portsmouth any time to see the rest of the family. If I know mother, she'll be round for the confinement. She won't miss that! Perhaps it will be a girl! We're all here to help you as much as we can. You've had a terrible time. Get the first passage back you can.'

Relief! Support! A return to the people and places I knew! It was Gwenny's kindness at that time which reduced me to a crumpled mess. It was then I wept. I wept for the children, I wept for myself, I wept for the world. Until then I felt only anger and disbelief.

I had to escape from this alien land.

Before I had even finished reading Gwenny's letter I had made up my mind.

When I journeyed to see the boys I took her letter with me to show them. I was surprised to see how grown-up Mo had become. It was as if, as the eldest, he naturally assumed that he was my chief helper and advisor.

'That'll be best, mum. That would be what Dad would have wanted you to do. Austen and I and Gug have all got to go to school, and you'll need someone around like Auntie Gwenny, to be with you. That's the best for us all.'

'She's having a baby, too, I said.'

'Well! That's perfect! You'll be good company for each other.' He sounded so sensible and grown up, it brought me to tears.

By that November, we had packed all our things, and were being winched up at Port Elizabeth onto the 'Cape Star'.

Dead Guy lay forever in the earth of the Traskei.

1928

ONE

Every year at Christmas Gwenny sent Neil a Christmas card. It was a ritual: one to her brother in Melbourne and one to Neil in Assam. She felt sorry for them not being in England at this special time. She always added a scribble or two, but this time she added the shocking news that Guy Hall had died in September.

Christmas mail from England was usually a pretty special event in Jorhat with all the parcels and cards from 'Home'. This Christmas, however, Neil had other, more important considerations, so his packet of mail was still in a pile on his desk for at least a couple of days after it had arrived.

Celia. Engagement ring. Celia. The Wedding! Guest lists, impossible not to invite the whole club. Best-man? Flower-girls, Celia, Matron of honour, Dodo of course. Celia was very systematic with a list which seemed to get longer every day. He hadn't had a moment to himself.

In the Ladies' room at the Club, Edith, Betty and Eulalie, enjoying all Celia's and Neil's goings-on were chatting over a drink.

'Soon, I should think,' Betty was saying

'Can't be too soon for some,' remarked Eulalie, laughing. 'She's a hazard for some of the wives! Too loose a cannon,' she added, removing a biscuit crumb from her upper lip.

'There's absolutely no reason to make it a long engagement. It's not as if either of them are in the first flush!'

'I guess you've seen the ring,' put in Betty.

'Not much chance of not seeing it,' replied Edith. 'She positively flashes it about.'

'It's a pretty good one,' remarked Eulalie, taking up her glass to sip her drink and settling back in her chair as she reflected. 'Solitaire diamond! She has very good taste. Mind you, Neil's not short of a few bob after his parents' death.'

'Cora was the one who had the money.' Edith smiled. 'She let you know she had, didn't she.'

'Celia knew all that. From Ada.'

'Celia's not stupid. She knows which side her bread is buttered.'

'So does her mother. Think how pleased she'll be that Celia's brought it off. She had little time for some affair that had been dragging on in London.'

'Married man of course.'

'The war. Not enough men to go round,' Betty sighed. Eyes widened for a moment in acknowledgement.

'Celia's really keen to go ahead as soon as possible. And what's to stop them?'

'I know a certain person who won't like it very much.'

They all laughed and Betty raised her eyebrows.

'He's got to sort out that one.'

'Good job they're not due back until March.'

'While the cat's away the mice will play!' There were peals of laughter.

'Neil's not good at sorting things out.'

'Celia will make him, don't you worry!'

It was true. Pam was and had been one of Neil's on-going 'complications'. The last thing he wanted was any awkward intensification or scenes. He and Pam had always had an unspoken arrangement. They both knew the consequences of marital infidelity, particularly within the confines of their small society. He had never made false promises and she had never asked for any. They made the most of the times when Roger went away on 'business' as, in fact, it turned out, so did he.

'We've all been pretty decent turning a blind eye,' said Eulalie, 'and it is just as well the Carters have been away. All that had to come to an end sometime.'

'So when's the wedding going to be?'

'Soon. Celia was talking about early in the New Year.'

'We haven't had a wedding at the club for ages.'

The thought of the fun and the dressing up enlivened them.

'Bridesmaids? All the pretty-pretties?'

'Hardly. They're a bit old for that. But Celia mentioned that she was asking Dodo to be her Maid of Honour. Dodo's been very good to her over the past months she deserves a treat.'

'Perfect setting. St. Mary's. And dear old Canon Ashcroft?'

'Absolutely.'

'She's already been discussing it with you?'

'Well, a bit.' Edith looked slightly smug.

'A proper wedding! How lovely.'

'No question. Neil's never been married and Celia's a widow. We all want a proper wedding, best hats, the works!'

In Neil's bedroom at Tinkharia some twelve miles away, a similar conversation had been going on.

Celia was sitting on the edge of Neil's mother's large bed, semi-draped solely in a corner of the sheet, while to her increasing annoyance, Titus' wet nose was exploring bits of her Neil would never have dared.

She had been having far more success with the master than the dog, she reflected, and Titus had not been hoodwinked with the occasional rub behind the ears by her cool white hand. She actually did not like dogs; their fishy breath, purple gums and warm saliva.

She was thinking 'bloody dog', but she said with only the slightest touch of irritation in her voice, 'Oh, darling, help! Titus is embarrassing me,' which indeed he was, 'and we've so much to talk about. We have to make plans.' She drew her legs back up onto the bed, tucked the sheet firmly round herself authoritatively, and sat up against the pillows.

'Now, no argument, the simplest and nicest thing will be a church wedding. No! No protests, please. The girls all want a church wedding and Canon Ashcroft's already whispered in my ear, that he'd like nothing better than to marry us. He remembers your parents, and mine, from all those years ago.'

Neil was listening and with his right hand stroking Titus, who had moved to the other side of the bed.

'Well?' Celia arched her eyebrows.

He looked at her and smiled. His years in Assam had caused him to bury deep his youthful emotional passions and taught him the value of inactivity and apparent nonchalance.

'Well? Say something!'

He stretched out his left hand towards her, and stopped fondling his dog.

'I'm not very religious.'

'Don't be silly! Nor am I. Religion's got nothing to do with it. It's the social importance. A church adds an absolute something. Adrian and I didn't have time to have a social wedding in the war, but here at the Club, the girls are all longing for new hats and dresses, and they really think we owe it to them for having brought us together. You don't seem to realise.'

Neil stroked her arm.

'Organise it just how you like, but not too many speeches.'

It had been Celia's turn to smile. 'Good. You agree.' She picked up his hand and kissed his fingers to register approval.

'Next.' She sat up higher, then turned on her elbow towards him. 'When?'

Neil lay back and reached out for Titus. He didn't speak.

'You say when. Before Christmas or after?'

'You choose.'

'I think it had better be after. Early in the New year.'

Neil nodded gently.

'And where shall we go for our honeymoon?'

'You choose that too.'

That had been two days ago. All that time the mail had been sitting on Neil's desk and Neil had allowed himself to start to accept the idea that he was to marry like everybody else. No reason not to. Pam? How would he handle Pam? Just as well she wasn't around. He didn't want scenes, and she did have her two boys, and, yes there would be some uncomfortable and awkward moments but she would have to accept a fait accompli. Yes he was fond of her, but she was ten years older and... well Celia? Celia was? What was she, exactly? She was something he couldn't explain. She was. He shrugged inwardly. That was the thing about her. This was what it was to be a lucky chap.

It was at this point that he started to finger through the letters in a pile on his desk and immediately recognised Gwenny's handwriting. He turned the envelope over. A new address on the back. Southampton he noticed, not Portsmouth. He smiled. Her annual card. She never forgot.

He opened the envelope, the card showed a typical English village scene with snow and carol singers with lanterns. That was when the piece of paper fell out which altered his life.

His eyes fixed themselves on the words. He sat motionless. He was hardly breathing. His insides changed gear.

His mind went white, froze, then burst into a thousand simultaneous pieces.

She...? She would need help. In Africa? On a Missionary station? Is that what Gwenny had said? Now, of all times. Just in time. Dessa was a widow. He hadn't married yet, nor could he now. Not possibly. The card, sitting there for days. The ironies. Celia, he couldn't think about Celia. Extraordinary to hear just when...

A seismic tremor seized him.

He swallowed.

He drew a deep breath, unable to take in the reality. The past came surging back.

He stood up, leaned against the door, his eyes not taking in what stood around him, but probing within his head.

Dead! Her husband dead. The war had been over years ago, why now?

She had several children didn't she? Did that matter?

He had to know more. He had to write to Gwenny, no, cable her. He had to cable her straight away, a pre-paid reply. The present was collapsing round him. He had to know something definite. Why? He couldn't think. He only knew what he couldn't do.

'Anxious, stop, Send details, stop, Urgent, stop, Letter following, Neil.'

In his mind he had pictures of a keen little girl with a too-large tennis racquet at Alexandra Park. With his parents no longer alive her annual card had continued to give him feedback from the past. And now?

Yes, last year, the mission station, South Africa! He hadn't been able to believe it. Dessa the Spreader of the Word! He had almost laughed out loud.

But this. This was serious.

How long ago? How long? Thirteen years. An unlucky number. A dreadful accident?

There was the world before Gwenny's news and the world after. Present plans were utterly out of the question. He couldn't marry Celia if... He couldn't, now, not possibly. He had to hear details.

He whistled for Titus and took off for the drying sheds to give himself time to think. Whatever could he say to her? Celia, that is. He took a deep breath and patted his dog.

When she arrived that afternoon he was at his desk in his study. He had heard the sound of car wheels in the drive, but before he could collect himself Vikram had shown her in and before he could take in her presence she was sitting on the edge of his leather-topped desk making little kissing noises through pursed lips accompanied by finger-pinches the quicker to get on with the business of the day.

'All white, shades of white that is, or bright colours against the green? What do you think? For the church and the Club. I think they should match.'

Neil sat straight, not speaking. The torrent of words went on.

'Darling, wake up. Flowers, I'm talking flowers. We've got to decide. Christmas will be on us all too soon. We've got to make arrangements now. I think white would be more dramatic. I mean everyone goes for colour these days, but I think white is classier, more original.'

Neil moved his left fingers to the edge of his desk. Celia was tracing her pencil down the list in her hand, not looking at him.

'Well? Come on, what do you think?' She looked at him and laughed. 'I don't want you to say that I've made all the decisions. It's your wedding as well, darling.'

Neil took a deep breath.

'Something's happened.'

Celia was in her element, smiling and organising everything. She was too pre-occupied to look directly at Neil. 'I must give you your hug,' she said, moving round behind him and putting her arms round his shoulder to give him a quick kiss on the top of his head. 'Now come on, what do you think?'

She was so full of plans she hardly felt Neil's stiffness, and as she had only glanced at him cursorily she had no possible thought that he might be any different from yesterday. 'Besides,' she went on, 'quite apart from amusing things like décor, you need to make some basic decisions. You do realise, don't you, that you are keeping everyone on tenterhooks because you won't make up your mind who to have for your best man. You've got to decide, or I'll decide for you. I know it's an awkward choice between Angus and Quentin, but on balance I'd settle for Angus and let Quentin be master of ceremonies, then neither can feel put out.'

She stopped talking suddenly.

'Are you listening?' she asked. 'I don't believe you've heard a word I've said. Look at me. What's happened?'

Neil turned his chair round to face her. She looked down at him.

'You didn't hear what I said. I can't. Not now.'

'Can't what?' She looked bemused. 'What are you talking about? Can't what?'

Neil looked at her straight. He stretched out his hand to take hers.

'I don't know how to say it. I can't go through with it. The wedding.'

Celia smiled disbelievingly. 'Rubbish. Of course you can.'

Neil shook his head.

'Can't? Why?'

He was sitting erect in his desk chair. 'It's news from England. It's changed everything. Dessa's husband's dead.'

Celia pursed her lips, repressing a smile.

'And? So what? My husband's dead. What possible difference can that make to us?'

'You don't understand.'

'No. Tell me.'

'Somehow I can't. It's something that ...' He was lost for words.

'You mean it's all off, just because..' Celia broke off and drew herself to her full height. 'I don't understand. You mean...? Oh Neil! What rubbish.'

For a long moment she paused and then she realised. She looked at Neil. There was a curious, elusive determination about him. This man whom she thought to be putty in her hands was meaning exactly what he said.

She gave out a deep breath of frustration and disgust.

'I don't believe a word you're saying, and nor do you.'

She smiled inwardly. That's what it was. He was getting cold feet. He needed re-assurance

'Come on Neil. This is now. How can what happens to her affect you now? We've got the chance of a life together....This is our wedding we're planning.'

Neil's strength at that moment was his silence. He sat, impervious.

Celia straightened slowly in total disbelief. She had worked hard for this marriage. It suited her well. Surely, he couldn't be such a hopeless case. Had she wasted all this time?

She raised her head slowly, took in a breath which squared her shoulders firmly. With eyes indignant and fixed, she stared at him, frozen in the moment.

Neil continued to sit. His stillness said what words could not.

Celia's nostrils dilated. Her eyes fired with disgust.

'God, man, think again! What are you? A louse? I cannot believe what you are telling me. After everything! Now?'

Her voice was hard and brittle.

'Don't worry,' she went on. 'I know all that stuff about her doing the dirt on you but I can't believe that after all these years you'd go grovelling. Even you.'

Her eyes narrowed as she looked at him.

His silence continued to engulf the room.

Celia realised that Neil, for once, actually meant what he was saying.

Along with this growing realisation, her tone became increasingly detached.

'But that's what you're going to do, isn't it?' Her look sharpened. 'It's written all over your face.'

Still Neil said nothing.

Celia drew herself to her full height.

Sparks flew from her eyes.

'Gutless man!'

Neil looked as if he was about to speak Celia gave him no chance.

'You've said quite enough. I don't grovel. Let me make that plain. If that's how you want it, it's your choice.' She gave out a snort. 'After everything! But your choice.'

She looked around, head high. 'No point wasting any more of my time here, I can see.' She swung around taking in the shapes of all Cora's massive furniture.

'Never liked this old stuff anyway. Stew in it. Better still, burn it.'

With that, turning on her heel, erect, she left.

Neil heard the car tyres spin in the gravel.

The wedding never happened, and the 'girls' didn't indulge in new clothes. Early in the new year of 1929, Celia went off to Hong Kong and for weeks, conversations in the Club centred on her sudden departure.

As for Neil, he made arrangements with the Company for a four month furlough in the June of that year and went back to England.

TWO

B ack in England!
Neil stepped off the train from London at Portsmouth's Town station. He hadn't been able to book a passage directly to Southampton and in a way this pleased him because he had no idea how he was going to organise himself or manage this chancy adventure once he had arrived. Landing in London meant he could play for time and get in gear for what he had come to do.

Via Gwenny, he had written a brief letter of condolence to Dessa weeks ago, to which he had not received a reply, nor expected one. All he knew was that she was a widow, that she had come back from South Africa with her four children, and was heavily pregnant with a fifth. Little as he knew about families and children he could appreciate the strange feelings a mother must have producing a new life from a bereaved partnership. How was she managing? She surely needed all her resources at this time.

Questions, questions.

Would he be welcome or not? Was his coming for better or for worse?

Why was he making this journey back to see her?

Could there be anything left of the times they had shared together?

This might be a fool's errand. Either way he had to find out. He couldn't settle back in his old life or contemplate a new, unless he completed, what was for him, unfinished business. Try as he might he had never been free from her, and he had had to come.

He found himself out of the station on the pavement, staring at the stone lions on the Town Hall steps. So familiar! It was as if he had never been away.

His break-up with Celia had caused him no emotion whatsoever, whereas now he was vulnerable, excited, alive and stirred.

Dessa, alone, no husband.

Might she need him?

He couldn't neglect this totally unforeseen shift of fortune.

Who could ever have foretold such shakes of the kaleidoscope? He couldn't risk not coming. He felt purposeful, unlike his usual indecisive self.

However much the backlash, the talk, the advice, he had broken off from his drifting way of life with Pam and Celia. Pam's quivering lip had been far harder to bear than Celia's disgust. Basically Pam had cared for him, Celia for herself.

True. She had had every reason to fulminate. He smiled to himself as he heard her clipped voice.

'I hope you like children, Neil. Five, did you say? She's welcome to you, if she'll have you, or haven't you thought of that? She'll use you, you know. She's used you once, and she'll do so again. Your mother had her sized up!'

Perhaps she would be proved right. He knew he was taking a chance. All too well Neil knew the repercussions of breaking off an engagement, but with Celia he was fully aware that his actions had only caused cracks to her pride and prospects. Their being thrown together had been fun and convenient for both of them at the time, but that was, well, before..... and this was after.

Besides, in reality, how long would it have taken for Celia to get bored with him and the small-time life of the community at Jorhat? How long would living in 'Tinkharia' have amused her, and then what? In such circumstances he could see himself turning into another version of old Gordon, doddering the years away collecting butterflies and moths, and drinking more and more. With Dessa? Well, that was why he was here.

It was to put it mildly to say that shock waves had reverberated through the Club with Neil 'doing the dirt' on Celia! It was unthinkable, Neil, of all people! Neil, a fading 'young' man deliberately missing out on a great opportunity! He knew exactly what they must all have been saying.

He had come in for a mountain of criticism. Not just remarks, but confrontations and advice. Dodo had taken him on one side and told him in no uncertain terms what a mistake he was making. Comments ranged from 'he had to be out of his mind', to cryptic, unsavoury allusions concerning his relationship with Vikram. Everybody was disappointed that the wedding they had so looked forward to wasn't to take place.

In the face of this Neil surprised himself by the way he remained unmoved. He knew what he had to do, which was why he was here, at this moment, looking straight at Portsmouth's splendid Palladian Town Hall.

It was strange to be back. In a sense it was as if he had died and returned to haunt his past. He was utterly immaterial to people around him, such a contrast with Jorhat where every other person knew him and acknowledged him. Here the thousand invisible threads which connected him with these streets made sense only to himself.

It was with a surprising sense of warmth that so many corners he turned revealed familiar facades, like uncovering the faces of friends at a masked ball. New buildings, new shops, new names jarred temporarily, as did the simple motion of walking, for steep kerbstones interrupted his gait; and there were no kerbstones in Jorhat.

A feeling of excitement and promise came over him, Irrational, he admitted, but nevertheless encouraging. He was back on familiar ground and enriched by the security of past, unforgettable experiences.

What should he do? No. What should he do first? He had time. Eat, sleep, get himself a hotel and think about that when fresh in the morning.

He rose early to take a walk by the sea. No sea anywhere near 'Tinkharia'. The South Parade Pier, the Common, the stone walls of Henry VIII's castle, splashed, not lashed, by high-tide waves for it was a mild, summer morning.

He walked.

Here were the Edwardian seats where they had had serious talks and he had longed to touch her hand; here were those machines with a claw-like crane inside which you manoeuvred to pick up a stuffed toy and usually ended up with only a sprinkle of licorice bullets. None of such memories had ever buried themselves successfully.

On he walked, towards the Clarence Pier.

Something new stood up high, a huge monument. He walked round it. Name after name after name of all those naval men killed in the war. Celia's Adrian's name would be there. He crossed the road to walk right round it. Back on the promenade was another new feature, a tank, an army tank from the Western Front. No forgetting the horrors of that far-reaching war. And there was Nelson's anchor from the 'Victory'! That was still there.

He hadn't yet gone to Craneswater to inspect his parents' old house, now long-sold. Just the memory of the word awoke the time when he first had taken Dessa to meet his parents. That had not been a success. How his mother's sceptical scrutiny had contrasted with his father's warmth! It had always been the same; his mother's ill-disguised hostility to Dessa and his father's support.

He stood still to take in the view and smell of the sea. The Island was exactly the same as he remembered. You could make out the buildings going up the hill towards the Church spire in Ryde. He walked on. Not far away were the tennis courts. The tournament! That had been enormous fun. How long ago? Years. Sixteen years since he had left England. Five children later.

He found himself wandering down to the shore-line. Like a schoolboy he bent down, selected a flat stone and skimmed it, ricocheting across the water. He did it again, the second stone travelling further than the first.

That was it! That's what he'd do! Why ever hadn't he thought of it before! So simple! He'd visit the old lady. Malins Road, forty-one. If she was still alive, that is.

The morning was a good time for someone elderly who might have a siesta in the afternoon. He recollected Sarah, who, by now must be in her seventies.

He took a tram to Commercial Road, alighting by Dicken's birthplace. It gratified him that that the surroundings here seemed totally unchanged. Just along the road was where he would meet Dessa on his way to school. He smiled to think of her tossing her head with indifference whether he rode with her or not.

The sight of these little streets around him did seem very shabby and run-down, he had to admit. He had forgotten how much of England still looked grubby, with rows of workers' tunnel backed houses which should have been condemned years ago. No wonder Sarah had loved her allotment! No trace of a garden here. He remembered his mother's snobbish disgust at the word!

He looked up at the street names. Yes. Malins Road. He had remembered his way well. Forty-one was at the far end.

He found himself standing outside the once-familiar front-door. How small it seemed and how worn! Not that he was to be put off. He hadn't come all this way to be put off.

He knocked on the door.

No answer.

He hadn't prepared himself for no answer.

He knocked again, more firmly and louder.

Perhaps the old lady was deaf. He waited.

Still no response.

A voice made him turn round.

'You'll be lucky. She keeps more to herself than ever these days. Won't open the door to no-one. It's been like that since Morris went away. She misses him. Doesn't like being on her own. Not that she'd let on. Not 'er.'

The local accent struck his ear.

'Then her daughter's not with her?'

'Which one?'

'The one who came back from Africa?'

'She's in Southampton. Had another baby. Mrs. Humby went round for the birth, but that was months ago. You a member of the family or something?'

'Not exactly. I've come from abroad. I've been away a long time. I knew the family years ago. I thought I would look up Mrs.Humby.' He smiled by way of explanation. 'For old times' sake,' he added.

'Knock again. If she doesn't answer, call through the letter-box. She's not deaf although she don't see too well these days.'

Neil knocked again.

That same letter-box through which all those letters he'd written years ago had passed. Then he remembered. They always kept a key on a string. You put your hand through the letter-box, grabbed the string and let yourself in. He was on the point of putting his hand into the letter-box when a muffled sound stopped him. Someone was coming to the door. It sounded like a nocturnal animal making its way warily out of its burrow. He thought he could hear shuffling footsteps. He straightened.

The bolts were being drawn, one up and one down.

From the inside the door was opening slowly, about six inches.

He could see a shine of light on the pebble-glasses.

'Mrs. Humby, its me, Neil.' He paused, repeating himself because the figure at the door couldn't possibly have any inkling as to who the strange visitor might be. 'It's, me, Neil, from India. I've come to see you.'

The door opened slowly to its full extent.

There was a pause.

'Neil, Neil Langford,' he repeated.

'Come inside,' she replied simply. No fuss. No surprise.

In the narrow, dark passage he felt taller than he really was. His eyes looked up and recognised the moulding on the ceiling, and the brown faded lincrusta wall-paper half-way up the walls. Nothing had changed. It was just as if....

She half-turned back to him as she was leading him through to the family room.

'I guessed you'd come,' she said simply.

Down the passage, past the bead curtain, now kept looped to one side. On, past the stairs round whose corner Daisy, Gwenny and Morris had hidden, giggling at the sight of the young man Dessa was bringing home. On past the pegs, now empty, where once hung bulging layers of scarves and coats, thence into the kitchen's eerie green filtered light from Henry's fernery. Without the screams and laughter and the slamming of doors the house was sepulchral, but the fire still burned and the kettle was on the hob.

'Let me make you a cup of tea,' she said.

Sarah's chair seemed larger than ever. This was because the old lady had shrunk into a woolly sphere from which hands and feet protruded. He would never have recognised her if she hadn't been on her own ground. Her thick glasses peered up to him from beneath a mass of strong, very white hair.

'I know the voice,' she exclaimed, smiling. 'Why, I still have the photo you sent me all those years ago in my front parlour. I wouldn't have recognised you but for the voice' she added.

'How is she?

'Managing.'

'Where is she?

'Southampton. She's recently moved into a new house. She's had another baby, did you know? This time a girl. I went round for the birth. I sold her house here, which fetched a good price, and the Mission helped her buy a house in a good area. She's close to the common, and it's plenty large enough for five children. They've been very kind to her, the Brothers. If they hadn't I don't know how she would have managed.' She paused. 'But you know all about it don't you?'

'Only what Gwenny told me in her letter. She told me that Dessa's husband had been killed in an accident.'

Sarah sniffed. 'Worse than that.'

'Worse?'

'He killed himself.'

The news made Neil take a deep breath. He stared into the fernery in disbelief. Suicide! Her husband had committed suicide? Why? What had been wrong? Questions, simultaneous questions flooded his mind, but he said simply, 'I didn't know.'

'No-one's supposed to know.'

Sarah took off her spectacles, and looked Neil straight in the eye. She rubbed them carefully with the lace shawl round her shoulders, and put them back on again.

Neil swallowed. He'd imagined some awful accident or some weird tropical disease, but never suicide. What had happened? How had this ever happened? What had she been through? Why?

'And Dessa?'

'She won't talk about it.'

'It's dreadful.'

'You can't worry about "dreadful" when you've got five children to look after.'

'Five. I was forgetting.'

'The daughter's called Alice.'

Neil was silent, stunned.

Sarah went on. 'Bill, that's Gwenny's husband, took me round to help with the birth. He and Gwenny have been wonderful. They looked after them when they first got back. Bill can't get over how dreadful they looked when he met them off the boat. He'll never forget, he says. Such a sad little group. People all round them laughing and meeting friends, and Dessa all strained and white. Mo was taking charge of the little ones, like the father of the family. Austen was guarding the luggage. They're both big boys now.'

'Killed himself. Why?'

Sarah shook her head. 'It's not for me to ask. She'll tell me when she's ready, if she wants to.'

'And having a baby on top of it all.'

'In a way that's kept her going.' She shook her head in sympathy and smiled briefly, then paused and sat silent. Neil, stunned, waited for her to go on.

'Terrible. A miserable homecoming.' She paused again, reflecting. She took off her spectacles wiped them carefully, then resettled them to look carefully at Neil.

'Yes. Bill and Gwenny have been marvellous. Bill says they were all shivering with cold in those horrible grey, cargo sheds after Africa. Those docks are depressing at the best of times,' she added.

Neil nodded.

'They were so thankful to see Bill's cheery face and the boys liked Bill's new car. I offered them to come here but Dessa was too worn out. She needed looking after. Not like herself at all. Bill's been doing all the cooking. Gwen's not very good at that, besides she's only just had a baby herself.'

'What a terrible mess.'

'It is. Life can be. Don't we all know. What can anyone do? You just have to deal with it.' She bit her lip and folded one hand inside the other. 'What else? A new life. The baby.' Sarah shook her head. 'So much sadness.'

It wasn't the time to speak more.

The old lady sat silent for a moment, her hands in her lap.

'It's better now than it was. The little girl's a pretty baby, and they're in a nice house. That helps. It was a terrible squash to start with at Gwenny's, and there was so much to fix up, the boys' schooling. The pensions; all that.'

'And how is Dessa?'

'Hard to say.'

Sarah took Neil's cup and placed it on the table. She looked at him hard.

'I think you can really help her.'

'I want to. That's why I've come.'

'Give her a surprise.'

'Not write? Prepare the ground?'

The old lady shook her head. She looked up, adjusting her spectacles.

'The shock might do her good.'

'I came to ask your advice. I wasn't sure what to do for the best.'

Sarah smiled.

'Who can say? Mind you she'll be proud, because she let you down, but don't let that put you off. She really needs support. She's had a bad time. She'll be amazed and glad to see you. Something needs to go right for her.'

'Should I leave it a bit?'

The old lady laughed and shook her head.

'How many years is it? My advice? Give her a surprise!'

THREE

T o-morrow was today.

Neil had decided to hire a car, not to impress but to give himself something to do. He didn't know how he would be able to sit still in a train. Moreover, if the meeting were a disaster he could escape at high speed.

He had hired a dark green Citroen from Haig's garage, quite a classy car, with a foldaway roof. He put on his gloves and cap, and giving himself a passing look in the hotel mirror behind the reception desk, he decided he looked promising.

Seated high and commanding a sweeping view, he drove out of Portsmouth, past Wymering, Fareham and Titchfield on his way to Southampton. As he proceeded the day cleared. Patches of blue sky came and went, reflecting the highs and lows of his own excitement and anxiety. Heads turned as he passed and he was still boyish enough to enjoy being behind the wheel of a rather splendid machine. Cars were still a cynosure in 1929.

'On the open road she'll do forty, easy,' the mechanic had said, and she was. Neil reined her in a bit because he didn't want to arrive too soon.

In his mind he was constructing yet another scene which he could not envisage with any accuracy. What might happen? What would a thirty seven or eight-year old Dessa look like? Five children would surely destroy the figure. He found himself thinking about the svelte Celia. She took good care that the slings and arrows wouldn't spoil hers. And children? He had decided long ago that he wasn't cut out for small children. He remembered some of those ratty little boys at St. Bartholemew's all those years ago. As for babies, he didn't know the first thing about babies, and didn't want to. That's where nannies and ayahs came in.

He could hear himself uttering romantic phrases he'd heard in moving pictures; phrases like 'Darling, I have come for you,' but such images faded when faced with practical realities like finding the place and standing at the front door.

He'd had a dream about a front-door with no knocker. He'd been glad to wake up from it.

A honk from a car behind him alerted him to the fact that the level-crossing gates had opened and he was holding up the traffic. He wasn't on Tinkharia roads here. He needed to find a pub, grab a snack and a glass of beer, to set him up for arrival in the early afternoon.

The address. He had it on a bit of paper. Funny name for a house 'Tsolo'. Trust Dessa to give her house a weird name. He was now driving along a wide road of houses which backed on to a common.

These were all new houses. 'Kirkhills', 'Mayfield', 'Verona'; people gave their houses strange names. At least "Tinkharia" meant 'place of peace and fruitfulness'. Whatever did 'Tsolo' mean?

Slow down.

That one must be it. Brick. Quite large. Modern. A fashionable diagonal wall at the end. Oriel windows. He would park the car here, a distance away, and walk through the gateway to the brown door set back inside a porchway.

He took a big breath. It was the biggest gamble of his life.

A bronze knocker and letter box eyed him from beneath an oval high leadlight of coloured glass. This door might prove either a barrier or a way into Dessa's life.

He knocked.

A man came to the door. A man! This was the last thing Neil had ever expected. A man!

She had got herself a man already! Another man! He was too late!

He wanted to turn away and escape but he found himself blinking and locked from movement. He cleared his throat.

'I was given this address for Dessa , Dessa Hall.'

'Then you've come to the right place,' the man replied. 'She's in the garden. Come in.'

Neil still couldn't move. Turmoil, futility, confusion, embarrassment, stupidity, and worst of all, disappointment, paralysed him. Facing him was another man. Neither Sarah nor Gwenny had even hinted at another man. He blinked again and changed feet to balance himself.

Before he had time even to swallow, the man was still talking. The buzz in Neil's head made him scarcely able to register what was being said.

'Wait a minute,' the voice continued, 'I'm sure I know you. From before the war. Your face is familiar. Aren't you Neil, Neil Langford? Remember me? I'm Morris.' He gave Neil a spontaneous welcoming smile. 'You've come to see Dessa? She'll be so pleased to see you.' The voice was affable, delighted! Neil couldn't believe his luck.

'Morris!'

'You wouldn't remember me. I was only a schoolboy at the time.'

Neil looked into the face. Morris! Yes, he could see now it was Morris. Relief! He took a large breath. So much relief that he felt a total weakening! The unreality of it all!

Neil is shaking Morris's hand. He is crossing the threshold. The house is hollow. It smells of new wood. Morris is leading the way, talking. Neil thinks he can hear himself talking, but he isn't aware of what he is saying, rather he senses that he is being watched, for out of the tail of his eye he can see an almost life-sized portrait of a man in naval uniform on the wall by the stairs. Morris is saying something about the baby. Neil finds himself at the top of some steps outside a French-window, overlooking a garden, behind which is a dip with a ditch and a blackberry hedge, beyond it trees and the green of the common.

A woman and a pram.

She is bending over a pram with her back to them.

Neil goes down the steps towards her, slowly. The blood drains from him with each step. He hesitates.

She turns round. She does not react.

Neil stops.

Initially perhaps she thinks it's Morris, then Neil can see her tightening. She stands up straight and narrows her eyes. She sees two people, yes, two. Everything stops.

'Neil,' she says, quietly, without moving.

His feet take him to her, and his hand takes hers.

Neither moves nor speaks. Time and space stop.

Morris's smiling descent down the steps finally melts the moment. Suddenly all three are laughing. Morris is saying 'you should see your face,' to Dessa. Dessa is saying 'you look so young,' to Neil. Neil is the only one who cannot bring himself to make words, only noises. The two small boys who have climbed over onto the common, come back because of the laughter. Mercifully the baby stays asleep.

No-one knows what to do next. Nothing normal is good enough.

'I'll make some tea,' says Morris. Dessa puts her arms round Neil and gives him a huge kiss. The boys are jumping up and down asking who Neil is. Nothing but Questions. How did he get here? The explanations are immaterial. There is too much excitement, Southsea, Sarah, Assam. The boys hear the word 'car'. They want to see the car.

'Why don't we go round to see Gwenny?' says Dessa.

They all say 'why didn't we think of that before'. Morris says he'll stay with the baby, and before they realise it the rest are in the green car going round to Gwenny's. The boys toot the horn. The car arrives at Gwenny's like a fire-engine, causing comment in the street. Why not! It's that sort of day.

'You knock on the door, Neil, to give her a surprise,' says Dessa.

The door half-opens, and there is Gwenny wiping her floury hands on a tea-towel. She flings her white hands round Neil's neck. The boys jump out from behind the porch pretending to be red-Indians. They all collapse in the back garden onto deck-chairs and a rug.

Neil can't remember when he last felt so carefree. Everything is spontaneous and natural.

'This feels like the best day of my life,' he says, amazed that he can burst out with such impulse.

But this is only a start. He has to meet the only baby girl ever-born, Marigold, Gwenny's wonder-baby, and, later, Bill of course, Gwenny's husband. Later he has also to meet properly Dessa's special, only daughter, Alice, as well as her two big sons Mowbray and Austen, who are at school until after four o'clock.

'You can stay here with us,' suggests Gwenny to Neil. 'Since Dessa got her new house, our house feels positively empty, and we'd love a visitor. And you two ought to have the evening together. We'll come over and mind the baby.'

'I'd like to take you all out,' says Neil.

'Not to-night,' says Gwenny who isn't a schoolteacher for nothing. She looks at Dessa firmly. 'I suggest the "Black Swan", by the Itchen. Take Dessa out. You two will have heaps to talk about.'

A moment of silence. The understatement of a decade!

Neil looks questioning at Dessa.

'Yes,' she replies. 'I should like that.'

The 'Black Swan' is on the edge of the New Forest, an historic muted-red brick, gabled building. Dessa and Neil are as at ease with each other as they are at odds, a strange feeling.

'There's so much to say I can't talk,' says Dessa.

'No need. I'm here for three whole months.'

They are sitting at one of the tables, outside by the river. It is a fine summer evening, and they have the privacy of anonymity among the other score of patrons.

'I've ordered champagne,' he tells her. 'I don't drink,' says Dessa.

'I've ordered it for me not for you,' he says jokingly. 'I feel nervous seeing you again.'

'How do you think I feel?' she replies.

She smiles. Across the table her eyes slowly re-acquaint themselves with his face.

Neil speaks again. 'Just on this one occasion you should have a small glass,' he pauses, 'it will make us both feel more relaxed.'

He looks at her. She feels it.

She gives a little laugh. 'Wrinkles,' she says. 'They all tell a story.'

'You still look like you,' he says.

'You don't have any.'

'Wrinkles? My loss. I haven't done anything of any importance. You've had five children. I've got nothing to show for thirteen years.'

They fall silent and sip their drinks.

Neil takes Dessa's hand across the table.

'Why did you come?' she asks, as she looks into his eyes, directly.

'You know why,' he says.

'I don't want you to be here because you're sorry for me.'

He smiles. 'Quite the contrary. I'm sorry for myself. I came because I wanted to be with you again. Simple. I'm fed up with being on my own. You're one of the very few people in the world that I feel myself with. Is that a fair answer?'

She nods.

'We can start again. I couldn't risk not having that chance.'

'I have so many responsibilities.'

'I know. Perhaps I can help share them. We have time on our side. No rush. Time to work things out. In our own way.'

'You might find all my obligations too heavy a price.'

'That's my choice. They'd be two of us.'

'You don't know about children.'

'But I can learn. You must teach me.'

'I can't believe this is happening. After everything.'

'That's the champagne talking.'

'No.'

'Time for dinner. All the excitement makes me feel terribly hungry.'

'Me too.'

Neil stands up and offers Dessa his hand. He puts his arm round her shoulders. She closes her eyes with release.

'I haven't felt happy for a very long time,' she says.

Neil gives her a squeeze. 'That's why I came. Me, too.'

FOUR

'Why's he here again?'

Austen shrugged.

'We never come home without him here. First Uncle Morris, and now him.'

'Uncle Morris is O.K. Pity he's had to go to London.'

'S'pose.' It was Mo's turn to shrug.

'Uncle Morris is jolly decent. He chucks balls and that kind of thing. So does Uncle Neil, come to that.'

'But he's not our uncle and I'm not going to call him "uncle".'

'He gave you a fiver.'

'He gave you one too.'

'It's a lot of money.'

'It doesn't make any difference. He can't buy me.'

'You don't like him because he beat you at tennis.'

'He beat you too.'

'He's coaching us. I mean you wouldn't expect him to coach if he wasn't any good at it. He thinks you're good. I heard him telling mum.'

This piece of flattery didn't mollify Mo.

'He may be good at tennis, but he doesn't know much, and he's s'posed to have been a teacher. I asked him about utilitarianism and John Stuart Mill and he just laughed.'

But Austen had lost interest. He was fishing under his bed for his Meccano.

Mo hadn't finished. He felt Neil to be an intruder, just when they were all starting to settle down. The sooner he went back to Assam the better for them all.

'At least when Uncle Morris is here, he goes off to work, but he's here all day. And now he's come to stay.'

Austen looked up from the floor 'So what? You're in school all day. Besides he hasn't anywhere else to go.'

'Furlough! How much longer? I want to get back to normal.'

Austen didn't like to admit that he didn't know what 'furlough' was. He grinned. 'Sounds like a disease!'

'He is a disease, a disease I don't want to catch! I've had to move in here with you because of him. And how much longer? Nowhere to put anything. And you're not to touch my things. And stop making that daft clicking noise. Shut up!'

Austen was now lying on his iron bed on his back, making noises and kicking the new green distemper. Already there were patterns of rubber heel marks on the newly painted wall.

'Mum'll be furious. Stop it! On her green paint.'

'It's just as bad for me, sharing a room with an owl.

But by this time Mo was into his book and had shut out the world No reply.

'I said 'owl'.

Still no reply.

'Fancy having a brother who is an owl. That's what they call you at school. Stop reading your beastly book, owl.'

'Birdly.' Mo cast him a glance, and smiled a bit as he settled into a new chapter.

The smile was what did it. Austen whipped off his bed suddenly and lunged at Mo's spectacles. This guaranteed a fight. Mo retained his glasses but at a cost, because Austen, though younger, was larger than himself and had managed to grab the book which he threw up on top of the wardrobe. Mo, irritatingly, could always score verbally which frustrated Austen intensely. He found it hard having a brother one year older than himself who was something of a prodigy. It made him feel mentally backward. In Grahamstown Mo had to be put into a high class because he was so brainy. And now, back here in England he had won a top scholarship to their Grammar school already, and was two classes ahead.

Mo, constantly, thought, read, gleaned ideas from every possible source. He picked up languages without even trying. From Austen's point of view there was little advantage in having a walking encyclopoedia for a brother, and to have to share a bedroom with him was even worse. His nickname 'owl' was pretty apt. Mo's large head seemed larger than it was on account of his mass of thick curly hair. And his silver rimmed spectacles made him look like the caricature of a brainy schoolboy. Although he was slight and could move quickly, he was nowhere near so stylish and debonair as Austen. As to cricket which Austen loved, Mo preferred to make a Wisden of his left leg with an indelible pencil, in preference to trying to hit boundaries.

Since his father's untimely death he took his responsibilities as the eldest very seriously. He was Dessa's confidante and right-hand man. He adored his mother and his little baby sister, and had great patience with the two young boys. Austen was different, and although they were close together in age, maybe because they were so close, they frequently had the odd spat.

At this moment a sticky Gug invaded. He spotted Austen's box of cigarette cards and made a bee-line for them. Austen, guessing what he was going to do was too quick for him. He picked them up and held them high out of Gug's reach.

'Jump for them! Jump for them,' he teased. 'Higher, higher!'

'Give me one,' Gug pleaded in vain. Finally he hurled himself as high as he could, knocking the box out of Austen's hands and scattering the cards all over the floor.

'Idiot! Now pick them up! All of them, bed-wetter!'

Gug sat down on the floor, oblivious of all but the picture cards.

'Put them back into the box or a skeleton will come and get you in the middle of the night.'

Gug burst into tears.

Mo came to his rescue, and rolled him over in a bear hug till he giggled.

'We'll both do it,' he said. He could be touchingly tender, just like a father to the little ones.

Their mother's voice came up the stairs.

'Mo! Keep an eye on Gug for half-an hour. Neil and I are taking Alice out to the common in the pram with Henry, O.K? There's some bread and jam on the kitchen table.'

Austen, having put away his cards happened to look out of the window. Mo, getting himself organised to go downstairs, picked up Gug and sat him on the wide window ledge. As he did he could see his mother laughing and smiling at 'Uncle Neil' as she pushed the pram. Next they saw 'Uncle Neil' put an arm round her shoulders.

Mo took a deep breath.

'See that?' he said.

Austen nodded.

'Mum likes him. The sooner he goes back to India the better. We don't need a new father. We're alright as we are. He'll muck up everything.'

'No,' Neil was saying. It's much too soon. You've got plenty to think about with the boys and the baby. When it's the right time for you. My concern is you. You work it out. I'm not going anywhere.'

'Except back to Assam.' Dessa smiled.

'You know what I mean.'

'You've turned things round for me. I could never have guessed! You've made me feel human again.'

Neil widened his eyes. 'Same.' They both laughed. 'If you could have said to me six months ago, that I'd be in Southampton pushing a baby in a pram, well!' Their eyes met with amusement.

'You've been a lifeline. I'm not exaggerating.'

'I've got a vested interest.' He squeezed her hand.

'Three more weeks.'

'The days have gone so fast.'

'I'll be back next leave. Four years. 1934. Alice will be—

'Five and Mo, eighteen.'

'And?'

'Well, the family should be sorting itself out by then.

'And?'

'Then we'll see. After all these years I really do want to see 'Tinkharia.' Be there. Help you. Look how you've helped me!'

'I've learned to wash up! No end to my expertise.'

By this time they were strolling back to the house, and Alice was making noises.

At supper that night, Mo asked his mother when Uncle Morris was coming back from London.

'In three weeks,' she replied. 'When Uncle Neil goes back to India.'

Dessa thought she saw Mo and Austen exchange a look.

FIVE

If Celia could see me now!

The ironies compounded, Neil thought, as he found himself doing his best to adapt to a household of children and a baby! He, who had been looked after for years by the stalwart, dependable Vikram was now wiping high chairs, tearing up newspapers to thread them on a string for the lavatory, and hanging nappies on the line. His well-meaning ineptitude was the means to his strange, new, courtship. A little smile would hover round Dessa's lips as he struggled with peeling a potato or wiping the mouth of a protesting baby, but secretly she was as pleased as she was amused.

'Covent garden? Wimbledon? The Albert Hall?'

He could hear Betty and Edith and Eulalie asking him what he did on his leave. How they would fall apart laughing!

'Watching Dessa perform conjuring tricks,' he might have told them. Simultaneously she could talk John Stuart Mill with Mo, extricate Henry from the honey pot, make Gug read words from objects on the breakfast table, pick up the baby, and iron Austen's one cricket shirt, ready for a match. Neil decided he was most use taking Henry and Gug over to the Common to play around with a ball. At least that meant two less pestering Dessa round the house. He did his best to make friends with the two older boys, but they looked at him and through him with a deliberate detachment which he found embarrassing.

There was always the portrait in the hallway. The eyes seemed to track his movements up and down the stairs.

'He's our father,' Austen said proudly to Neil one day. 'We've still got his uniform and medals. They're in the sitting room, in the cabinet. D.S.C AND Bar. That means he got it twice. What were you in the war?' he asked.

'I wasn't in the war,' said Neil, 'I was in India.'

'Didn't you volunteer?' asked Austen. 'Daddy told me that almost everybody volunteered, all round the Empire.'

'Neil wasn't allowed to volunteer,' said Dessa, sensing Neil's embarrassment. 'The government had to have people growing tea. The army depended on its tea.'

But Austen was far from impressed. 'I'd have sent him white feathers,' he told Mo, in a not very soft whisper behind his hand.

Despite the incessant and tiring daily family tasks, these days for Neil were precious and airy. Dessa and he laughed a lot together with shared memories of his motorbike, her room up those outside steps at the Macdonalds, his fury at Colonel Parson's clandestine overtures, and far from least, the soft sands of Hayling. Unforgettable. They both smiled with relaxed warmth.

'I'm so glad you came,' she told him gently one evening, when at last they were on their own. 'You've made me feel human again. You, of all people. I don't deserve it.'

They were sipping whiskies. Neil liked his neat in England, whereas Dessa's was very weak, quite undrinkable, dissolved in tepid soda water, for she didn't 'drink' often. Too many bad associations.

'I can't believe this is happening' she said, lying back and drawing her feet up on the settee. 'Come to that I can't believe anything that's happened.'

Neil had kept off questioning of any kind, not wanting to destroy their present rapport. He and Dessa had created an extraordinary normality in these past weeks born curiously from the whole unlikelihood.

Whatever were they doing, here together, twenty-nine years after they had first met? It was extraordinary. Keeping to the present and working towards a future was the only feasible thing. The past had to be accepted and put behind them. Now was a time for support, not questions.

That evening Neil needed his whisky to relax. The boys' unfriendly candour had upset him. He didn't want them spoiling his and Dessa's limited time together. Encouraged by her acknowledging how glad she was that he had come, he asked her whether Guy had known much about him. 'Just curious,' he said.

'Very little,' was her reply. 'You were my business, not his. Nor did I enquire about his past. Just as well, I guess. And then so many things were happening. The war, the continual moving from one crisis to another, dealing with the children, all these things. What we had shared was a world apart.' She took his hand and kissed it. She continued. 'People like to think that you can forget and move on but you can't avoid being part of what you have been. It's impossible. That doesn't mean you have to drown in the disasters. It means you have to go on swimming. You're my lifebelt, when I least expected one.' She smiled. 'We must make the most of each other.'

'And have we enough now, together, do you think?

She nodded slowly. 'I think so.'

Both fell silent. Dessa was the first to speak.

'No rush,' she said. 'I have to get the children settled. It takes time to establish some normality after all that's happened.'

Neil understood.

'Mo and Austen are my biggest worry. I want them to settle into their school and into Southampton. Mo, specially. He feels responsible for the family.'

Neil hesitated. 'I think Mo looks on me as an intruder. I feel it. Austen isn't so bad, although both of them seem to look at me through the eyes of their father. They make me sense his presence. You do realise, don't you, Dess, the last thing I would ever want is to take you away from them. Reassure them.'

'The portrait?' She had guessed.

'I put it up deliberately to give them something to hold on to. I want them to grow up with respect for him. They don't know what happened, and I never want them to know. For them their father is a hero. I want it to stay that way.'

This was the first time Dessa had mentioned any of the complications and details of Guy's death.

'It was a good thing they were away at school,' she went on. 'I've always been thankful for that. Gug and Henry, luckily, were too young to have any real understanding, although I think sometimes Gug's need for affection has doubled since his father's death. I can tell from the way he always wants to get near Bill and Morris and now you.'

Gug was simple and affectionate, not like Mo and Austen. He liked Neil giving him piggy backs and taking him to the common. 'Guy always did those sorts of things with him,' Dessa added.

'And you?' Neil fingered her cheek gently. 'Three more weeks and I've got to go back.'

'I'm not facing up to that yet.' She stretched out her arms to him. 'I like things as they are. You've been wonderful. It's all been far better than I ever could have expected, or deserved!'

'Deserving doesn't come into it.'

Dessa's face broke into a smile as she looked into his face. 'You still look so young,' she added. 'I'm sorry about me. At least you don't love me for my looks! I'm a haystack these days.'

'And I've been shut up in a drawer for twenty years. At least you've lived.'

'And died sometimes. Or it felt like it.'

She sat back and drew breath. 'You do know about Guy.'

'Only what your mother told me'.

'That's not half of it. But I want you to know.'

She twisted her hands tightly between her knees. She started to talk and then stopped. She looked into Neil's eyes, then down again at the floor.

'That morning,' she began, and broke off. She took a deep breath, biting her lips to make herself have the courage to tell the story. She began again.

'That morning we had a terrible row. I was angry, hurt, disbelieving, utterly disgusted. I lost my temper. I flew at him and hit him round the head, hard. That was when he left, white faced. And---- Well you know what happened. If I hadn't been so furious he might never have...'

She closed her eyes.

'It must have been some row.'

'He had been drinking again. Not that morning, I don't think. But certainly several weeks before I had sensed that he was, although he had promised not to. He took good care that the Brothers didn't know. That would have been the end in any case. He knew that.'

Neil listened. Dessa was still, her eyes fixed on the floor. Then she took another deep breath, sat up holding her knees, staring ahead.

'There's something else. No-one knows, no-one. It was the last straw.'

She paused.

'He had got our nanny pregnant.'

Neil swallowed.

'I couldn't believe it! She was there when I came home with Gug. They were there in the house together.'

Dessa unclasped her knees and closed her eyes.

'It was her manner which made me furious. She was proud. Seventeen! A girl. A black girl. She was in love with him; that was plain. He had been playing around with her all those months. And I was pregnant. And he had got her pregnant too. This had been going on behind my back. I had no idea. All his fine words. His cajolings, his secret anxieties whispered to me, and all the time he was...'

Neil could barely hear her words, intense and muted as they were with recollection of the memory.

'If I hadn't been so sickened. If I hadn't felt so violated. If I hadn't flown at him so violently... he might never have killed himself.'

She sat upright.

'You see, Neil, I feel partly to blame.'

He took her into his arms. He nursed her in silence.

The clock ticked.

'It was his guilt which killed him, not you.'

But Dessa, lost in her thoughts, barely heard his words.

She turned towards him.

'It's as if it can never end. Alice looks just like him.'

Neither could speak. Neil stretched his hand to take hers.

'Alice deserves a future. She's yours too.'

SIX

Was Dessa different?

Yes and no he thought.

Neil had plenty of time on his return journey to Calcutta to mull over their extraordinary weeks together. The Guy years had raised her up and put her down. The owner of those eyes in the portrait and his five live children may have sapped her energy, diluted her wilfulness and divided her determination, but her nature, ravaged as it had been, still showed spirit and individuality. Dessa, once wife, and now mother and father to her children, had not lost the intrinsic marks of herself, those marks he had always remembered. Sarah had been right. The surprise had worked. His sudden and unexpected arrival had taken her by storm at the time when she most needed love and support. He found himself humming a tune and smiling. What were the words? 'Nothing venture, nothing win.' Exactly right. A new chapter had opened for them both.

For Dessa, Neil's coming, whatever else, had proved a lifeline. She had felt so alone, so cheated, so angry. Seeing Alice every day, never failed to remind her that somewhere in the Transkei lived a half-caste brother or sister. This fuelled, and continued to fuel, her innate fury and jealousy. Never could she forget that look of triumph on Sala's face. Continually it brought out a degree of savagery in her, the power of which, ironically, helped her to get through those cataclysmic days after Guy's death and at the inquest. Now, in a sense, accepting Neil's attentions was a pay-back, a pay-back at Guy, which would give her feelings of satisfaction for the rest of her life.

There were to be four years before Neil came back on leave again.

They sat back together to sort out a future.

There were two realities; her children, his job. She argued that there was little point in taking her large family 'out there' as there was equally little point in Guy's abandoning 'Tinkharia' and leaving Mason-Webb.

'We're middle-aged. We have to be practical. It's not a question of proving that you love me more than your life in Assam. This is no time for heroics.'

The year was 1929. The New-York Exchange had suddenly collapsed with resulting world-wide bankruptcies. Even the Bank of England had come off the gold standard. There was widespread slump and unemployment. For Neil even to consider leaving a job which he loved and did well was insanity.

'I want to share your life,' she told him, 'not have you abandon it, and if you were to give it up and come back here what would you do?'

'I could have my own business, run a nursery, something on those lines, perhaps.'

'Yes,' I replied, 'and invest your capital in it and work like hell to get established and make endless losses with no customers and end up another bankrupt!'

What Neil was doing in Assam, was pretty gilt-edged. Producing tea could hold its own even in times of 'poverty within plenty'. For him to leave what had been his father's and was now his tea-garden at such a time was unthinkable. 'We're hardly naïve,' I told him. 'In four years time the children will be that much older and we can sort out a feasible plan.' If he came back now and tried to set up a business, the misery of hard work and no rewards would eat into our daily lives and drag us both down.

No, no and no.

We both agreed that now wasn't the time for me to go out to Assam. This would mean splitting the family I was doing my best to hold together. We were still all reeling from the all-too recent drama of Guy's death. At last, with the new house, the two big boys settled at their Grammar School, Gug, happy at the little school up the road, and Henry enjoying kindergarten we had a good routine. Neil knew that. He had been part of setting it up. Four more years of family stability were essential. For the time being he was better off maintaining the life he knew. The three youngest children invading 'Tinkharia' was out of the question. As it was he needed to go back to Assam 'for a rest' I told him.

We talked and talked, facing the problems and discussing solutions. Finally, yes, he would go back as planned and return in four years on his next leave. By then we could really make plans for our future. That was our understanding as the day came for him to leave. Gwenny and Bill, Marigold, Alice, Henry, Gregory and I gave him a real family send-off. For a surprise, I had ordered him a special pair of heavy gold cufflinks, an 'N' for one cuff, an 'L' for the other, specially made. He in turn gave me beautiful diamond-drop earrings and an amber necklace. Also, on a more practical level, he had insisted on paying me a quarterly sum which would enable me to have some help in the house. His weeks of being an 'au-pair' had made him realise how invaluable another pair of hands could be! I was glad of this generosity.

Four years to surmount and we were back to letters. The ironies!

'Marvellous to have Winnie,' I wrote. 'She's a great investment! How shall I put it, she is more predictable round the house than you, and pegs out the washing more systematically! The boys like her for the pudding special she makes. She calls it "haystack in a flood". It's full of golden syrup and milk and pastry and the boys can't get enough of it. She takes Alice to the park in the afternoons. That's now, so I can write you a letter.'

The months passed. Dessa's weekly letters kept Neil au fait with family news, and vice-versa.

There had been camping at Lulworth Cove that summer holiday. Morris and Bill 'were marvellous with the boys, taking them fishing.' Alice and Marigold played happily for hours together, on the beach. 'Find enclosed a photo of us all, including Morris's new girlfriend, Poppy. She's the one you won't recognise. She's a dancer. They met at the stage door. They're smitten with each other. As you can see we were all sitting on a five-barred gate.'

In turn Neil sent photographs mostly of his garden and of Titus. He was very busy developing the tea terraces to enlarge the property. More planting, more building, more workers; there was no slump in the tea industry. 'Quite the reverse', he wrote. As well as day-to-day changes there were retirements of old friends, and deaths. Canon Ashcroft had died. Dodo and Angus had retired to the Channel Islands, Betty and Peter 'of all things' had decided to go to New Zealand. 'He has a sister there.' Also there were new people in 'Rituparna', who had moved on from Ceylon. They were Isabel and John Beynon. Dessa would like them. They were 'roughly our age and had similar interests. I've had them to dinner twice and told them all about you.'

Back in Southampton Mo and Austen were getting larger and their lives more complicated, Dessa wrote. Trips to the Continent are now a 'must'.

'Our Gallic experience took the shape of a fifteen year old Parisienne girl, Lucette.' Austen, apparently, had quite suddenly taken up a major interest in French.

'I hadn't realised how fast he was growing, and believe me she taught him a thing or two about you know what! I hesitate to think what they got up to when he went over to her family on exchange, but his French marks at school went up astronomically!'

Then it was Germany. 'Gehrhart Glombig stayed with us in the summer holidays. He and Mo got on very well and went cycling together. They are arranging to have a cycling holiday in Bavaria after their last term at school.'

Increasingly, Mo proved to have a gift for languages. He had been doing Greek and Latin at St. Paul's in Grahamstown and now he was fluent in French and German. 'His teachers were very impressed, and it was at their suggestion that he sat for an open scholarship to Balliol college, even though he was only sixteen.' She wrote in utter delight when he won it, 'although', she added, the headmaster advised that he shouldn't 'go up' too young, 'so he is having a third year in the V1th form, He really is an academic, I think,' wrote Dessa. 'He's got his father's brains, and he's the first member of the family ever to go to university.' Proud as she was, she had been relieved to learn that his full scholarship would cover fees and living in college, 'which was a blessing.'

'When you're next here,' she wrote, 'we must go to Oxford and stay for a few days. I want us to enjoy it together. Bill took us up in the holidays and it's a wonderful city.'

Three years, two years, one year.

The years of family life swelled with the changing demands of growing children at different stages, their sore throats, chicken pox and broken arms, their crazes of darts, jacks, yo-yos, and stamp collections, their adventures with the go-kart Morris made. And now, already, Alice had started at the little school down the road.

Neil was soon to arrive, this time at Southhampton direct. We would all be on the quayside to meet him, I told him.

I was preparing one of the bedrooms for him when something unnerving happened.

Austen had already gone over to France, 'to perfect his French,' which was how he put it. It was the 'long vac' and Mo, along with the younger ones, was still in the house until he went away to Cornwall on a reading holiday. I had already given the children their tea, and Mo and I were to have supper together later.

I called up the stairs to him.

No answer.

I didn't think any more of it. I heard Gug's usual evening reading, because he always had a bit of difficulty and stammered a bit when he got nervous. Then I read them a story, sent them upstairs to get undressed and called Mo again. Still no answer.

I put Henry and Alice to bed, and let Gug stay up to get on with the model of a boat he was making.

'Supper in half-an-hour,' I called.

Puzzled by his not answering, I went upstairs and tapped on his door.

'Mo? Can I come in?'

He didn't reply so I tried the door. It was locked.

That surprised me. I didn't even know if any of the doors inside the house actually locked. We weren't that sort of family.

'Mo. Open the door. Why is it locked? Anything wrong?'

Silence.

'What's the matter?'

Still silence.

'Are you in there or aren't you? Open the door.'

Nothing. No reply.

'Mo, I know you're there, what's up?'

Finally Mo replied.

'I'm not coming out if he's coming.'

'Mo? We've been through this before. I thought we had an understanding.'

'I've changed my mind. I don't want him in this house.'

'I've invited him. He's coming to see us.'

'See you, you mean.'

'Come on.'

'This is my father's house, not your lover's.'

'This is my house too.' I felt angry and vulnerable.

'Don't pretend. I know what you're up to. You just want to sleep with him, I know.'

'Mo, let me in. You're not being fair.'

'You're the one who's not being fair. You're wrecking the family.'

'Neil's an old, old friend.'

'Yours, maybe, not ours. If he comes here I'm leaving.'

'Now who's breaking up the family?'

'D'you think I want to be in the same house with him in your bed every night?'

'That's enough. Unlock this door. Come downstairs and discuss this properly. What's got into you? I do all I can to support you. It's time you supported me.'

'What do you think I've always tried to do? Ever since Dad died.'

'I'm not arguing with you. Come downstairs and have some supper, and let's sort this out. Unlock the door, please. I'm going downstairs. I've got to put Gug to bed.'

I was worried. No one in my experience in our family had ever locked themselves in their rooms before. Gug, once had jammed the bolt in the outside lavatory, but that was totally different.

I tried to get on with the supper. Eventually Mo did come down but I could tell he was in a strange mood. He stood, leaning against the doorway.

'I don't want anything to eat.'

'Don't be like that. If you feel so strongly about Neil's coming, we must talk about it and sort something out. I'm not going to marry him and disappear, and abandon you all.'

'I don't want him here in our house. Isn't that plain?'

'Then we'll make other arrangements.' When I said this I had the feeling that at last that he was becoming less confrontational.

'Like what?'

'He can stay somewhere else. I'll ask Gwenny to have him. His being here needn't affect you. You're off to Cornwall, you're going youth hostelling in Italy; Neil's arrival need not upset you. I certainly don't want to upset you. I know you don't like him, but Neil is a good friend to me. We've known each other for a long time, and, yes, we like each other. But that's not a crime. Dad's death has been tough on us all and you've been a real support to me.'

I could tell that this remark had mollified him a little, but he was still angry.

'You're grown-up now, away at university and you have a life of your own. I'm proud of all you've done and you've got your life ahead of you. But just think, I need to have a life ahead of me. Neil's only here on leave, and then he's back in Assam. Surely you don't grudge me any bit of pleasure we might have while he's here?'

'You're being disloyal to Dad.'

'For God's sake, Mo, Neil's been living on the other side of the world for four years. How can you say I'm being disloyal to Dad? I've got to go on living as well as you.'

'Aren't we enough for you?'

'You'll all leave home and I'll be left on my own. Neil's been good to me. Aren't I allowed any pleasure in life? Don't I do my best for you all?'

He was starting to calm down, I could tell by the way he bit his lip and looked at the floor.

'Mothers have to have some life to keep themselves going.'

At that point I went into the kitchen to clear up. I was worried and hurt by the things he'd said.

He stood in the doorway.

'I don't want to quarrel with you.'

'Then don't.'

'I don't want you to forget Dad.'

'As if I ever could,' I took a deep breath and faced him.

'I don't want anyone to replace him.'

'No-one could. You should realise that. Your dad was utterly unforgettable.'

'I loved him.'

'I loved him too. Don't forget.'

Finally he came round. We gave each other a hug. It was a kind of truce, I thought.

The last thing I wanted was a scene between Mo and Neil. Neil couldn't cope with scenes. He didn't know enough about families. I fixed up for Neil to stay with Gwenny and Bill who were pretty good to me. They looked after the children on more than one occasion so that Neil and I could have time together. We had a whole memorable week in the Isle of Wight on our own and three days in and around Oxford. Mo was away for more than a month, so that was a relief. When he came back I was careful to avoid any confrontations. The incident with Mo made me realise that now was not the time to make major changes.

One evening when Neil and I were on our own away together, he asked me when we might be married. 'There's still a few problems,' I said, 'which is putting it mildly.'

We had been enjoying an evening walk all across Port Meadow, and had sat on the river bank looking at the barges moored on the Thames.

'This isn't easy for me. If you want the truth.'

'No point in anything else.' He smiled wryly. 'I wouldn't want to spoil what we have after everything. Tell me.'

I told him. He listened with quiet patience.

'I think I'll need another two years. I'm not joking. Mo's being very difficult. Two more years sounds terrible, and I can hardly bring myself to ask you to wait that long. I don't know how to be fair to everybody.'

We had been sitting, each assuming the presence of the other as one does with people who are close. At this point I couldn't help but sigh. I turned to him.

'It's impossible, Neil. Can you go on waiting? I can't pretend it can be less. I don't like trading continually on your good nature, but what can I do?'

'If I have to, I have to.'

'You're wonderful to me, Neil. No, more than wonderful. I don't know how I can possibly be worth it.' She leaned her head into his shoulder and embraced him closely.

He kissed her forehead gently. 'You're worth waiting for,' he said simply. As he kissed Dessa a mother duck took to the water, followed frantically by two ducklings one of whom somersaulted comically and ineptly down the bank in desperation.

They both laughed. 'See how it is, Neil?' He nodded.

'Two years. By then Gregory and Henry will be old enough to go to boarding school, Austen and Mo will be basically off my hands, and more importantly Alice will be seven. The Jesuits say that in seven years they can shape a child's character for life. What do you think? If they can do it so can I.'

'Third time lucky,' he said.

1936

ONE

When Austen got an Exhibition at St. John's College, Oxford, Dessa at last decided she could make arrangements to go out to Neil.

The two eldest boys were at university. They were grown up with independent lives, not her worry any more. They still needed some financial help and the house in Southampton could be kept going for them as a base in vacations, so now was the time that Dessa could really start to work out a future for herself.

The next two; Gregory and Henry.

They would have to go to boarding school. People who worked in India naturally sent their children to boarding schools. It was a way of life, squeamishness didn't come into it. Dessa's situation was identical except for being the other way round. Neil had been sent from Assam to board at Petersfield and had survived, as had heaps of children whose parents worked abroad. She was now going abroad to Assam.

Besides, the children had each other, and there were her sisters and brother. They were hardly orphans.

One trouble was cost. Neil was prepared to help Dessa financially but he was not prepared to spend his money on Guy's children. She made enquiries. There were some schools which gave free education to the children of Naval officers killed in the war. Guy hadn't been killed in the war but he had been awarded two medals for bravery. That should surely count for something. Dessa argued her case with the naval authorities sufficiently to convince them, and Gug, now a grown up ' Gregory', and Henry were awarded places at a well-known Public School, Henry in the prep department, and Gregory in the Senior school.

That settled that problem.

Next. Holidays.

Surely her brothers and sisters would have the children to stay, on and off, and the house in Southampton would be there in between.

Next, Alice.

Should she take Alice with her or not?

How would Alice make out with few children of her own age in Jorhat? 'Tinkharia' was actually about seventeen miles out of Jorhat, so she would be pretty isolated. At seven she was too young for boarding school. This problem needed careful thought.

What other options were there? Gwenny? Marigold? She couldn't really ask them to have her full-time.

Wait! An idea!

If she were to maintain the house in Southampton on a permanent basis it would be empty for most of the year. If on the other hand she employed a housekeeper, who could be a nanny to Alice as well, that might work.

What a sensible idea!

Dessa put an ad in the local paper and had twenty one replies. No trouble finding people in the present economic climate, besides there were all those lonely women over from the War. She sifted through the answers and interviewed five of the applicants. Free living and three pounds a week in wages. Duties: to maintain the house and garden, to look after Alice, to be responsible for Gregory and Henry in the holidays, and to give Mowbray and Austen a base when they needed it. 'Successful applicant needs to be able to take up this position in two months' time.'

The idea was that she could dovetail the person into her family routine before she actually left. She needed someone plain, hardworking, kind and trustworthy. She nearly chose a Mrs. Blackmore but her good looks and self-possession worked against her. The final choice was Edna, well into her forties, a widow from the war, with a young married daughter in Romsey. Edna was reliable and 'a find.' Alice took to her, which was the most important thing. She was used to children having grown up in a family of eight, five of whom were boys, so she got on well enough with Henry and Gug, and she treated Mowbray and Austen as 'real gentlemen'.

That big worry was over.

They had an unwritten contract for four years. Dessa worked out that she and Neil would be back 'on furlough' to see the family in four years time. That seemed to work out everything on the family front. It wasn't as if anything catastrophic was likely to happen in the big wide world, nothing like the war which had happened last time. Didn't she know! Ironic, really. If war hadn't broken out in 1914, her life would have worked out wholly differently. She would have gone out to marry Neil, or he would have come back to marry her. The whole Guy episode wouldn't have happened and she wouldn't be the mother of five children and all the hassles children entailed. What sort of shake of the dice was that! Anything going on in the Far East was hardly likely to affect India, despite the fact that Neil had drawn her attention once or twice to Japan's sabre rattling against China, but, as far as her own affairs were concerned, that was well off the map. Back home no-one had any intention of a repeat of the unrepeatable Western front. The hazards of submarine activity which she had known about all too well, was history. 1918 had been the war to end all wars, thank goodness! So, to realities.

1940, and they would be back.

Alice would be eleven, nearly ready for a good secondary school, and she and Neil would be there at that important time. In the interim her living with Edna would be the same as having a nanny. Edna would be her nanny, and what was so extraordinary about that!

Now some thought for herself. What would she need, living in Assam? She remembered all those basic things she had had to take with her to Africa. From all she'd heard and seen, life for the English in and around Jorhat was very civilised. Neil had told her about his friends and the people he worked with. She would love being part of the Club. Lots of activities. Pretty social really. She'd need dresses and a new tennis racquet and all the gear. She hadn't much knowledge of Bridge, but Neil could teach her. She'd love the play-readings and productions. She'd easily make friends. And she could be a big help with the workers. She could run classes for them and help them with their little children and the old people, a bit like the kind of things she had done in Africa. Not that the mission would be anything like the town of Jorhat.

She had one worry and that was dentistry.

Ordinary medical services in Jorhat were fine, Neil told her but 'see to your teeth before you come out.' Dr. Keane was an excellent Irish medical doctor who ran the local hospital and was a member of the Club, but dentists, well, better to get herself fixed up in Southampton. Dessa remembered the agony she had had with an abscess under a tooth at the Mission, the price of five pregnancies. She couldn't risk going through that again, no messing.

Decisive as ever she resolved to have every single one of her rather beautiful teeth out, all at once, at one sitting. Even the dentist protested, but she insisted that he make dentures for her instead. It was a small price to pay for her future with Neil. She withstood the bleeding mess with equanimity, and adapted herself to false teeth without complaint.

'Everything is working out well,' she wrote, telling him about all the arrangements she had made, including the teeth. I'm perhaps not quite as beautiful, but I'm making assurance double sure. I haven't quite squared Mo, yet, but I'm working on it. I also have to talk seriously to Gwenny and Daisy and explain to them how I've organised everything.'

Of all the children Mo was the most intransigent. 'I'm trying to make him see things from my point of view, our point of view, but all the time he keeps on about his father, and says I'm letting him down. If only he knew!'

Mo was continuing to be difficult. Dessa persisted in trying to reason with him.

'You've got to try to see it how I see it. I've had to struggle a lot to get through these past years, bringing you all up. No arrangement can be perfect but I've tried to think of the most important things. Edna is a very nice woman. Alice likes her. She'll have your room ready for you whenever you want it. Remember you're away for well over half the year, what with university and travelling in Europe, and it's not as if you spend a lot of time as it is with Alice yourself. Alice likes Edna and they get on well together. She's her nanny.'

Mo's expression did not change.

'What better arrangements can you think of?'

'There's one obvious answer,' was all he would say, and lapsed into silence.

Dessa felt cross. Mo was doing his best all the time to make her feel guilty. 'I've tried to think of everything. Remember, there's always Auntie Gwenny. She'll help out if there's a problem, and so will you, I hope.'

Mo wasn't at his best. Dessa's recitation took place at a time when he was rather worn and dishevelled having recently come back from yet another youth-hostel cycling trip in Germany. He had been amazed at the support for Hitler among the ordinary people, and the fast-growing prosperity under National Socialism. Hitler had defeated the Communists, and everywhere he went there was enthusiasm for what he was doing for a Germany, now well-risen from the ashes of the War. He had remained silent and blinking through all his mother's protestations.

'And you do realise, don't you, that I've managed to get Gregory and Henry into a very good school, and that whether I am here or not, they would be away for three quarters of the year. They'll only be home in the holidays and Uncle Morris and Uncle Bill are sure to take them off camping or fishing, like they did you. Next week I'm going to Portsmouth especially to discuss our plans with the family.'

'Our plans? Your plans you mean.'

Mo had looked stony-faced at Dessa all the time she was talking.

'Don't I deserve some happiness, Mo? Neil can't wait for me forever. We're both well into our forties.'

'You're our Mother,' was all he said.

'And I always will be,' Dessa added. 'But children grow up and lead their own lives. And it's not as if Neil isn't helping me to provide for you all. Where do you think the extra money comes from so that you can go abroad and explore Europe? Think about it. This is my chance of having some life of my own. I've given up everything to launch you children and now it's my turn.'

'Alice is only seven,' he said.

'Mo. You can help me. Why don't you? I've only ever tried to help you.'

'I don't think you should walk out on us all like this.'

'It's not as if I'm not coming back. Four years and I'll be here again.'

'Four years! Austen and I are quite able to look after ourselves but Gug, Henry and Alice need you. You're their mother. What would our father think?'

Dessa refused to be drawn.

'You didn't know as much about your father as I did. I never let him down. If he knew what I was going to do he'd be glad for me.'

And it was left at that.

It was shortly after this last exchange that Dessa needed to have a serious talk with Gwenny and Daisy before she went away. She hadn't seen her family since Mother's funeral some weeks earlier.

Yes, Mother had died. What an impossible thought that was. Mother had always been there, a stable life-force. Born in 1850 she had been this odd mixture of unconventionality and Victorian propriety. She wasn't the kind of person you could ever forget. Left in Malins Road on her own, finally she had agreed to sell and move in with Daisy and Desmond, newly back from their posting in Malta and set up in a large, three-storey house in Portsmouth.

Since then, that was only the first of a number of changes. Bill had been promoted by his company to run their office in Portsmouth, which meant their moving house, and Morris had a new job in the Isle-of-Wight. Everyone was on the move.

It was during the family get-together at Sarah's funeral that Daisy told Gwenny that the house next-door to them was up for sale. Gwenny was determined to have it, even though they couldn't easily afford it. Large, like Daisy's, Gwenny had the bright idea of turning it into two flats initially, to help with the money problem. Now, of all her brothers and sisters Dessa was the only one left in Southampton. She would have to go by train to Portsmouth to have this necessary talk.

To her great surprise, Mo said he would come with her.

At last he was facing up to the realities of her going away, she thought, and she was relieved and touched by his offer.

Bill picked them up from the station. Gwenny was very excited to show them the new flat and the alterations, he said, and Daisy was already there from next-door making coffee.

The flat was fresh with paint and smelled delightfully of coffee. Gwenny met them at the open front door, with hugs and kisses, keen to show them everything.

'We've even managed to get the baby-grand piano into our upstairs sitting room,' she exclaimed. 'They couldn't get it through the hall and stairway, so it had to be winched up through the window! That was a real performance! They're here,' she called to Daisy. 'Before we settle down for coffee I'll show them round.'

One of the bedrooms on the first floor had been converted into a kitchen. 'No problem with the bathroom for us,' she explained, but we've turned the downstairs cloakroom into a small bathroom for our tenant. She's an old friend of mine from teaching days and works at the school round the corner.' They then proceeded up a second staircase to a large attic room at the top of the house. 'Marigold's room, as you can see.' There were books and a dolls' house and a table with paints. 'This is a marvellous room for her. Our bedroom's on the same floor as the kitchen. Do you like it? We're very pleased with what we've done. Now come and see the sitting room and have some coffee.'

All of them heard but Bill was the only one who saw. Until that moment they hadn't realised that Mo wasn't in the room with them.

Dessa and Gwenny saw Bill's face. They were sitting on the sofa in the window facing him.

'Christ!'

He leapt to his feet.

'Mo.' He said and rushed out of the door.

Dessa, Daisy and Gwenny were staring at each other in horror. They had heard an unnatural dull thud. They followed Bill downstairs and out into the front garden.

Mo lay slumped in a grotesque pile on the grass.

He had missed the wide concrete-topped brick wall by inches, but the standard rose that Sarah had planted shortly before her death had been snapped in two, along with its supporting stake, somewhat breaking his fall.

'Don't touch him!' ordered Bill who was already on his knees by Mo's body.

Dessa, too, was on her knees, while Daisy and Gwenny looked on with disbelief.

'He's not dead. Unconscious but still breathing. Get an ambulance!'

TWO

'No question about it. She can't possibly go now.'

'Imagine if something like this had happened if she was miles away in India.'

'What a good job's she's here!' Daisy shook her head slowly in disbelief with what had happened. 'Not possibly.'

'He couldn't bear the thought of her going.'

Gwenny in her mind was seeing Mo's huddled figure on the ground.

'He really tried to kill himself.'

'It's terrible.'

'What next?'

Yesterday had been a terrifying day. I had gone in the ambulance with Mo to the hospital, the Royal Hospital, where my father had died with peritonitis. I had waited and waited and waited for news. Too much time to think. All my plans in a mess. My mind was darting about randomly.

So this was why he had wanted to come with me. He had planned it.

That didn't make sense. I had to think again.

He didn't even know that Gwenny and Bill lived in an upstairs flat. He had never been there before. He must have acted on the spur of the moment. Why, oh why hadn't he talked to me? He had been very silent in the train, but he never had been a casual talker so his behaviour hadn't struck me as odd. Now, of course, I realised that perhaps all he had been thinking about was how to stop me going. That was it. He was determined to stop me going.

If he wanted to punish me he had certainly succeeded.

What on earth could I do? What dreadful injuries did he have? How could I possibly go to Neil now?

It had been an age waiting for the ambulance. Now, nothing, more waiting.

Someone brought me a cup of tea.

No news.

I had a booking on the P&O line. Neil was expecting me. He was coming to Calcutta to meet me. I would have to cable to put him off. What would I tell him?

I wouldn't tell him the whole truth all at once. I could hardly bring myself to digest what had happened. That top-storey window. I felt sick and numb. We had just been looking round Gwenny's new flat. What had happened was unthinkable, impossible. What could I say to Neil? I didn't know how to realise what had happened myself. How should I break it to him? Questions,and more questions. But I had to tell him something. Yes, I would have to think of something. Yes, that was it .I would tell him that Mo had had a serious accident on his bike and was in hospital and I couldn't leave as planned. Would that do? I wasn't sure.I wasn't sure of anything anymore.

And Mo? His injuries. Perhaps he would be scarred for life and needing my total support? I tried to pull myself together. The tea was cold.

Mercifully Bill arrived in the waiting room. He put his arms round me.

'No news?

I shook my head and sighed. We sat side by side, waiting.

Eventually a doctor came to speak to us.

'Your son?' he inquired.

'Yes, yes.' We were anxious.

He was sorry. Weren't we all? But at least the news seemed better than we first thought. It was remarkable that Mo managed to survive with comparatively few injuries, 'as far as we can see,' the doctor said. Mo had a broken leg, a dislocated shoulder and a broken wrist. 'He's been very lucky,' said the doctor. 'Something, somehow, must have cushioned his fall. No obvious internal injuries.' Nor did his X-rays show any specific head injuries.

He assured us that he would operate as soon as he could.

He told us that there was no point in staying. That we should go home and telephone later. For the time being we couldn't do anything.

Bill squeezed me with relief, and I did my best to try to smile back. Nothing to be done, except think.

Back at Daisy's, where I was to sleep, Bill said, no question. We sat around looking at each other. All of us were pretty washed up.

Desmond had come home and brought in whiskies to calm us down.

'Thank goodness it wasn't worse,' I remember him saying.

'What will you tell Neil?' asked Daisy. 'You'll have to cancel your passage now.'

'To-morrow,' I said. And I couldn't talk about anything, or think about anything until I had had some sleep. They understood. We all felt shocked and numb.

Sleep! Some sleep!

Little chance of sleep.

Daisy had put out her best satin nightdress for me, and pink sheets, especially. I drew the curtains and lay on the elegant bed, eyes closed, but my mind was white with activity.

Mo.

I still could hardly believe what had happened. It had been so sudden, so unexpected, so ghastly.

I'd had a husband who'd killed himself and now a son who'd done his best to do the same.

But Mo hadn't known anything about that. He hadn't known all the lies I'd told in court for all their sakes. He hadn't known about Sala and all those thoughts I'd had about her.

So many ironies.

And why did he hate Neil so much? Or was it me he really hated? What psychological mix-up was that? Why was it that Austen could appreciate how I felt about Neil and Mo couldn't? Austen had accepted all the arrangements I had made and was pleased about having our house always available with Edna as housekeeper. He appreciated the fact, too, that my liaison with Neil meant that he had a more generous financial allowance than would otherwise have been possible.

Mo hadn't given any credit to Neil ever. It didn't occur to him to understand that his coming back into my life stabilized me when I needed it most. The schoolboy he then was could only see him as an interloper. That rancour had never left him, and now this. It was utter madness.

Thoughts crowded my mind and unnerved me. Finally I fell into fitful sleep disturbed by the prospect of the realities I would have to face on the following day.

Everything was in a state of flux. Next morning we telephoned the hospital.

Mo had regained consciousness but was in considerable pain and confused, they said. 'There was no point in trying to see him until late in the afternoon, and then only by special concession. At present he was heavily sedated.'

Hospitals in those days kept visitors and relatives at arm's length. Hours for visits were strictly adhered to. The sister in charge of the ward, starched in white headgear and severe stripes, guarded her patients from her desk at the ward's entrance with the vigilance of a Pluto. Visitors interfered with the running of the hospital and were not in the interests of the patient. That morning, as much as to have something to do, as we were all wholly skewed by Mo's 'accident', Bill had driven me back to Southampton to bring Alice back to Gwenny's. I packed clothes, made arrangements with Edna, for surely it would be a week, or two, or three, or more before Mo could possibly be moved. Everything was on hold.

Back in Daisy's sitting room Dessa's two sisters were still in shock.

'I'll never forget that dreadful thud.'

'Amazing that he is still alive.'

'Whatever next?'

'One day at a time.' They both sighed.

Daisy went on, 'I don't know what it's like to have children, but I just couldn't leave them, especially not now, I know I couldn't.'

Gwenny shook her head thoughtfully in agreement. 'What a lot she's had to deal with. Now this!'

'You know about Guy, don't you?'

'We all know, but it's not something we talk about.'

'It's weird that...'

'Don't say it. I know what you were going to say. It's lucky that Mo's still alive.'

'Was it?'

That evening I went to see Mo. Bill came with me. I was glad. The sister in charge of the ward took us to Mo's bedside.

'He looks worse than he is, but I'm sure he'll be glad to see you,' she said. As she drew back the thin white curtain surrounding the bed.

I had to close my eyes at the sight Mo presented. He had his eyes closed, too. I put my hand on his, the one piece of flesh visible amid the plaster, the bandages and the cradle over his leg.

He opened his eyes and looked at me. Then he closed them and did his best to turn away. I felt upset by this, but I drew up a chair to sit by him. Bill stood on the other side of the bed.

He opened his eyes to Bill.

'You gave us a bit of a shock, old boy,' said Bill. 'Thank goodness you're going to be O.K.'

I squeezed his hand very gently. 'I'll just sit by you darling.'

His lips moved. 'Go away.' What he said was barely audible but plain enough, and it upset me terribly.

He tried to take his hand away from mine.

I couldn't leave him. Of course I couldn't.

Bill had heard what he said and told me afterwards not to worry about it. He could hardly be himself after what had happened.

A full half-hour later he spoke again, turning away from me. 'Go away,' he repeated.

Worse. He refused to look at me and seemed visibly agitated by my presence.

The doctors were studying him closely. Physically, because of his natural health and youth, he was making good progress but his stress levels were high and much of what he said made no sense. Gwenny and Bill went along with Daisy. They had some desultory conversation with him, which was more than I was able to have. They took him grapes which he ate absent-mindedly. He was polite to them but pretty monosyllabic, they said. One day he did speak but they couldn't make sense of what he said; something about the 'Queen's countersigning his criticisms', and his concern with British politics. It sounded crazy.

They had looked at each other in bewilderment they told me.

After that he started to talk frequently but very quietly and things were obviously going on in his mind about Germany. Hitler was wanting him to sign a death warrant against himself. We couldn't make head or tail of what he said.

I talked to the doctors and described how only recently he had visited Germany and had been amazed by what was happening, but the mixture of things he was saying gave no clue as to what was going on in his mind.

We were all getting more and more anxious.

'It must have been the fall,' Daisy said. He's damaged his brain. You can't see that sort of damage. He's talking rubbish. Whatever can they do?'

What could they do?

He seemed to be confusing his injuries with imagined attacks. I had the feeling that he knew perfectly well who I was but had written me out of his life.

It was now a full four weeks after the accident, and the doctors decided that Mo should be moved to St. Leonard's Hospital for psychiatric tests and treatment. With all his plasters and bandages, he couldn't get physically violent but he was increasingly abusive and disturbed the other patients with roaring noises and uncontrollable outbursts of tears. He was now complaining of hearing voices. The doctors asked him to write down the kind of things the voices said.

He did. They didn't make sense either.

In his small precise writing he wrote down incoherent, jumbled, mixed phrases.

'I didn't make her in my beautiful reporting.'

'You'll scream my programme in my beautiful homework's windows.'

'They keep talking to me. They give me no peace. They make me want to scream,' he told the doctors.

Besides this he was under the impression that any thoughts in his head were being read by radio waves. He told the doctors such thoughts could only condition him, not dictate his life, that he had poetry to write and that dark political forces were imprisoning him.

I was summoned.

Apparently the doctors had come to a cul-de sac of a decision. Mo had been diagnosed as schizophrenic. Apart from the mess of words in his brain he was definitely suicidal and of 'unsound and disturbed mind'.

For his own good, he would have to be kept indefinitely in a mental institution. Had I been able to think of anything, any behaviour recently which was unlike himself? Had anything been worrying him, his examinations perhaps?

That last almost brought a smile to my face. Mo loved exams, they were his element and absolutely the last thing to cause him stress.

Were there other worries?

I didn't feel it was their business to know that he hadn't liked the reality of my going to India.

Where did this diagnosis put me? Somehow I had to come to terms with the reality that my son Mo was mad and that he had tried to kill himself.

He had to be locked up for his own good.

I didn't seem able to help him in any way. To me he was particularly abusive, never acknowledging me as his mother but calling me whore and worse.

None of us liked to acknowledge the reality of this socially unacceptable fact. It was spoken of in whispers and with hushed innuendo even by Bill, Daisy and Gwenny.

Who wanted to be related to anyone with mental illness?

My own family sympathised with me and thought it very sad, but it wasn't a topic to dwell on and particularly not one to blazon abroad. This was a skeleton in the cupboard. Nothing less. It came into the class of 'unmentionable' and should only be alluded to in euphemistic language. I told Austen and Gregory and Henry that their brother was in hospital, and that he had had a nervous breakdown. That description was acceptable whereas schizophrenia wasn't.

Who liked the idea of having mad relatives?

According to Gwenny this was the result of Mo's brains. Mo had been too brainy, unnaturally brainy. And, looking back, hadn't he always been a bit peculiar, posed Daisy? What could anyone do? He was his mother's responsibility. Daisy and Gwenny agreed that the one thing that was utterly plain was that their sister couldn't go off to India. She certainly couldn't go now.

THREE

The street was a cul-de sac.

Small, terraced houses hemmed the straight, narrow road. At the end was a long, blank, stone wall. Following the wall at right angles, stood a confronting pair of iron gates. This was St Leonard's hospital.

The buildings were set far back from the street and hidden behind a thicket of bushes and some surprisingly tall and leafy horse chestnut trees. A curving drive kept them out of sight adding to their isolation. The cries of the people in this hospital may have been faintly audible, but their shapes were never seen.

The buildings themselves were gaunt and grey, surmounted by a four-sided stone tower with four steeply sloping tiled roofs culminating at the top in a dog-toothed pinnacle. Double and single gothic style windows broke up the stone walls which let in light but were too high ever to allow a human face inside to look out.

It had taken Dessa and Gwenny more than twenty minutes of firm walking to reach the hospital from the main road bus stop. The central doors looked firmly closed but there was an arrow to the left which said 'Reception'.

They were directed to Mo's ward. 'Ground floor, to the left and right at the end. Security Ward 12.'

The heels of their shoes echoed sharply on the tiled and patterned Victorian stone floor as they receded to the far end of the building. They pressed the buzzer. A male nurse in a blue cotton suit let them inside.

'Mowbray Hall, How is he?' Dessa asked.

'He's alright, now,' the nurse answered. 'We've got him well sedated, because he kept kicking up a fuss, quite violent at times, and pretty abusive, but he's settled in a bit more. We've got him in bed, mostly to keep him quiet. He's in the third bed on the right.'

There were fourteen beds in the ward. They were largely occupied, but one or two patients were in dressing gowns at a long deal table in the centre where they were reading newspapers.

Mo didn't look up as they walked towards him. He was concentrating on bits of coloured tissue paper, as was the greying man in the next bed. They had spoons and trays and they were making petals for paper flowers by stretching the paper into petals with the back-side of the spoon.

Dessa and Gwenny each drew up a chair to sit by him.

Mo still hadn't noticed them.

'Mo?'

Preoccupied with the bits of tissue paper, Mo looked at them and smiled, without speaking.

'How's the leg?' Dessa asked.

'Where they shot me?'

She nodded. 'You've got the plaster off.'

'I was lucky to escape.' He put down the spoon on the tray and leaned forward, almost whispering. 'They were out to get me. They thought I was a spy.'

'Can you walk now?'

'It's a bit stiff, but it's getting easier. They brought me here because it's safe. I've been in great danger.'

'We've brought you these,' said Gwenny, producing a bag of bananas and apples.

'How did you know where to find me?'

'They told us. The hospital.'

Mo took out a banana peeled it and ate it as he was talking.

'I was very scared. They so nearly got me. They rushed up behind me and pushed me into a van. I didn't know where I was.'

'But you're feeling better now.'

'Yes,' he said through a mouthful of banana. 'It's safe here.'

'I've brought you some of your books from home,' said Dessa, producing 'Hermann und Dorothea', 'Peter Schlemil' and some Guy de Maupassant. Something to go on with. I'll bring you more later. And here are some peppermints. I know you like those. What else would you like me to bring from home?'

'I don't have a home. They mustn't know where I am.'

'Would you like pens and paper?'

'Paper and pencils. They don't allow pens here. I have a lot to write. The voices tell me, and they warn me about Hitler's windows.'

'You're looking a lot more like yourself, Mo,' Gwenny said. 'That's good.'

'How is Marigold?' he said.

A bell rang. Time for the few visitors to leave.

Dessa got up and kissed Mo's head. Gwenny kissed his hands. Mo picked up his bits of tissue paper and pressed the spoon into them.

'Give your mother and me a kiss,' said Gwenny.

'I have no mother,' Mo said.

Which was worse, death or madness? Dessa wasn't sure.

'You heard him,' she said to Gwenny. 'It seems I'm the last person he needs. It's beyond my control! I can't do anything for him. He's a ward of the State. How many people have you ever heard of who got out?'

'But you can't go to the other side of the world for four years and leave him.' Daisy was incredulous.

'If Mo's... accident... had resulted in his getting better, it would be different. As it is what can I possibly do for him?'

'You could be here. You could visit. He'll need you.'

'He hardly looks at me. Gwenny heard him, didn't you Gwenny! He says he hasn't got a mother. How do you think that makes me feel?' Dessa was hurt and angry. What did Daisy know about life!

Gwenny nodded. 'It was awful. I can't bear to think about it.'

'You can't bear to think about it! How do you think I feel when they tell me he's insane. I've never known an insane person before, and now my son, my gifted, clever son is insane.'

'That doesn't mean he won't need you.'

'Daisy, I'm at my wits' end. I don't know what it means. Insane people are off their heads. They aren't the people they were. He's certainly not the person he was any more. He's not talking sense. It hasn't needed the doctors to tell me that. You haven't any children, you don't know what it's like. I've had him shut himself away in his room, for long periods, not knowing what was going on, simply presuming he was studying, but how could I possibly pick that he was going off his head or wanting to kill himself?'

'Face it Dess, he's always been a bit odd. I mean he's so brainy.'

'Brainy doesn't mean mad. Austen's brainy too, but he's as normal as anyone can be.'

'That's not the point. You can't just walk out on him.'

'She's got to work it out for herself, Daisy.' Gwenny was trying to calm everyone down. She could see that Dessa was near to tears.

Daisy had made her feel bad. She wanted support, not these awful arguments.

'Of course I'm not sure what to do for the best, but I've had a pretty bloody awful life ever since Mo went into that hospital. And now this! You've helped a lot and I'm grateful. It hasn't been easy, but Neil's always been my hope. I've waited all this time. I've made all these arrangements. I've been planning them for ages. I've got the boys' uniforms. I'm due to take them to their new school in a couple of weeks. Originally I came here specially to ask you and Desmond and Gwenny and Bill to keep an eye on everyone for me while I'm away. If I don't go now, I can't ask Neil to wait for me any longer. It isn't fair on him.'

'Have you told him everything, Neil I mean?'

'No. Well, yes and no.'

'You should tell him.'

'Who are you to tell me! Of course I'll explain everything, but in my own time.'

'You've surely got to tell him about Mo. He must realise that something very major must have happened for you to postpone your going. If he knew the truth he might come up with a solution.'

'I've cabled. You know I've cabled. And I've written. You know I have. I've told him that there has been an unforeseen accident which meant I'd have to make different arrangements and that I've had to postpone my passage. What was I to tell him? Mo's off his head and in an asylum?'

'Well that's the truth. You've got to face it.'

'I am facing it.'

'But you're still intending to go?'

'I'm still making up my mind. I don't want to upset Neil too much. As it is he's had to put off all his arrangements for coming down to Calcutta to meet me. We're supposed to be getting married, remember?'

Daisy looked serious.

'I think that was the trigger. Mo didn't want you to marry again.'

'Oh, Daisy, you're making me feel worse. It's hardly a crime to re-marry, surely? The other children have been pleased about it. And you, you and Gwenny have always known. It hasn't been a secret.'

'Yes, but none of us could ever have forseen that Mo...' Daisy hesitated.

'That's just it. Could any of us?' Dessa bit her lip. 'Could we?'

'I still can't believe that in the circumstance your going out to India is the right thing to do. Anything could happen while you're away.'

Dessa felt that her sisters had no idea of all she'd been through. Why, even Gwenny was looking at her straight. She obviously agreed with Daisy.

'It's already happened, hasn't it,' she retorted. 'What could be worse than hearing that your son is insane? How do you think that makes me feel?'

'It's just that India is on the other side of the world,' replied Gwenny. 'It's not as if you could get back here in a matter of days, if you needed to. It takes weeks. Look what happened when Neil went away before the war.'

'That was the war. That was then.'

'Desmond says that the War Office is worried about Hitler and the Rhineland now. And look at Spain,' continued Daisy.

'That's Spain's own civil war. Nothing to do with us. We've all had enough of war. That's the last thing I worry about. The moon's not going to fall out of the sky. I've made all the arrangements I can. I'm only asking you to help if something serious happens with the children themselves. That's all. I would do the same for you; we're family, aren't we?'

'Of course we are. But you've got your priorities wrong, this time, Dessa.'

'Then we'll have to agree to differ,' their sister replied.

FOUR

Neither Gwenny nor Daisy could understand how, despite everything, Dessa was still set on going out to Neil. They were making lunch together in the kitchen.

'Anything could happen. She's virtually turning her back on us all. It's not as if she were going up north or to Scotland. I mean she's going miles away. Ships sink, there are natural disasters, I mean, who knows? And five children and...' Gwenny stopped chopping and looked straight at her sister. 'Four years is a very long time. It doesn't make sense.'

'I'm sorry for those little kids. Alice is only seven. Imagine. No mother.'

'I can't bear to think about it. Four years! Alice and Marigold will be eleven when she gets back! No matter how nice Edna is it's not the same. I couldn't do it. Somehow it's not quite right.'

'It's right for her! What's good for Dessa! Come on, Gwenny, Dessa's always set out to get her own way.'

Daisy and Dessa had frequently fought over the years.

Daisy went on, 'I would have thought now this has happened she really would put her children first. It's terrible about Mo. To leave him when he's so sick is beyond belief.' She stopped again, this time in the middle of slicing up the tomatoes.

'It's interesting that she hasn't told Neil the whole story.' She looked at Gwenny straight. 'It's struck me that if he really knew about Mo he might decide to retire early, and come back here instead, and that would solve everything.'

Gwenny shook her head, 'I'm not too sure about that. We don't know half. I know Dessa a bit better than you. It's awful of me to think beyond poor Mo, but I believe Dessa knows that Neil would never agree to come back here and give up his job. Of course going out to him spells escape for her, but it's also money. Neil's generous to Dessa, but he's stayed with us for weeks on end over the years, and I know that he's pretty careful when it comes to cash. His financial retirement arrangements at this stage wouldn't be nearly as much as they'd both like. Besides, there's always...' Gwenny broke off.

'What?'

'It's an awful thought, I feel awful for having thought it, but there might be some truth in it.'

Daisy opened her eyes questioningly.

'Think of Maud.'

'What's Maud got to do with it?'

Gwenny bit her thumb reflectively and looked up at her sister. 'I wish it had never occurred to me.'

'You've got to tell me now.'

'Think about it. Maud's had the sense not to marry again, because she'd lose her pension. It's crossed my mind that the last thing Dessa wants to lose is her large naval pension and when she and Neil are halfway round the world who's to know whether they're really married or not?'

Daisy started a kind of laugh in disbelief.

'You mean?'

'I don't mean anything. But if they were living together back in England people might ask unsavoury questions, legal questions, whereas out there who cares? I'm not minimising Dessa's frustration or need to escape but I am suggesting that she might have more than one agenda! The trouble is, now, Mo's illness has really put her on the spot.'

Back in Southampton, having fixed up the boys in their new school and having made the household comfortable for Alice and Edna, Dessa, increasingly, felt that she had more reason than ever for persisting with her plans. It was her due. If she could have been any real help to Mo she would stay, but now? She took a deep breath.

Daisy, she couldn't win over, but Gwenny had been more understanding. Gwenny and Dessa had shared far more than Dessa and Daisy ever had. Gwenny had been part of that harrowing time when Dessa had returned, racked and dislocated, from South Africa. She had been welcoming when they had most needed welcome. Dessa and the children had felt like bedraggled refugees arriving on that draughty, gloomy dockside, where there had been nothing cheerful save for Bill's face to put new life into them. Bill had made them all smile then, and when he came back from work and at weekends when he took the big boys out to see castles, or to the New Forest to get away from babies and washing lines heavy with nappies. And Alice! Alice had actually been born in Gwenny's house. Compared to Gwenny, Daisy never could understand enough what she, Dessa, had been through, having lived a carefree social life at the naval base in Malta. Perhaps that was at the root of it, that, and her inability to have children. The nice thing about Gwenny was that even though she did not see eye to eye, she had still reassured her that if she went, she'd watch out for the children. Her last words had been, 'you must make your own choice. You don't want our advice. It's your family and your children. Of course we'll help out whenever we can.' Those words had reassured Dessa and re-echoed not only on the long sea journey out to Neil, but in Tinkharia, isolated back in Assam over the next ten years, when to everyone's horror Hitler invaded Poland and World War Two began.

Surely she had done everything she could. She'd written that awkward letter to the Master of Balliol, explaining Mo's nervous breakdown. She had sent colourful postcards to the children. She had explained in letters to Daisy and Gwenny how she needed some happiness in life and expressed her gratitude for help given and any help which might be needed in the future.

What more could she do?

Forty-eight hours and they would be docking in Calcutta. Dessa resettled herself comfortably in her low deck-chair and sipped her Pimm's. Nothing like time for ones-self to recapture flourish and aplomb! Those days of ironed-flat spirit had not destroyed her essential self; it had not been annihilated, only suppressed, wrung out, and waiting for enlivening hydration. She was not a new woman in the sense of a different woman, but the luxuries of the voyage had revitalised the Dessa she had always felt herself to be. She was feeling how she used to feel years ago, confident, alive, how she had felt when she had flashed wicked looks at Colonel Parsons and when she had flirted mildly with the curate at West Meon. Life was for living! Choice and chance had brought her to life again. This voyage had made the metamorphosis possible. No point in dwelling on the past. She had done all she could.

Children gnawed you, decimated you, claimed you.

Now, no longer.

Ahead lay a life with Neil.

That last-minute cancellation had been Fate's hand. She would have spent the rest of her life full of regret if she had not taken the opportunity. The sea had washed away her anxieties. The secure small world of shipboard life had restored her sense of self as each nautical mile had distanced her from the frustrations of family.

And Neil. If not already in Calcutta, it was only a matter of hours before he would be there. He would be immaculate in a pale grey suit. She would wear her blue linen and a chic fine-straw hat she had bought in a fit of extravagance at Tyrrel and Green. They had days of liberated holiday ahead of them before the return to Jorhat. A honeymoon.

The last night aboard had been a party night, dining, dancing, drinking, promising to meet again, exchanging names and addresses; those hothouse shipboard friendships as intimate as they were brief and transient.

Less than an hour to go. Cabin baggage packed and checked. Good-byes to Heather Winthrop who had proved to be the perfect cabin partner from the outset as Dessa had guessed. On deck now, for the moments of docking. From this height, invulnerable, she watched the sideways swirling of the water as 'The Britannia' eased herself into her berth.

There were crowds on the quayside. Dessa was certain she had spotted Neil.

Had he spotted her?

He knew she would be waving a pink silk scarf.

Yes! He had seen her. She was sure he had seen her.

Yes! He was wearing a pale grey suit, and waving his topi.

She returned his wave with high, unhurried elegance.

New hat, new teeth, new smile, Dessa emerged as new from the covered gangway, shards of the past, discarded.

THE END

www.ingramcontent.com/pod-product-compliance
Lightning Source LLC
Chambersburg PA
CBHW070216030726
47505CB00006B/1702

* 9 7 8 0 6 4 6 5 5 8 0 9 7 *